Frankenstein and
the Vampire Countess
(The Empire of the
Necromancers 2)

Frankenstein and the Vampire Countess
(The Empire of the Necromancers 2)

by

Brian Stableford

A Black Coat Press Book

Introduction

In Paul Féval's *John Devil*,[1] that legendary pseudonym is adopted by Comte Henri de Belcamp in support of his mother's career as a notorious member of London's underworld, where she is known by her maiden name, Helen Brown. After attempting unsuccessfully to rescue her from an Australian prison camp, Henri takes news of her death to his long-estranged father, the Marquis de Belcamp, in the small town of Miremont, and is reconciled with him. Meanwhile, he is secretly engaged in financing the construction of an unprecedentedly powerful steamship with which he intends to rescue Napoleon from St. Helena and conquer India; in pursuit of this plan, he takes over a secret Bonapartist organization, the Knights of the Deliverance. Henri is assisted in this project by his long-term companion, Sarah O'Brien, the daughter of a murdered Irish general.

When a potential traitor to the Deliverance, the opera singer Constance Bartolozzi, is murdered in London, the case is investigated by Gregory Temple, the senior detective at Scotland Yard, assisted by his junior, James Davy. John Devil is identified as the murderer. Temple strongly suspects that the person behind that name is Helen Brown's son, known to him as Tom

---

[1] Black Coat Press, 2005, ISBN 978-1-932983-15-9.

Brown, but the accumulated evidence seems to point to Temple's former assistant, Richard Thompson (who is secretly married to Temple's daughter, Suzanne). Actually, James Davy–who is another of Henri de Belcamp's many aliases–has framed his predecessor, exploiting the account of his methods Temple has published in a book on the art of detection. Henri/Davy persuades Thompson to flee to France, where Suzanne is a guest at the Château Belcamp, but he is captured and convicted of the Bartolozzi murder.

When Henri is reconciled with his father, Sarah rents the so-called "new château" on the Belcamp estate under the name of Lady Frances Elphinstone. Henri commissions the murders of his dead mother's wealthy brothers but there is one further obstacle to the fortune he intends to collect by this means, in the name of Tom Brown: Constance Bertolozzi's daughter, Jeanne Herbet, who also lives in Miremont. Jeanne is the designated heir of both brothers, neither of whom knows which of them is her father. Henri falls in love with Jeanne after impulsively saving her life, and decides to marry her fortune rather than murdering her.

Henri eventually marries Jeanne under the alias of an English entrepreneur, Percy Balcomb, in which guise he slips out of the jail where he is supposedly confined. Henri is in prison because the obsessive Temple, having failed to prove that he murdered General O'Brien or Constance Bartolozzi, found out where the bodies of his hired killers were buried. Temple obtained thus information from the drunken mistress of the vertically-challenged petty criminal Ned Knob, who was a witness to the murders and disposed of the bodies. Ned also schooled the false witnesses at Richard Thompson's trial, using members of a troupe of vagabond actors.

On the eve of Thompson's execution, Henri inveigles his way into Newgate Prison, helping him to escape by taking his place. When Temple tries the same trick, Henri confronts his nemesis in the condemned cell, almost driving him insane by telling him that Tom Brown is not, after all, one of his pseudonyms but an actual half-brother, sired by Temple. After escaping in Temple's place, however, Henri finds that everything is going awry. The Deliverance is betrayed, his new steamship is destroyed, and his mother has returned from Australia, accusing him of having abandoned her. He finds it politic to commit suicide–or, at least, to appear to do so.

Part One of *The Empire of the Necromancers* picks up the story four years later, in November 1821. Ned Knob, now directing the acting troupe, is unexpectedly confronted with his predecessor in that role, "Sawney" Ross, who has been hanged but now appears to be alive again, though somewhat slow-witted. When the reanimated Ross is collected by a diminutive French physician, Germain Patou,[2] Ned follows them to a boat where they are met by a man in a Quaker hat like the one Henri wore in his guise as John Devil.

After being knocked unconscious, Ned wakes up in Newgate and is interrogated by Gregory Temple, now working for the secret police. Temple is supposed to be investigating a series of body-snatching incidents, but his attention has been caught by a report of the Quaker hat. Following his release, Ned tracks Patou to a house in Purfleet. There he renews his acquaintance with Henri and witnesses the resurrection of a man from the dead

---

[2] A character introduced in Paul Féval's *The Vampire Countess* (Black Coat Press, 2003, ISBN 978-0-9740711-5-2).

using an elaborate electrical technique recently discovered by a Swiss scientist.

The demonstration is interrupted when Henri's ship is attacked by a rival group under the command of the only one of the reanimated "Grey Men" to have recovered all his faculties: a person who styles himself "General Mortdieu." Mortdieu's hirelings seize the electrical apparatus from the house, taking it to their own ship, the *Outremort*. Ned is arrested again, but makes a deal with Temple.

As the *Outremort* is about to depart from her berth in Greenhithe, a three-cornered battle develops between Mortdieu's hirelings, Henri's followers and Temple's men. The fight eventually arrives at an impasse, but a hastily-contrived treaty permits Mortdieu to sail away, taking Patou with him.

Later, Gregory Temple is woken one night by Henri, who tells him that they must join forces, at least temporarily. Temple's grandson has been kidnapped from the Château Belcamp, where Thompson and Suzanne are now resident, along with two younger children of much richer parents; one is the son of Henri and Jeanne, the other the son of the former Sarah O'Brien, now the widow of a German Count.

Temple and Henri set out to make their separate ways to Miremont, where Temple has to break the news to Jeanne that she is not a widow. Henri is delayed and Temple has to respond to the first ransom note with no one to help him but Ned Knob. He is taken prisoner in his turn. Temple's captors are members of a long-dormant society of heretic monks known as *Civitas Solis*, seemingly led by Giuseppe Balsamo, who are more interested in securing the secret of resurrection than in the ransom money that will help finance their exploitation of it.

Henri's delay has been caused by his traveling under the name George Palmer, in which guise he was involved with a vehm (a secret society of vigilantes) at the time of General O'Brien's murder, and in whose eyes he is still a wanted man. Having made his peace with the *vehmgerichte*, however, Henri is able to attack *Civitas Solis* and liberate Temple and the captive children before disappearing again, intent on joining forces with *Civitas Solis* in the expectation of using them as he had formerly used the Deliverance.

Now read on...

Bran Stableford

PART ONE: THE RETURN OF FRANKENSTEIN

Chapter One
Sleepless in Spezia

Having written his report out in longhand on the rickety table in his hotel room, Ned Knob began the tiresome work of translating it into two different ciphers, using two different keywords.

The clear version of the report read: *More laboratory equipment delivered today to house rented by Walton, including Voltaic cells and apothecary's supplies. His companion remains hidden; will continue attempts to confirm identification. Other spy seen watching house not present today. Have identified visitor previously mentioned as Edward Trelawny, temporary resident at Casa Magni, San Terenzo, present home of Percy Shelley and Edward Williams. Town gossip associates Shelley and Williams with larger group including Lord Byron, Tom Medwin, Capt. John Hay, Leigh Hunt, John Taaffe, rumored to be involved in conspiracy. Agenda of conspiracy unknown, but company apparently has enemies. Several members recently involved in conflict; Shelley and Hay injured, their attacker, Stefano Masi, badly wounded; legal investigation proceeding. Will travel San Terenzo tomorrow to make further inquiries.*

Having transcribed this screed twice, in the coded versions, Ned immediately put the original to his candle-flame and made sure that it was thoroughly incinerated. Taking great care not to mix them up, he put the two coded versions into envelopes, addressed them different- ly and applied two different seals to the wax that secured them. Then he took one of them downstairs, where the courier that would initiate its transmission to Gregory Temple of the King George's Secret Service was waiting to receive it beneath the arch of the coaching entrance.

Having watched the courier ride off into the night on a coal black mare, Ned left the hotel and hurried down the steep hill to the shore, where a second courier was waiting discreetly on the approach to the quays. Ned gave him the second envelope, and watched him hurry away. There was a yacht waiting in the harbor that would bear the courier and the letter away in the direc- tion of Marseilles; thereafter, it would eventually make its way into the safe hands of Henri de Belcamp, whe- rever he might be and whatever alias he was presently using.

Fortunately for Ned, Henri paid a good deal better for the information he received than the King of Eng- land's Secret Service, which expected its operatives to be primarily motivated by patriotism. Ned was not devo- id of patriotism, but he was proud to maintain an authen- tic radical conscience beneath his carefully-turned coat. He had no qualms about accepting the King's secret shil- ling, but he had no qualms either about accepting Henri de Belcamp's secret half-crown. He did not think of his double-dealing as a mere matter of trade; he obtained a whimsical delight from the knowledge that he was work- ing for two mortal enemies at the same time, owing no particular loyalty to either, but he was also glad to be in- volved in a sequence of events that had the potential to change the world. His gladness had been redoubled by the discovery, earlier that day, that there was a direct and immediate link between the house he had been set to watch and one of the men he admired most in all the world.

However comical or despicable he might appear to the world, by virtue of his dwarfish stature and his criminal tendencies, Ned Knob saw himself as a giant of sorts, and a Romantic above all else. He thought that working as an agent for Gregory Temple's branch of the secret police was Romantic in itself, and that his casual betrayal of the secrets he collected on Temple's behalf to Henri de Belcamp was more Romantic still, but the fact that his labors in that regard now promised to bring him into contact with Percy Bysshe Shelley, the author of the recent *Prometheus Unbound and Other Poems*, was definitely the icing on his own Romantic cake. Ordinarily, given that Ned's short legs were naturally ill-equipped for such work, the trek back up the hill to the establishment that was known throughout Spezia as "the English hotel" would have been a tedious one, but there as a spring in his step tonight.

When he arrived back at the hotel, Ned ate a little late supper in the hotel's meager dining-room. A party of young Englishmen from Sussex, sent away by their parents to improve themselves by taking the Grand Tour, was drinking wine a little too abundantly, as was their habit. They invited him to join them, partly because of the democratic spirit that comes upon young men in a foreign land, when even the humblest of their countrymen seems nearer in station than a disapproving native, and partly because they found Ned almost as innately amusing as an authentic dwarf, but Ned declined. He had already sucked all the information from them that they had; it was their propensity for eager rumor that had given him the names of Shelley's local acquaintances, although none knew the name of Robert Walton's mysterious companion.

They did not take his refusal gracefully. One of the young aristocrats grabbed his arm as he attempted to leave. "Don't go, Master Knob," he said. "We're going whoring later–I'm sure that we can find you a midget, or a little girl, to suit your stature."

"That's very kind of you, milord," Ned said, speaking with conspicuous mildness, although he met the young man's bleary gaze with a basilisk stare. "But I've been down to the lower town already this evening, and I'm tired."

The fool was too drunk to take the hint provided by Ned's expression. "Hear that, fellows!" he said. "The little chap's already been a-whoring, and he's tired." The young man tightened his grip on Ned's right wrist.

Ned used his left hand to pluck the drunkard's hand away, squeezing the fingers so hard that the man's drink-flushed face turned ghastly white–but Ned smiled at the other members of the party as he said, with exaggerated softness: "I hope you have a good time, gentlemen."

He went directly to his bed, intending to be up early to make the trek to San Terenzo, to see what he could discover for himself about the group of like-minded men that seemed to be forming around the two English poets. Despite the remarks about consorting with *Carbonari* and fomenting revolution that the young gentlemen from Sussex had bandied about while laughing sardonically, Ned thought it perfectly possible that at least some of the men he had named in his report had come to Italy with none but literary interests in mind, and quite probable that all of them had far more interest in a potential scientific revolution than any petty political upheaval, but he knew that Gregory Temple would expect more details in any case. Indeed, he felt sure that Temple and his superiors would be very grateful for any information he could provide on the potentially seditious activities of "Jacobin exiles," because it would soothe the suspicions of his Parliamentary masters that his and Ned's present endeavors might be entirely futile. He frowned as he wondered exactly how he could fabricate some such details without causing any difficulties for Byron and Shelley additional to those that already haunted them.

Once he was in his bed, Ned found that he could not sleep, and not because his encounter with the young men from Sussex had been slightly discomfiting. His sense of anticipation was too teasing. This was not merely because he expected that his spying mission—which he so far proved rather dull—might suddenly become more thrilling, or even because the prospect of "renewing his acquaintance" with one of the great minds of his generation was so delicious, but because certain implications were beginning to sink in of what it might signify if Byron and Shelley really were intimately involved in the project that seemed to be taking shape in Robert Walton's rented house.

Like every other man in England who considered himself a connoisseur of Gothic fiction, Ned had read *Frankenstein*, which purported to be based on letters sent by one Robert Walton to his sister and a manuscript transmitted with one of those letters. Because "Robert Walton" was such a common name, Ned had at first regarded the fact that he had been sent to watch a man of that name as insignificant, but the sight of the equipment that was being imported into the house, and his awareness of what it might be used for, had quickly convinced him otherwise. He had already guessed that Walton's

mysterious companion must have been Victor Frankenstein–or the individual called by that name in the novel–
before he had any inkling of Shelley's potential involvement, but he had also heard it rumored in London,
long before Gregory Temple had sent him to Italy, that
Shelley was the author of *Frankenstein*. He had dismissed the rumor at the time, because he was well used
to the tactics employed by unscrupulous publishers to
boost the marketability of works they published anonymously, but now he was forced to consider the matter
anew.

Suppose, he thought, that there really as a connection between Shelley and Walton–that they had, in fact,
known one another for some time, and that it was Shelley and Byron who had persuaded the inventor of the resurrection process to resume his experiments. His first
success had obviously proved traumatic for the Swiss
scientist, who, if even part of the manuscript reproduced
in the novel was authentic, might well have suffered
some kind of delusional breakdown. In the meantime,
the exploitation of his discovery had been continued by
other hands–but now, it seemed, he was ready to begin
again. How secure, though, was his return to sanity and
resolution? And what had become of his first experimental subject: the very first "Grey Man?" These were the
thoughts that buzzed in Ned's head as he twisted and
turned on his pillow.

According to the gossip relayed with such relish by
the young gentlemen, the rumors circulating in Pisa regarding the "Byronic conspiracy" were ridiculously
wild. Some of the leaning tower's more credulous
neighbors alleged that the recent brawl had been caused
by their leading an armed insurrection, presumably on
behalf of the *Carbonari*, against the city gate. That was

certainly untrue, in Ned's judgment, but even the better-informed natives of Pisa seemed unprepared to accept that the gathering of the English company was what its members contended: a mere matter of assembling a company of literary men to found a new literary journal to provide a worthy showcase for their philosophically-inclined works. Given that Trelawny seemed to be an adventurer who had sought his fortune unsuccessfully in India, while Hay was an experienced military man, the explanation that Byron had put about did seem to be a trifle disingenuous.

Ned's Italian was still patchy, and he found it far easier to communicate with other English and French visitors than with the local population, so he was by no means ideally equipped to be a spy in these parts. His unsteady command of the tongue had, however, enabled him to understand that the gossips in Spezia devoted the greater part of their consideration to the imagined conspiracies of the Roman Church and the *Carbonari*, often mingling rumors of either sort with perennial whispers about notorious *banditti*. Despite San Terenzo's proximity to Spezia, and Lord Byron's frequent comings-and-goings in the *Bolivar*, no one in the immediate vicinity seemed to care a fig about Percy Shelley having taken up residence within comfortable walking distance of Spezia's harbor, and everyone seemed quite oblivious to the existence of Robert Walton–except for the other spy, who seemed to have been keeping watch on Walton's house as interestedly as Ned, albeit from the opposite side.

Spezia's "upper town" was much more generously distributed than the dense cluster of streets near the shore; it was arranged on a series of natural terraces on the jagged slope. Walton's house was set in a covert of its own, isolated from any other by at least 100 paces. The ledge on which it stood had once been a hive of industry, accommodating a small olive grove, which curled around the house on the eastern and northern sides, and a healthy herb garden as well as a rank of vines set against the wooded face of the hill, which reared up almost vertically 30 yards or so in rear of the building, but the war had put an end to its cultivation and the tiny estate had run wild while the house had stood empty for almost a decade. It was now very overgrown, the hedge along the road that ran past it having grown to more than seven feet in height. Ned's natural approach to the house from the hotel was on the eastern side, so he usually stationed himself in a gap in the hedge, from which he could see through the olive-trees. The other spy, by contrast, set himself up to the west, often positioning himself high on the slope at a point where it was not so steep, hiding behind a rock. Thus far, they had only caught glimpses of one another in the distance, but Ned was sure that the other man had marked his presence just as interestedly as he had marked the other man's.

Ned did not waste time wondering who his rival might be. Under the pressure of his insomnia, he did, however, waste time regretting that he did not have a copy of *Frankenstein* with him, and wishing that he had read it more attentively when he had borrowed its three volumes, one by one, from the circulating library. He had read the volumes swiftly and returned them quickly, in order to make the most of his subscription. That had, alas, been two full years before Sawney Ross had wandered into Jenny Paddock's gin-shop, so Ned had not had the slightest grounds for suspecting that the novel might be based on fact. Now, he cursed himself for the haziness of his memory of the text.

In the story, he knew, Frankenstein had died on Walton's ship in the Arctic, but that was obviously not true of the actual person on whom the character was based. The real man of science had vanished from sight, but his research notes must have been taken to Paris, where they had come into the custody of German Patou, then to Portugal, where Patou and Henri had conducted a considerable series of experiments but had failed to restore more than the most meager mental facilities to the vast majority of their resurrectees; nor had they enjoyed much greater success in that regard when they had transferred their operation to Purfleet. Had Frankenstein made any significant progress in the meantime? His single experiment had apparently been more successful than most of Patou's, although it might also have gone seriously awry, if the accusations labeled at the Grey Man featured by the novel were actually true rather than the result of Frankenstein's delirium or some ghost writer's penchant for melodrama. Had the originator any grounds to expect, or at least to hope, that his new venture would produce far better results than Patou's? If so...

Suppose, Ned thought, as he continued to turn over and over in his bed, his thoughts becoming wilder all the while, that he were able to insinuate himself into the conspiracy of English exiles. Suppose that the conspiracy extended much further than its presently-visible members, to include such "Jacobin scientists" as Humphry Davy, Joseph Priestley and Erasmus Darwin. Suppose that he could get himself onto Lord Byron's payroll, reporting to the conspiracy on the activities of the English secret service and *Civitas Solis*. What a player he might then become, instead of the pawn his employers presently considered him to be! And why should he not prefer the conspiracy mounted by Walton and Trelawny to those to which he was currently affiliated, if they already had a better version of the secret of resurrection and the apparatus to begin a new series of successful experiments? They might, after all, be the destined custodians of a glorious future in which death's sting was comprehensively drawn...

The man who now styled himself "Mortdieu" had evidently wrestled with the problem that had confounded his own maker, but his insider's view of it had apparently given him no advantage. Now that he and Patou had joined forces, they might be able to succeed where each had separately failed, but that depended on the *Outremort* having found a haven safe from fearful and prying eyes, and the material means to continue their research. That could not have been easy, Ned judged–and in the meantime, the original discoverer of resurrection might well have laboring with all his might to make further improvements in his process. Even if the Swiss scientist really had been vengefully harassed, as the published narrative implied, by his first experimental subject, the fact remained that the subject in question had obviously recovered more intelligence than any of Patou's subjects, save Mortdieu, and might well have offered Frankenstein a valuable clue to the means of generalizing that achievement...

Chapter Two
An Alliance of Spies

Eventually, sheer exhaustion forced Ned to be still. He finally dozed off, but his sleep was very light–fortunately so, as it turned out. Some little while after he drifted off into a quiet state, he heard a slight noise from the direction of his window.

Instead of sitting up and parting the curtains of his alcove in order that he might look towards the window, Ned remained exactly as he was, carefully feigning unconsciousness. He used his ears to measure what was happening.

Although his room was on the second floor of the hotel, Ned knew that its balcony was not inaccessible to a skillful climber, and that the shutters securing the window would not be difficult to unlatch from without. He listened to the tripping of the catch and the faint creak of the hinges as one batten of the shutter was drawn back. He heard the unobtrusive scrape of cloth on painted wood as the intruder slipped through the unglazed window, and the almost-imperceptible tread of slippered feet on the wooden floor.

Ned took firm hold of the dagger hidden beneath his pillow. Its blade was short, but that would not be to his disadvantage in the circumstances; the weapon would be easy to draw clear with a single fluid motion, ready for use. He had no idea whether the intruder was holding a weapon of his own, but he had to assume, for safety's sake, that he was, and that it would be ready to thrust home at a moment's notice.

Ned was not afraid, not because he had no respect for deadly weapons, but because he knew how ready other men were to underestimate him. Because he was only five feet tall, people who did not know him invariably assumed that he was both awkward and puny, but he was neither.

When the time came for him to move, he moved with great speed and great skill. He swept the other man's legs out from under him and had him flat on the ground within a second. The intruder's right arm was firmly pinned to the ground, and the point of Ned's knife was pressed to his throat.

It was only then that Ned ascertained that the intruder had, indeed, been carrying a weapon: there was still a stiletto clutched in his right hand.

"Drop it!" Ned ordered, in crude Italian.

The captive obeyed, and Ned picked the weapon up.

In the wake of a single reflexive convulsion, the intruder had made no further attempt to resist, and now seemed disposed to be cooperative.

"You have the advantage of me, Monsieur Knob," the supine man observed, in French.

The comment was ironic, and Ned was as displeased by its tone as its content. The remark told Ned that the other spy he had observed watching Robert Walton's house had succeeded where he had so far failed, in identifying his rival. Not only did his adversary know Ned's name; he also knew that Ned could speak French. To judge by his accent, French was not the intruder's first language, but Ned–much to his chagrin–could not identify the man's nationality from the inflection.

"Did you come to kill or to steal?" Ned asked, gruffly, also speaking in French.

"I merely came to talk, my friend," the other assured him, implausibly. "The time has come to form an alliance. Since you showed no sign of approaching me, however discreetly, I decided..." He broke off as Ned's left hand began rummaging inside his jacket, and sighed when the little man pulled out a sheet of paper.

There was too little light filtering through the unshuttered window to illuminate the paper, but Ned only had to touch it to divine that it was one of his letters. His fingers sought the broken seal, and contrived to identify the broken half. It was the letter to Henri de Belcamp, which he had given to the courier on the approach to the quay. The other letter did not seem to be in the spy's possession.

"I did not hurt the man from whom I took it," the spy was quick to say, "although he was certainly annoyed to be relieved of it, and swore vengeance, as these Italians are ever-ready to do. I hoped that I might be able to read it, but I could not decipher it–the code must be a subtle one."

"So you came to ask me to translate it for you," Ned guessed, "bringing your stiletto to provide an incentive."

"No, no, my friend," his rival assured him. "I came to discuss a mutually advantageous division of labor. We are in the same business, after all. We cannot be everywhere at once, and while both of us are stuck watching Walton take delivery of everything he needs to furnish his bomb factory, who knows what Milord Byron and his Carbonarist friends are plotting? We need to find out where the bombs will be placed, and by whom. I am no more English than French, as you can surely tell, and I cannot speak to milord's associates as you can–but I

23

have information that you do not, and there is much that might be gained by our working together."

"Who are you?" Ned growled.

"My name is Guido," his captive said. "It does not matter who sent me, any more than it matters who puts money in your purse. We are two of a kind–I know that because I know that you sent a second report by a different route, presumably to a different master, although I was not in a position to interrupt the galloping horse to make sure. If we are to sell what we know to the highest bidder, we would do better to combine forces and act together."

Ned made sure that Guido had no other weapons about his person before allowing him to get up. He gathered both knives and the stolen letter in his left hand in the meantime, then used his right to strike a match and light the candle by the bed. When he stood up, Guido towered over Ned by an entire foot. He was no weakling, despite his leanness, but he made no attempt to renew their brief struggle.

Given his black hair, olive complexion and pointed beard, Guido could easily have been taken for an Italian or a Spaniard, but Ned suspected that he might be from somewhere further east, perhaps as far as the bounds of the Ottoman Empire.

"What do you know that I do not?" Ned demanded, expecting that he might get a few nuggets of information by way of inducement to enter into a compact.

"I know all about the boat," Guido replied, shortly.

Ned knew better than to confess ignorance by saying: "What boat?" Instead, he said: "I know all about the *Bolivar*'s movements." In fact, all he knew was that *Bolivar* was the name of Byron's yacht, and that it sometime docked in Spezia.

"Not the *Bolivar*," Guido countered. "The *Don Juan*. She set out from Genoa on May 10, but was not delivered to Lerici until May 12, having been driven back by bad weather. Shelley and Williams sailed out to the Isola del Tino on May 18. Byron brought the *Bolivar* to Lerici to meet the *Don Juan* on the June 13, and fired six cannon-shots by way of salute. Both vessels then set sail for Leghorn, where the *Don Juan* was put in for modifications, including a false stem and stern. She was brought to San Terenzo today, very discreetly; she is moored within 100 yards of Casa Magni at this moment."

"All that may be true," Ned conceded, "but I cannot see its relevance."

"Can you not?" Guido asked, raising a dark eyebrow. "I don't know exactly how the boat has been modified, or for what purpose, but I do not think that Monsieur Shelley is any common smuggler. I would dearly like to know what cargo it is intended to carry, and to what destination—you might be better able to find that out than I am. In order to ascertain all this, I had to leave you to watch Walton's house by yourself for a considerable period. Only you can tell me if anything significant occurred during that time."

"Indeed," said Ned, in a neutral tone. "What, exactly, are you proposing?"

"I speak Italian better than you do, and I am far better equipped to obtain information from Walton's neighbors and anyone making deliveries to his house. You, on the other hand, speak English better than I do, and are thus better equipped to obtain information from the wives and servants Shelley and Williams brought with them. Shelley's wife is confined to her bed, having fallen victim to a fever in the wake of a miscarriage; Madame Williams and the servants are in state of anguish. If Shelley and Williams are planning another expedition, I suspect that they will not be able to depart without an argument. What I propose is that I prowl around the Walton house for the next day or two, while you make inquiries at Casa Magni, and that we pool the information we glean."

This fitted in very well with the plan Ned had already made, but he was careful to give the appearance of being dubious. "I have been ordered to keep close watch on Walton's house," he said. "I need to find out more about his guest."

"I know that," Guido retorted. "I know, too, that you have been given Trelawny's name. You know that the conspiracy in which Walton, Shelley and Trelawny are involved extends much further than Spezia. One or other of your masters might send help, once they know that—but one, at least, will not receive your report in good time. I am already here—also alone, for the time being. Why should we not help one another?"

"That depends who your master is," Ned said, bluntly.

"Have I asked you to name yours?" the other retorted. "What does it matter? Neither of us is a common soldier, and if either of us is bound by oath to a nation, he is not the kind of man to offer oaths with any great sincerity."

Ned did not bother to complain about that unflattering estimation. "You mentioned bomb-making," he said. "Is that what you imagine Walton and his companion to be doing in their laboratory?"

"If they are working for the *Carbonari*," Guido said, "that is what they are highly likely to be doing. Infernal machines have become an important, if direly unreliable, instrument of modern politics. There is a new chemistry in the making, thanks to Messieurs Lavoisier and Priestley, and a new science of electricity too, thanks to Messieurs Galvani and Volta. Masters of artillery and ordnance all over Europe are taking a very keen interest in these new sciences. There are revolutions in progress in Spain and Portugal, while wars of unification are bubbling up in Germany and Italy. The Ottoman Empire will likely unravel completely if the Greeks win their independence, and the Americas are already in turmoil. Any man who can manufacture a more powerful explosive, or one subject to safer and more reliable detonation, is in a position to make a vast fortune."

"And that is what Walton's companion is doing with his apparatus, in your opinion?"

"I do not pretend to know the composition of all the compounds he has been importing by the barrel," Guido said, "but I know that your Monsieur Davy has used electricity to isolate new elements, and that some of them are so volatile that they explode in sudden contact with water. As you must know, Monsieur Walton's friend has a great many Voltaic piles at his disposal."

"Do you know his name?" Ned asked.

"Perhaps," was the guarded reply. "Do you?"

"Not for certain," Ned parried.

"Well?" the other demanded, abruptly. "What do you have to say to my proposition?"

Ned shrugged his shoulders. "I say yes," he said, "while reserving my judgment as to what you might have done had I not disarmed you as you drew nigh to my bed."

"You did not stab me," was Guido's response to that, "for which I am duly grateful. You have my word that I shall not attempt any violence against you, and will defend you vigorously if anyone should attack us while we go about our work. I will swear a blood oath to that effect if you require it."

Ned handed back the stiletto, but kept the stolen letter. "I'll go to Casa Magni tomorrow," he said, "while you keep watch on Walton. I'll find you when I have information to exchange–but you had best have something solid to offer me, for everything you've told me thus far is mere vapor."

"Agreed," said the rival spy, promptly, apparently having no suspicion of the fact that he had received no concession at all. "*Bonsoir, mon ami.*" He moved swiftly back to the window, and made his exit the same way he had come in.

Ned closed the shutter and went back to bed, even though he knew that he would not find sleep again before it was time to rise.

Henri will not be pleased when he finds out that his courier has been robbed, he thought, as he began turning this way and that on his pillow for a second time. *That will serve to arouse his interest more fully than the actual message I had sent. I shall wait until the next scheduled rendezvous to repeat the information–by which time I might have a great deal more to say... or a great deal less.*

Chapter Three
At Casa Magni

The first thing Ned Knob did on reaching San Terenzo was to make his way down to the shoreline so that he might approach Casa Magni along the strand, on the lookout for the *Don Juan*. There were dozens of small boats pulled up on to the shore, some with masts and some without, and a great many small huts built to contain fishing-tackle and apparatus for repairing timbers and canvas. These afforded him abundant cover as he approached the house that Shelley and Williams had rented.

Casa Magni was somewhat dilapidated, like many of the larger houses on the once-prosperous shore that had lost their former occupants to the effects of Napoleon's war. There had been no major battles fought in the vicinity, so Spezia and San Terenzo were unmarked by the scars of cannon-fire, which now pockmarked so many European towns and villages, but the lingering effects of the war were not entirely hidden beneath the surface. The absence of violent defacement only meant that the subtler ravages of long neglect became more evident, putting a face to the dispirited quality of post-war existence. Seven years after Bonaparte's fall, this region was still stunned, its convalescence hardly begun. The mere sight of Casa Magni would have made that obvious to the discerning eye, even had the mind behind the eye not known that the house had been rented to the English, whose tourist swarms had returned to their old haunts in greater numbers than before, exerting their strange cultural pressure with renewed force.

Ned had no difficulty at all identifying the *Don Juan* among the other boats berthed close to the house, although a tarpaulin had been placed to mask the place on her hull where the name had been painted. She was the only brand-new vessel to be seen on this relatively quiet stretch of shore. It was obvious that corrective work had been carried out on her hull, in spite of the fact that her timbers had scarcely been exposed to the sea. Even more remarkably, a large piece of canvas had been cut out of her brand new sail and replaced. Ned guessed that her name had been painted there by the boat-builder, but that Shelley had demanded its removal. If Guido knew that, it must have greatly increased his suspicion regarding the purpose for which the vessel was intended.

As Ned came close to the boat, moved by curiosity, three men emerged from her cabin on to the aft deck. Ned immediately recognized one of the three as Robert Walton, and took even greater care to remain hidden thereafter; he knew that Walton had had numerous opportunities to catch sight of him while he was watching the house through the olive grove. The second man in clear view was unknown to Ned, and the third man was partly obscured by the mast. Ned had seen Shelley in London more than once, but only from a moderate distance; he had to creep even closer and find a better angle before he could be sure that the third man was, indeed, the celebrated poet.

To judge by their gestures, the three were arguing, though not very violently. Their body language suggested that Shelley, at least might have raised his voice to emphasize his case, but the other two seemed very anxious that he should keep his voice as low as theirs–this despite the fact that they were in a land where few would understand them if they shouted in English, which was certainly their native tongue.

Ned could only make out fragmentary phrases, but he gathered quickly enough that Walton and the other man were allied against Shelley, but more in sorrow than in anger. They were, apparently, intent on rejecting some proposal he had put to them or some demand that he had made that was contrary to a previous agreement, but they seemed to be doing so on someone else's behalf rather than their own. They seemed sympathetic to his distress, but were nevertheless unable or undisposed to make concessions to his request. The poet seemed to be on the brink of losing his temper, although he was struggling to control himself. He made more than one reference to his wife being ill, but Ned was unable to judge the exact relevance of that fact to the argument. His opponents were quite obdurate, though, despite their determination to soothe him with apologies and sincere regrets. In the end, they appeared to win his reluctant consent to whatever it was had previously been agreed.

Shelley evidently felt badly enough about the outcome of the argument to remain on the boat when his two companions jumped down to the shore and marched off, although their triumph in their petty victory was distinctly muted. At first, the poet stood in the stern watching them go, but then he stepped back towards the mast, apparently feeling very weary. He reached out a hand and managed to support himself for a minute or so, while the other two Englishmen passed out of sight. Then he slowly folded to his knees, eventually collapsing entirely, out of Ned's sight.

Ned had been instructed by Gregory Temple not to reveal himself to Robert Walton and his companion, but he had received no specific order in respect of Percy Shelley. Even if he had, it would not have stopped him going to the poet's aid. He did not hesitate for a second before running forward. He clambered up on to the *Don Juan*'s deck and dropped to his knees beside the stricken man.

Shelley was still breathing, but he was unconscious. He had fallen face-forwards, and Ned could see that the scab on an old wound on the back of his head had been breached by internal pressure. The fluid leaking from the breach had more yellow in it than red. Ned felt the poet's neck, and found the flesh hot. Then he measured Shelley's pulse, which was rapid.

The argument upset him more than he would consent to reveal to his friends, Ned thought, *but he must already have been ill, and was striving to conceal that too. Is this the wound he sustained in the brawl in which Masi was hurt? If so, it should have healed long ago—but if it ever did, it has now taken a turn for the worse and has begun to fester.*

Ned put his arms under Shelley's body and braced himself. The poet would have been a featherweight to Ned's once-beloved Pretty Molly, but was quite a burden to a man of his own size. Even so, he lifted the inert body up and carried it to the side of the boat. It was not easy to maneuver it down to the ground, but he managed to do it, and then set off towards the house at a steady walk. He managed to ring the bell without having to set his burden down.

The door was opened soon enough by a female servant. The look of astonishment that crossed her face when she looked down at the top of Ned's battered hat turned to horror when she saw what the little man was carrying. She let loose a little scream, and cried for help.

The only help that arrived was a sullen manservant; Walton and his companion obviously had not come into the house.

"We need to get him to bed immediately," Ned declared, authoritatively. "If one of you will show me the way, the other must fetch a doctor. If you have a kettle on the boil, you might fill a bowl with hot water and bring it to me, with some carbolic soap. An old wound on his head has opened, and it needs cleaning."

The manservant immediately stiffened, resentful of Ned's commanding tone, but he could obviously see the necessity of following Ned's advice. "Show the boy where the master's bedroom is, Jenny," he said to the maidservant. "I'll saddle a horse and ride to Pisa to fetch Dr. Todd."

"Yes, Mr. Gregory," Jenny replied.

"Is there no one closer?" Ned was quick to ask. "Surely there's a doctor in Spezia, if there's none in San Terenzo itself–the matter may be too urgent to allow you to prefer an Englishman."

The manservant was about to deny that there was a doctor in Spezia, but the girl chipped in: "I've heard the master say that the man staying with Mr. Walton knows more than any mere physician."

Gregory's expression became even more clouded, but all he said was: "I'll do what I can." As he strode off, the maidservant beckoned Ned toward the stairway.

Ned frowned at the necessity of climbing the stairs, but he did as he was bid, and was eventually able to lay Shelley's body down on a bed in a large room whose thick curtains were still closed, keeping the daylight at bay.

"The mistress is sick abed," Jenny told him, plaintively, "and Mrs. Williams has gone to Pisa with her husband. There's no one to help you but me–but there's a kettle in the kitchen."

"Put it on to boil," Ned said. "In the meantime, fetch me a jug of cold water and a glass," Ned said, "I think we might be able to revive him."

The maidservant raced away.

In the event, Shelley began to stir even before the water-jug arrived, and when Ned put a glass to the poet's lips, he was able to sit up. The poet did not look at Ned, though–it was the fluttering maidservant who caught his eye. Shelley frowned, and murmured: "You were ordered not to leave Mary's side, Jenny." The effort was too much, though, and he sank back on to the pillow, closing his eyes. He seemed far younger than his years– hardly more than a child–and his near-feminine beauty was strangely exaggerated by his distress.

The girl retreated, babbling apologies.

"Boil the water first," Ned called after her, "and fetch the carbolic soap." Then he turned back to the poet. "She was not at fault, sir," he said. "For the moment, your need is even more urgent than your wife's. The wound on your head has turned bad."

Shelley was still confused, but he opened his eyes again and peered at Ned through the gloom. "Is that you, Patou?" he whispered.

Ned controlled his astonishment. The opening seemed too promising to be neglected. "I am not Germain Patou," he said, smoothly, "although I had the honor of meeting him once, and I understand how the confusion might have arisen."

"You've met Patou?" Shelley murmured, still battling with confusion. "Where?"

34

"In London," Ned replied. "I've seen you there too, Mr. Shelley, on three separate occasions, but we were never introduced."

Shelley raised himself up to take another sip of water, propping himself up on his elbow so that he could stare at Ned more intently. His brow was furrowed with concentration. The effort seemed to help him, and his gaze became clearer.

"The Royal Institution," he said, eventually. "At Mr. Davy's lectures–twice, I believe."

Ned was genuinely impressed. Men of his extraordinarily short stature were a rarity at the meetings in question, always likely to attract more attention than individuals of ordinary height; even so, he was immensely flattered by the fact that he had been noticed by Percy Shelley. "That's true, sir," he said. "I suppose you noticed my resemblance to Monsieur Patou, if you are acquainted with him. The third occasion was one of Mr. Coleridge's lectures."

Shelley was still concentrating hard, perhaps focusing his thoughts as a defense against falling unconscious again. "In that case," he whispered, "there was a fourth occasion, which you have forgotten. You were in court when Tom Wooler was prosecuted for seditious libel in 1817. I marked you then, as a bantam who seemed ready to tear that rogue Shepherd limb from limb, for all that he outweighed you by several stones."

That took Ned's breath away. "I did not see you, sir," he admitted. "The public gallery was crowded that day, and I was thrown out for heckling the prosecutor too loudly. I missed Tom's speech in his own defense."

"It was historic," Shelley said. "I'm pleased to make your acquaintance again, if we might be said to be acquainted when I have no idea what your name is."

"I'm Edward Knob, sir, at your service," Ned said, automatically.

Shelley looked around, as if noticing for the first time where he was. "Have I been here long?" he asked. "I seem to remember that I was on the boat with Walton and Taaffe."

"You fainted, sir," Ned said. "I happened to be passing, saw you fall and carried you to the nearest house–which, it seems, is your own."

"*You* carried me?" the poet whispered, and then apparently felt ashamed of his own incredulity. "Well, sir," he added, "I'm grateful to you. I received a blow to the head some months ago. It seemed to get better, but it was never entirely right. It became vaguely troublesome again a few days ago, but the pain did not flare up until I was on the boat. It was a silly thing, to begin with–some fool of an officer in the Tuscan Light Horse picked a quarrel, and it blew up out of all proportion. I was sure that the headache would fade away again, and I dared not claim that I was suffering–poor Mary in a much worse state than I am."

Ned did not trust that judgment, although he understood that Shelley might have had little or no idea how his wound was faring, positioned as it was. "Was your injury examined by a doctor, sir?" he asked.

"Todd glanced at it, but he was more concerned about one of my companions, who was slashed in the face and bled fearfully."

"He should have done more than glance, sir," Ned opined. "The fact that wound has become infected probably has nothing to do with his neglect, though. Have you suffered another blow more recently?"

"Yes," Shelley admitted. "I lost my balance when Williams and I took the boat out to a nearby islet. I'm not much of as sailor yet, I fear. It was nothing–or seemed so."

"It might have been, had it not been for the earlier wound. I can clean it myself, if you'll permit, but I took the liberty of sending your manservant for a doctor, and told him that the matter was urgent. I hope he will not go all the way to Pisa if there is a doctor nearer at hand. Your Dr. Todd certainly would not be able to get here before nightfall, and would likely be delayed until tomorrow."

Shelley felt the back of his had with the fingers of his right hand, and winced. "Damn," he said, softly. "On the other hand, this might change..." He stopped, and looked at Ned again, studying him carefully.

"You're right, sir, in your estimation of me," Ned said, cheerfully. "I'm not a gentleman, alas–but I'm a man bent on self-education, and this is the 19th century. There's no reason why a man like me can't take the Grand Tour in his own fashion, just as his betters have been doing for a century and more. And there's no reason, too, why a man who has knowingly been in the same lecture-hall as Percy Shelley on three different occasions wouldn't take an interest in his welfare as well as his work. When I said that I happened to be passing, I wasn't entirely honest. The fact is that I came to see Casa Magni because I heard that the author of *Prometheus Unbound* was here–but I swear to you, sir, that I would not have dreamed of disturbing you had I not seen that you needed succor. You are a great man, in my opinion, and I would have been well content to catch a glimpse of you in the distance." He laid on the flattery with the utmost care, because he was perfectly sincere in his judgment of Shelley's worth as a radical poet.

"If you know me by repute," Shelley murmured, "and have read my work, you know that you have no need to apologize to me for not having been born a gentleman. We seem to have interests and sentiments in common, Mr. Knob, and I am glad to meet you in person, so far from home. Are you staying in Spezia, at the English hotel?"

Ned smiled at the assumption. "Yes sir," he said. "That is the ritual, is it not? We all stay in the *English hotel*, in the space marked out for us. It makes it easier for the townspeople to pretend that we do not really exist–that we inhabit some parallel world whose dimensions overlap with theirs, but somehow fails to intersect with it." He cursed himself silently for trying too hard to impress, even though his listener was sick and weak.

Shelley did not seem to mind at all. "Even here," the poet said, mildly, "one cannot fall down without being picked up to be a philosopher. You mistake the people though. They do not pretend that we do not exist, nor do the resent our presence. They are reserved by nature, and the legacy of the war has made them very careful. You might appreciate their discretion, if..." He broke off then, but not because he was too weak to continue. After a momentary pause, he resumed: "Thank you for bringing me home, Mr. Knob. I am in your debt."

"Never, sir," Ned was quick to say. "I remain in yours, as will every thinking man for centuries to come."

"You're too kind," Shelley said, giving the phrase a more earnest emphasis than was usually applied to it.

"If I might ask..." Ned began–but he did not get a chance to formulate his question. The bedroom door burst open at that moment, and Robert Walton strode in.

Chapter Four
The Man of Science

Walton was alone. Ned deduced that the manservant had encountered him and his companion on their way up the hill, and that Walton had sent Taaffe on up the hill to his own house, while he returned to see to Shelley.

As soon as he caught sight of Ned, Walton stopped dead. Ned judged that his earlier anxieties had been well-founded; Walton had indeed caught glimpses of him in the vicinity of his house. He could not know for sure that Ned had been spying on him, but he certainly suspected it.

"I'm sorry, Robert," Shelley murmured, while Walton was still dumbstruck. "I didn't realize..."

"Don't try to talk," Walton cut in, speaking more harshly than the ostensible sentiment of his words demanded. "Who is this man?"

"Edward Knob, sir, at your service," Ned was quick to say. "I know Mr. Shelley slightly, from brief acquaintance in London as well as admiration for his work. I'm staying at the English hotel in Spezia..."

"I've seen you there," Walton said, interrupting brusquely.

"Yes," Ned said, calmly. "You're the gentleman who lives in the house behind the olive grove. It's a shame, isn't it, that the terrace has been neglected of late. Perhaps you intend to restore its fortunes?"

"That's none of your business," Walton said, "and I'd be obliged if you'd keep away in future. I took that house in order to avoid all contact with tourists and locals alike."

"Don't be so harsh, Robert," Shelley said. "The man helped me. I know him–I saw him at Tom Wooler's trial, and he attends Davy's lectures."

The latter item of information did not diminish Walton's suspicions in the least. "You do not know him well enough to be sure of what he is doing here," Walton said, bluntly. "I do not accuse him of being a spy, but..."

Knowing that he was about to be more-or-less politely dismissed, and that Walton would try to make quite sure that he was never readmitted to Casa Magni, Ned decided to take a gamble.

"In fact, sir," he said, addressing himself to Shelley, "I suppose I *am* a spy, of sorts, although I am not here to spy on you. Everything I have told you is true, but I omitted to mention that I am in the employ of the government, directly answerable to Gregory Temple, of whom you might have heard."

"Temple!" Shelley exclaimed. "Isn't that..."

"The man who traveled with us on the night-coach to Dover some little while ago," Walton finished for him. "If he was watching us then, he put on a very good performance of utter disinterest." He frowned deeply. Ned was startled by the news that Gregory Temple had traveled on a coach with Shelley and Walton, but he had more urgent concerns on his mind than wondering whether the detective had really been as uninterested in his fellow passengers as he had seemed. The seafarer's mind was obviously working hard on the calculation of that probability, though.

Ned had to follow up on his decision. There seemed to be only one course of action open to him that might lead to considerable profit, and the knowledge that there was another spy interested in Walton and Shelley's project increased his sense of urgency. "There are some things you need to know, sir," he said, still speaking to the poet rather than the adventurer. "I mentioned to you just now that I met Germain Patou in London. I did not mention that I met him in the company of a *Grey Man*. I subsequently observed him in the process of resurrecting a man from the dead, and had the privilege thereafter of a brief interview with General Mortdieu. Mr. Walton has observed me taking an interest in his house, but he may not have observed the other man doing likewise. I cannot be sure, but it is possible that the other man is in the employ of the Sultan of Turkey; at any rate, he seems to believe that the research in which Mr. Walton's colleague is engaged is directed to the manufacture of some new explosive. I, of course, think differently."

The effect of this speech was, as Ned had anticipated, quite electrifying. Both men looked at him in frank amazement, mingled with desperate anxiety.

"Gregory Temple knows all this?" Walton whispered, his face having become very pallid. "And the English Parliament is sending spies to watch on us!"

Shelley's face was still flushed, and his eyes, already bright with fever, took on a new fire. "The Turks are watching us?" he said, incredulously. "They think we are manufacturing infernal machines?"

"I cannot be sure that the Turks sent him," Ned said, scrupulously, "but if not..."

"More likely the Italians," Walton growled. "I *knew* that Tuscan cavalryman was acting under orders..."

41

Shelley had already moved on. "Where is Patou now?" he demanded, excitedly, reaching out as if to grab Ned's sleeve, although he checked the impulse as soon as he realized what he was doing.

"I don't know," Ned told him. Looking up at Walton, he added: "Gregory Temple knows what Patou has accomplished and has seen the other Grey Men who were revived in London, but he knows little more than that. He sent me here to investigate a rumor, but I doubt that Parliament knows anything about it." He turned back to Shelley, thinking it more urgently necessary to elaborate his earlier reply. "I don't know where Patou and Mortdieu went when the *Outremort* sailed away from England, but their intention was to seek a quiet haven where they might establish a small colony. They probably headed for the Caribbean, but they might have decided to make their way to the Pacific."

"If the English police and the Turks are both on our track..." Shelley began.

Walton cut him off again. "Say no more, Percy," the seafarer instructed him, gruffly. "We must keep what secrets we still have."

"It is too late for that," Ned told him, gently. "Whoever sent the other spy may not know the truth, although it is entirely possible that his talk of bombs is deliberately deceptive, but Gregory Temple is not the only one who knows what your collaborator has accomplished. If the publication of a garish version of his apologia in the form of a Gothic novel was intended to deflect suspicion, the ploy failed. Any hope you might have cherished of resuming experiments in resurrection secretly was probably doomed from the start."

"We have to get away from here," Shelley said, in a low voice. "No matter how direly unsatisfactory the *Don*

Juan and my sailing skills may be, or how much more time and equipment our volatile friend thinks he needs, we must act without delay. Byron must be told to bring the *Bolivar*."

"Say no more!" Walton repeated. "I will show this man out." He took a step forward, apparently more intent on throwing Ned out than showing him out. Ned instinctively braced himself, although he had no intention of putting up a fight.

"You shall not lay a finger on him, Robert," Shelley said, with a slight hiss of anger in his voice. "This is my house, and the man came to my aid. I know him. I am prepared to swear that he was not at Tom Wooler's trial as a government agent. He may be in Temple's employ now, but he is not our enemy, else he would not have told us all this."

"I am certainly not your enemy, sir," Ned said, eager to confirm the fact, "and I think that you might find more friends than you know, if you care to stay here."

"Alas," Shelley said, in a low voice, "we already have more enemies than *you* know. Suspicious Turks fearful of Lord Byron's intentions are the least of our worries. Can you be certain that the *Outremort* did not head for the Mediterranean?"

"No, I can't," Ned admitted. "That was not Patou's intention, but if General Mortdieu is the man I took him to be..."

"No Grey Man is the man his dearest friends once took him to be, it seems," Shelley said mournfully. "Did you, by any chance, encounter one in London named John?"

"This is foolish," Walton complained. The expression on his face implied that it was not Shelley's question that had upset him, but some other thought or expectation. Ned had guessed what his particular anxiety must be before the door opened again, to admit Shelley's manservant and a second man. The manservant was carrying the bowl of hot water that Ned had requested, but he made no move to give it to Ned; indeed, he seemed determined to hold on to it.

Ned had only caught fleeting glimpses of Walton's mysterious house-guest, but he had no doubt at all as to the identity of the man who came in behind the servant. This, he knew, was the greatest inventor of the 19th century: the modern Prometheus who had begun the conquest of death. The modern Prometheus was not, however, an imposing sight at present. It was obvious that he had once been handsome, and Ned knew that he could not be more than 30 years old, but his features had been rough-hewn by strain and he was showing signs of premature aging. He was the very image of a man not yet recovered from some long and taxing illness or some profound and enduring anguish. There was a touch of Bedlam about him; his eyes were haunted and his hands tremulous.

The man of science seemed more anxious about Shelley's condition than Shelley was–but not, Ned judged, because he feared the imminent loss to the world of a great poet. The modern Prometheus seemed to be anxious for himself, afraid of the pressure that Shelley's illness, if it were serious, might bring to bear on him. He seemed, to Ned's curious eyes, to be *extremely* anxious about the possibility of being forced to action by Shelley's misfortune.

If Robert Walton, Lord Byron and their co-conspirators believed that Victor Frankenstein was yet ready to resume his experiments with due mental objectivity and clinical efficiency, Ned concluded, they were reckless optimists. This seemed to Ned to be a man un-ready for anything at all: a man still firmly in the grip of an ongoing nervous complaint that had just taken the latest of many turns for the worse.

The newcomer barely glanced at Ned as he went to the bed and attempted to put on a show of examining his patient. The tremulous hands made a tentative gesture towards Shelley's head, and the poet obligingly turned round to display the renewed wound–but the man who knew more than any mere physician barely glanced at it before stepping away, biting his lip. "If that infection should spread to your brain," he muttered, in faintly-accented English, "the consequences would be serious. If the skull is actually fractured...."

"I do not think the skull is fractured, sir," Ned said, quietly. "The infection needs to be contained, though, if possible. The wound must be properly cleaned and dressed, and the patient must rest thereafter."

"It's not serious, Victor," Shelley put in, addressing the nervous man of science. "I wish you would go to see Mary, though. I fear that her condition may be considerably worse than worse than mine. That's why..."

"I told Walton and Taaffe that I cannot do anything more for your wife," Frankenstein said, petulantly, "and certainly cannot do anything for her if... but yes, when I've cleaned and dressed your injury, I'll look in on Mary, although I'm certain that she won't be glad to see me, and I'll do whatever I can to make her more comfortable. That's all I can do, for the time being, no matter what happens. I can make no promises to you, either, on your own behalf. Patou went at the business with all the reckless force of a steam engine, it seems, and it did far more harm than good. I need to be careful."

"There comes a point," Shelley stated, quietly, "when there is no more harm to be done, saved by pusillanimous inaction."

Ned had deduced by now what the argument on the boat had been about. "If you will pardon me for continuing to play the spy, gentlemen," he said, "there is a question I still need to ask you. It's evident that you are all perfectly familiar with Monsieur Patou, but do you know the man who brought him to London, and directed his operation there?"

All three pairs of eyes were turned to him, although Ned was convinced that the thoughts behind them were still elsewhere. "Are you referring to the Comte?" Shelley said.

"Yes," Ned replied. "He is usually a Comte in Paris, although he is not always the same one. In London, he plays a different part, and he has other guises for use in Germany and Australia. I know that he is not involved in your own project, but I firmly believe that he would be more than ready to take an interest in it. If you need a useful friend, he..." He left the sentence dangling.

"The reckless force of a steam engine," Frankenstein repeated, grimly. "Patou, I think, was merely caught up in the toils of the mechanism. Lord Byron..."

"*Say no more, God damn it!*" This time, Walton barked the phrase as an order, with all the force of a ship's master. "Whether this wretched dwarf is the King's spy or some mischief-making imp strayed from Satan's kingdom, he has sown abundant seeds of worry and potential discord in our midst. Whatever we are to do, we must first get rid of him."

Shelley seemed disposed to disagree fervently, but Ned raised a hand to forestall his intervention. "Captain Walton is right, sir, at least for the moment," he said, politely. "You cannot trust me fully, since I am admittedly in the employ of Gregory Temple. I can understand, too, why you might be unready to trust our mutual friend the Comte–but if, as you say, you have more enemies than I know, you might be well advised to seek further assistance from those most sympathetic to your cause. I shall go now, but I will come back, if you will grant me permission, when your wound has been properly dressed and you have had a chance to discuss the matter."

He paused until Shelley nodded to give him the permission he had requested, and then continued: "In the meantime, I might be able to do you one small service by removing the Turks from the list of your potential enemies. The other spy who has been watching your house may well have followed your friend here from Walton's house. If so, I shall seek him out. I'll do my very best to persuade him that you are not, in fact, engaged in the manufacture of explosives, and that you have no hostile intentions in respect of the Ottoman masters of Greece or anyone else."

Walton and Frankenstein were still looking at Ned with alarm and frank distrust. Shelley, on the other hand, seemed to be clinging stubbornly to the good opinion he had formed in advance of the unexpected cataract of revelations. "Thank you for your kind assistance, Mr. Knob," the poet said, formally. "I shall look forward to seeing you again. Gregory will show you out."

Gregory scowled, but set down the bowl and gestured towards the door. Ned went lightly down the stairs ahead of the manservant, and allowed himself to be ushered out of the door that let out on to the road behind the house. He went unreluctantly, feeling that he had set the stage well enough for another, hopefully more productive, encounter.

Chapter Five
The Skirmish on the Strand

Ned had little difficulty locating the man who called himself Guido, who had indeed followed the man of science from Walton's house, and was now inspecting the *Don Juan* very carefully. He saw Ned coming towards him, and made no particular attempt to hide himself. On the slope that led down to the strand, however, 100 yards behind Guido, another person was trying as best he could to conceal himself, although the cover offered by the desiccated bushes was not quite adequate to the task. Ned did his best to hide the fact that he had seen this new spy from both Guido and the man in question.

"They should not have hired a fool like Roberts to build her," Guido observed, as Ned drew near. "The English are so stupid, always preferring their own countrymen, however inept, to local craftsmen. This vessel is not suitable for pleasure-trips within the gulf, let alone for carrying armaments all the way around the boot of Italy to the Greek islands."

"That is not her purpose," Ned said. "I have spoken to Shelley, and I am certain that he has no intention of doing anything so silly. If ever Lord Byron decides to lend material aid to the Greeks in their war of independence, he will take a more direct route. For the moment, he has other concerns in mind."

"The *Carbonari*, you mean?" Guido guessed, giving the impression that he would not mind at all if Byron's mind were focused on Italy's domestic problems.

The bright daylight gave Ned a much better opportunity to measure his adversary than he had had the previous night, but he could not find any tell-tale sign to indicate whether his inference that Guido was a Turkish spy was correct. It remained possible that he had been sent by the Spanish authorities, who had cause enough to be anxious about their own revolutionaries and the possibility of their gaining foreign support, but Ned still suspected that he had come from the east rather than the west. "No," Ned said. "Shelley and his friends are not involved in anything of immediate interest to the *Carbonari*. What concerns them at present is a private and personal matter, with no political implications." That was not entirely true, of course, but Ned felt perfectly justified in giving a narrow meaning to the "political implications" of the project in which Shelley and Byron had involved themselves.

"You're telling me that I'm wasting my time here," Guido said, skeptically. "You know that I can't take your word for that. We're pooling information, remember. I need to hear something useful, something new, if we're to continue our friendly association."

"I don't know who you're working for," Ned said, in a neutral tone, "but I feel confident that I don't have anything to tell you that would be useful to them."

"Why don't you let me be the judge of that?" Guido said, instead of responding to Ned's tacit information to name his employers.

Ned sighed. "You were right about the boat having been modified," he said, nodding his head in the direction of the *Don Juan* "but you must have seen enough by now to know that it was a mere matter of correcting faults of construction. The boat has not been adapted for smuggling anything."

"To speak of correction is overgenerous," Guido said, gesturing contemptuously at the *Don Juan*. "The vessel is a death-trap. The Mediterranean has the reputation of being placid, by comparison with the Atlantic, but the Ligurian Sea can be exceedingly treacherous. I agree with you, though–the adaptations were not made with the purpose I suspected."

"Shelley is not in need of any further death-traps at present," Ned told him. "He and his wife are both ill. Whatever plans he and his friends had in hand this morning will have to be shelved for the time being. The cavalry officer who was sent by the authorities in Pisa to put a spoke in their wheel succeeded all to well–the wound he inflicted on Shelley has been reopened and the injury has become serious."

"He seems likely to die himself," Guido observed. "These Italian hot-heads always take such projects a little too far. It would be amusing if the affair were to escalate into a vendetta, but this is not Sicily, and Masi was, as you say, acting under orders–however ineptly. Will Walton's associate be able to save Shelley's life, do you think?"

That, Ned knew, was the crux of the matter. What he did not know was whether Guido knew, or suspected, how exactly crucial it was. He glanced surreptitiously at the bushes on the slope, but he could not make out any detail of the person watching them, save that he was dressed in drab grey clothes, with a broad-brimmed hat pulled down over his brows and a scarf masking the lower part of his face. Given the scarf, and the gaucherie of his attempt to hide himself, the big man might as well have been carrying a flag bearing the word SPY, but there was something about him that unsettled Ned.

"They told me that they had more enemies than I knew," Ned told his immediate rival, risking one more small revelation in the hope of obtaining something in return. "Do you, perchance, know of any enemies they have, apart from you?"

"I am no one's enemy, my friend," was the reply he got. "But I do know of at least other party which might be ill-disposed toward Walton's companion. Circumstances sometimes conspire to set the most virtuous of men at one another's throats. Do *you*, perchance, know who the man on the slope might be, who is watching us at this moment? His presence seems to be disturbing you."

Ned cursed his own carelessness silently, but contented himself with replying: "I don't believe that I've ever seen him before, although it's difficult to be sure while he's muffled up like that–but there is something disconcerting about him, is there not?"

"Yes, there is," Guido agreed. "He followed me from Walton's house, as furtively as he could, but he's far too awkward to be unobtrusive. Even had he been a tiny mouse like you, I'd have seen him easily enough. Given that he's so bulky as well as so clumsy, and so carefully wrapped up in spite of the summer heat, I would have had to be blind and stupid not to be aware of his proximity. Is *he* one of the enemies of whom your countrymen are fearful, do you suppose?"

"I don't know," Ned said. "Shall we follow him home and sneak into his bedroom tonight, daggers in hand, to propose that we all join forces?"

Guido laughed. "I like you, my friend," he said, "despite your reluctance to share what you know."

"This business is becoming far too complicated for my simple tastes," Ned told him. "When too many spies become involved in a matter, they're bound to waste their time fencing with one another, as we are doing now." So saying, he turned round, intending to march straight towards the bushes on the hillside where the third would-be spy was attempting to conceal himself.

Ned's primary objective was to get a closer look at the man, in order to assuage the nagging suspicion that had taken hold of him, for no reason of which he was conscious. Hardly had he taken two strides, however, when he saw that a number of other men were now heading towards the crouching man's hiding-place from the top of the slope. They were moving stealthily, and they were armed. Some had poniards in their hands, others pistols.

If the situation had seemed complicated before, it now seemed utterly chaotic. Ned looked to his right and left along the shore. There were several other people visible within 100 yards, all of whom seemed innocently busy about their boats, but none had yet taken alarm. He did not know whether he ought to resist the temptation to call out a warning to the tall man, but his hesitation in that regard was momentary. No warning was necessary.

The man who had been hiding in the bushes stood up suddenly, having realized that there were people behind him. To Ned's astonishment, it was the big man who called out a warning to him.

"Take cover," the masked man shouted, in French, just before the first shot was fired.

Ned was astonished that the big man's pursuers were prepared to fire their guns in broad daylight, for they were certainly not policemen or militiamen; they looked for all the world like a gang of bandits. Tuscany had no shortage of such robber bands, but they were very rarely seen this close to a town as large as Spezia. Although the shore of San Terenzo was relatively quiet, save for the hours at which the fishermen habitually set sail and returned, it was unusual in the extreme for bandits to call attention to themselves in such a location. The other men on the strand had all taken alarm now, and several had begun to run along the shoreline in one direction or the other.

Now that the man who had been hiding was out in the open, running down the hill with great leaping strides, it was possible to make a much better estimation of his size, build and gait–but Ned observed, with a slight sinking feeling, that it was still impossible to judge the color of his skin. His waving hands were gloved.

Because he was coming down the slope as fast as he could the fugitive was, perforce, heading almost directly towards Ned and Guido, putting them both in the line of fire. Only three pistol-shots had been released, but Guido needed no further provocation; he dived behind the stern of a fishing-smack drawn up on the strand parallel to the *Don Juan*, ducking low as he passed out of Ned's sight. Ned ran the other way, into the shelter of the *Don Juan*'s prow, but he remained on his feet and went right around the boat to the stern, eager to keep track of the fleeing man.

More men had already appeared at the top of the slope, some of whom were already raising muskets–but they did not fire, perhaps because they were fearful that too many detonations would be sure to attract attention and perhaps because they were fearful of hitting their fellows instead of their intended target. Ned could not tell where the three pistol-shots had gone–for all he knew, they might have been fired into the air by way of warning rather than aimed to kill–but the pursuers chasing the big man certainly seemed determined, and were evidently not afraid to use their weapons.

Once he was on the level ground of the strand, the hunted man turned aside, running in the opposite direction to Casa Magni, towards Spezia's harbor. The boats drawn up on the shore provided far better shelter than the bushes on the slope, and he was soon lost to sight. No more shots had been fired after him, perhaps because the pistoliers thought that he was too far away to permit them to take aim, but perhaps also because they feared that a stray shot might hit some innocent party, and did not want that to happen. Ned glanced back at Casa Magni, and saw a face–almost certainly Walton's–at one of the first floor windows, staring out anxiously. The spectacle seemed sure to excite the conspirators' anxieties even further.

The men who were chasing the fugitive were all in plain view now. They were at least a dozen in number. Their well-worn clothes might have marked them as peasants had it not been for their weapons, but they were obviously well-used to bearing arms. Although the war had, in theory, been over for seven years, Ned knew that the desultory fighting in these parts was unlikely to have been stilled immediately by news of Waterloo. He knew, too, that many of the *banditti* in the northern provinces of Italy had joined forces with anti-Bonapartist resistance-fighters, rebranding themselves as patriots, and had thus obtained far greater license to steal and kill than they had ever enjoyed before. It was possible that these men still enjoyed a local reputation as heroes, and thus felt free to parade themselves, but Ned could not believe that the man they were chasing was merely a left-over

Bonapartist who might be considered fair game by the townsfolk of San Terenzo and Spezia.

Within five minutes, the hunt and its quarry had passed out of sight and hearing. The bandits if such they were, had paid no more attention to Ned than to any of the fishermen they had briefly disturbed.

"This is a madhouse," Ned muttered, as he went to look for his rival.

Guido was lying down where he had taken cover, but he was not about to get up. His head was bleeding. For a second or two, Ned thought that he might have been grazed by a stray pistol-shot, but then a head appeared over the side of the fishing-boat, its face wearing a broad grin. A hand appeared, still clutching the short club with which the spy had been struck down. Ned recognized the courier to whom he had given the coded letter destined for Henri de Belcamp–the man that Guido had robbed on the previous evening, and who had sworn vengeance in the customary Italian style.

The courier jumped down and began to rummage through Guido's pockets, expectantly. Ned took the letter out of his own jacket, but paused before handing it over in case the courier found anything else of interest while searching for it. Eventually, though, the courier looked up and shook his head.

Ned handed him the folded paper with the broken seal. "I've no time to write out a supplementary report and encode it," he said. "Have you enough English to take and transmit a verbal report?"

"Yes," said the courier, "but..."

"No buts," Ned said, "unless you can tell me who that man was who fled just now, and why the others are hunting him."

The courier shook his head, but grinned again. The chase had provided him with the distraction he needed to get close to his own quarry, but he had no idea what it was about.

"In that case," Ned went on, "I must make shift to find out. Do you know who *this* man is?" He pointed at the unconscious Guido, expecting another shake of the head.

"Dirty magyar," the courier supplied, spitting on the sand beside the bleeding head.

"In the pay of the Turks, you think?" Ned said.

The courier shook his head. "No Turks here," he said, confidently. "Vampire's minion."

Ned looked at the courier in amazement. "You can't mean that literally," he said.

The courier shrugged. "Dirty magyar," he repeated. "Be careful. Great danger, if vampire comes. Strange things. I make report too."

"By all means do so," Ned said. "Make sure, though, that you keep it distinct from mine, which is this: *Shelley is injured, perhaps mortally. His wife is ill. Frankenstein is ill too, in a different way. He is extremely hesitant in the matter of resuming his experiments. Shelley and his companions know that I am here in the name of the English crown, but they know nothing of my other master. They are afraid of some enemy, but are reluctant to seek the help they may need.* That will do–can you repeat all that when you pass on the letter?"

"Yes," said the courier, "but..."

"He will not approve. I know that–but the time for codes and ciphers is past; events are moving too rapidly. If he decides to take a hand in this, he had best come quickly. Now go."

The courier made no further objection. He moved off rapidly along the shore, in the same direction that the fugitive had taken. Ned looked down briefly at the unconscious man, then shrugged his own shoulders and followed the courier at a slower pace, looking for signs of the pursuit.

The trail was very evident, and easy to follow whle the hunters and their quarry were moving along the shore towards Spezia. When the tracks turned inland again, however, they became more difficult to follow, and they twisted and turned as the hunted man attempted to evade his pursuers. They finally evaporated on the hard and busy pavements of the town.

After searching for some time, Ned eventually caught sight of eight of the hunters outside a tavern. They had evidently abandoned the chase, at least until one of their scouts could obtain another sighting of their prey. They had put their weapons away, but they were making no attempt to hide themselves from the eyes of passers-by. On the contrary, they often offered salutes that implied recognition, although not all the greetings were returned. The eight men seemed to be adopting a swaggering attitude, whose bravado did not seem to be exaggerated by insecurity. *Banditti* though they presumably were, the men were evidently familiar to the port's inhabitants, and had no fear of arrest or molestation. The day when they could pass for heroic veterans of a fierce guerilla war against Bonaparte's allies was evidently not yet done. There was no sign of any uniform whose wearer might be duty-bound to object to their armed presence.

Ned began to make his weary way back to his hotel, deep in thought. His priority now had to be to make contact with Shelley again as soon as possible, if possible in confidence, in order to build on the sympathy that had sprung into being between them.

He had to insinuate himself into the conspiracy, if he possibly could. If he could not convince its members that he was a friend–and they seemed far too mistrustful, at present, for that–then he had to persuade them that he could be useful to them in some way. They knew now that he knew the bare bones of their secret, but they did not know how much he knew.

Perhaps, he thought, he could persuade them that he knew more, and that he might be a useful assistant if the man of science were, indeed, forced by circumstance to use his new apparatus before he was ready, on Percy Shelley or his wife.

Chapter Six
Science's Adam

Deep in thought as he was, Ned was not long unaware of the fact when someone began following him. Nor had he any doubt as to the identity of his tracker. He was not in the least worried for his own safety, but he was anxious for the safety of his follower. Guido must have recovered consciousness by this time, and the *banditti* must still have scouts scouring the town. The man who was taking so much trouble to hide his face was only drawing attention to himself by so doing.

Fortunately, the Sun was past its zenith now, and the inhabitants of Spezia tended to be as strict in their observance of the *siesta* as any Catalonian. The streets were not yet deserted, but the people who were still about were mostly in a hurry to be elsewhere, and they walked with their heads bowed. Everyone sought the available shade, averting their eyes from the brightly-lit paving stones.

Ned hurried his paces, not because he was trying to evade the pursuit but because he wanted to draw the other man into a safer vicinity as soon as was humanly possible. He took as roundabout a route as the hill would permit back to the hotel, taking time to make sure, as best he could, that there was no one dogging his immediate pursuer's footsteps. When he reached the hotel, he was glad to find it silent, with no sign of anyone moving within. When he turned the corner of the stone arch that formed its coaching entrance, he stopped dead and waited for his pursuer to catch up.

As soon as the tall man with the muffled face turned the corner, Ned raised a hand. "We'd best hurry up to my room," he said. "You should be safe there, if no one has seen us. Fortunately, the *banditti* cannot have many friends in this part of town, no matter how many they have about the docks."

The other stared down at him, evidently surprised by this matter-of-fact greeting. The Sun was high and the big man's broad-brimmed hat cast a black shadow over his partly-veiled face, but Ned was almost certain now that the man's skin was grey. General Mortdieu was obviously not the only Grey Man ever made who had retained all or most of his mental faculties.

"Who are you?" growled the reanimated man, speaking English with a guttural accent that might have been Switzer-Deutsch.

"I believe that's the question I ought to be asking you," Ned said. "Either way, let's get out of sight first. This way–and be as careful as you can, in case any of the servants is still on the prowl."

Ned and his companion took the back staircase up to his room. They met no one as they climbed, and Ned sighed with relief as he shut the door behind them. The water jug on the dressing-table had been refilled since he had gone out; he filled two cups, offering one to his guest and drinking deeply from the other. The morning's exertions had given him a fearful thirst.

"You can remove the layers of protective clothing now," Ned said. "I've seen your kind before, and talked to them. I didn't get much out of poor Sawney Ross, but General Mortdieu was much more forthcoming, though not very polite to begin with."

The Grey Man took off his hat and headband, and then unwound the silk scarf that covered the lower part of his face. His movements were deliberate, but not particularly awkward. The resurrected man seemed to be challenging Ned, measuring his face to see if he were really as brave and well-prepared as he pretended.

Eventually, seemingly satisfied by Ned's composure, the Grey Man sat down into the armchair, accepted the proffered cup and drank even more thirstily than Ned had done. Ned filled both cups again, while he studied his guest carefully.

His heart had begun to race as he accustomed himself to the idea of who this man must be. In *Frankenstein*, he remembered, the man of science had called his subject a "daemon" or a "creature," never a *man*. Ned knew that much of what was said about the creature there must be the pure product of madness or the literary imagination, but it would be foolish to assume that it was all false. After all, General Mortdieu had given the impression of being a wrathful and violent individual, and it seemed not unlikely that waking up from the sleep of death to find oneself reincarnate as a slate-grey walking corpse might be a intrinsically embittering experience.

"Since you asked first," Ned said, as he continued to study the grey features anxiously, "I'm Edward Knob, an Englishman. I thank you for the warning you shouted to me on the shore, but I wonder why you were watching me from hiding before your pursuers chased you away."

"Do you really know what I am?" the Grey Man asked. "I was about to assure you that you had no need to be afraid, but perhaps there is no need. Have you seen many others of my kind?"

"Yes, I know what you are and how you were brought back from the dead," Ned said. "I am certainly willing to assume, until I have evidence to the contrary, that I do not need to be afraid of you. I have seen several dozen others of your kind, but I fear that all but a few were imbeciles, and only one seemed as articulate as you. May I take my turn to ask some questions now?"

"You were in that house on the shore," the Grey Man stated, guardedly. "You must, therefore, know... my maker."

"Ah," said Ned. "You were following *him*, of course, although that also obliged you to follow Guido, who was also following him. You are his first subject, then–the infamous *daemon* of *Frankenstein*?"

The Grey Man's dull eyes did not flare up at that, but his broad mouth curled in distaste. "My maker should not have described me thus," he said, softly, "if, in fact, he did. Nor should he have written his memoirs while he was still sick enough to mistake his fears and delusions for reality. In either case, Walton's sister should not have given the letters and the manuscript to a publisher. All of that has done us both a severe disservice. Walton was very angry with her, I think, when he found out–but it was too late."

"In all probability," Ned said, currying favor shamelessly, "the worst of the horrors supplying the story with a plot were grafted on to the original by some hired hack instructed to bring out the tale's inherent melodrama–I cannot believe the rumor that Shelley was responsible, but, whatever the truth of the matter, I agree with you it would have been better for everyone concerned had the book not appeared."

"I am entitled to compensation for that, if nothing else," the Grey Man murmured. "I am certainly not eight feet tall, as the text alleged, and I was certainly not patched together from the refuse of slaughterhouses, although I presume that my body was plucked intact from a fresh grave. However ugly I may seem, I am certainly not a demon."

"You're not so very ugly," Ned assured his visitor. "Your color is a little unusual, but it's preferable to the hideous yellow that was if my memory serves me rightly, cited in the published text. Actually, I'm not personally acquainted with your maker, although I knew *of* him before meeting him for the first time this morning. He is quietly famous, in his way, quite apart from what I feel sure is a gross misrepresentation of his character in the pages of the novel named after him. Germain Patou's continuation of his clandestine work has not provided the best of supplementary advertisements, but it has served to attract a good deal of fascinated attention from various interested parties. Why were the *banditti* trying to kill you?"

The Grey Man shook his head slightly. "I'm not sure," he murmured. "I've encountered their kind before, in a quarrelsome fashion, but I had hoped that the disagreement was long-forgotten, given that it dates back to the years when men of that sort fancied themselves revolutionaries–but Italians hold grudges. It was their fellows who attacked me all those years ago; I merely defended myself a little too well for their liking. Coming back to the region was always a risk for me, I suppose–that fact might have figured in my maker's calculations when he decided to establish himself in Spezia. It was a risk I needed to take, though. If my maker is about to resume his work, at last, then I am entitled to play my part. He owes me that–and his fears are groundless."

"What fears?" Ned demanded.

"He wants to reserve the privilege of educating his subjects and directing their lives to himself. He would have guarded the privilege of supervising my own education very jealously had he not fallen victim to illness and dire anxiety, and he bitterly resents the fact that he lost control of me–but once I had recovered self-consciousness, I was my own man; we were bound to quarrel. He fears, I think, that I might have more ready-made moral authority over other people of my kind than he would be able to retain for himself. That is true, or so I hope and believe–but he need have no fear of what I might do with that authority. My intentions are benign."

"In the novel," Ned observed, "the so-called creature demands that Frankenstein make him a bride, and becomes murderous when thwarted."

"Melodramatic embellishment," said the Grey Man, sipping water from his cup with affected delicacy. "My maker always intended to repeat his experiment, when he was well enough, and tried more than once. I was his natural partner–but he rejected me, as he lost his grip on reality, and fled from me. If I have pursued him ever since, it is only with the determination to make my peace with him. I have never murdered anyone. He might have loved his little cousin, I suppose, but he certainly never married her, and I certainly did not kill her, any more than I killed his brother or his friend Clerval."

Ned nodded, anxious to give every visible indication that he believed what the Grey Man was telling him, no matter what private reservations he was careful to make. In fact, he was perfectly prepared to believe that the Grey Man was no Hellish fiend, but he was a spy now, and it was his duty to withhold his judgment. "Your maker might be forced to resume his work sooner than he wanted to, if Shelley has his way," Ned observed. "He seems reluctant to press forward, but he might have no choice if he wishes to retain the good opinion of his friends."

"Is one of them dying, then?" the Grey Man guessed.

"Shelley is worried about his wife," Ned said. "I am worried about him. Do you know Shelley?"

"We have met," the Grey Man said, a trifle guardedly.

"As I said, I mistrust the rumor that he wrote the published version of Walton's story," Ned said, in case that was the reason for the other's caution. "It was probably falsely credited to him by a rumor put about by the publisher. Lord Byron was once said to have written a famous tale about vampires, but that ascription turned out to be false."

"I have met Byron too," the Grey Man said, mildly. "I know more of vampires now than he ever did."

Ned frowned at that. "Do you, indeed?" he murmured. "The man you followed from Walton's house is rumored to be a vampire's minion, it seems. Is that likely, do you think?"

"Quite likely," said the Grey Man, casually–but he was not unobservant, for he immediately added: "You did not believe it when you heard it, I suppose? You were testing me–but vampires are not what you think, if you have taken your notion of them from Polidori's tale."

"What are they, then?" Ned asked.

"Nature's Grey Men," his guest replied. "The accidentally reanimated dead. Most are mere brutes, even if decay leaves them relatively unravaged, but on occasion... I am not alone, you see, even though I was the first of my kind to be deliberately made. A new Adam I

65

may be, but the world beyond my meager Eden was not empty. There are more avid hunters looking out for me than the ones you saw today. Is Shelley really in danger of dying? I had thought Byron far the more reckless of the two, and hence more likely to die first."

"He was injured in a brawl, it seems," Ned said. "The wound was not serious at first, but it was aggravated by an accident on his boat and it has become infected."

"Did he aggravate it deliberately, do you think?" the Grey Man asked, surprising Ned yet again.

This time, Ned did not attempt to hide his surprise. "I cannot believe that," he said. "Do you really think that he might be courting death deliberately, in order to force your maker's hand? I don't think so—although I do believe that he tried to win an agreement from his friends to subject his wife to the treatment, should she fail to recover from her present fever."

"Is she very ill?" the Grey Man asked.

"I haven't seen her, but Shelley was obviously very anxious."

"*She* would not have endangered herself deliberately," the Grey Man said, bleakly. "She did not like me at all, although I was never anything but courteous to her, and she did not take to my maker either, although he was still handsome when they first met. She could almost have believed that farrago of nonsense that the publisher put out—her nightmares were worse than my maker's."

"Where did you meet her?" Ned asked, curiously.

"At the Villa Diodati, on the shore of Lake Geneva, six years ago. My maker had a house not far from Cologny; Byron and Shelley became acquainted with him there. He and I were on better terms in those days, but he was still determined to hide me away. Inevitably, his secrecy only piqued their curiosity, and they persuaded him to let them in on his secret, swearing to keep it. He probably did not take much persuading–he was still proud of his accomplishment, as much in the process of my initial education as my reanimation. It was shortly thereafter that he fell prey to the delirious fever that induced his panic and caused our estrangement. That was not entirely a disaster for me, though, for it forced me to take charge of my own education–not in the bizarre fashion represented in that silly romance, but with far greater success."

"I'm a self-educated man myself," Ned told him. "I pride myself on having made a better job of it than many schools would have done–but I suppose that men like us are bound to think that."

Grey Men did not, in Ned's experience, have expressive faces, but the Adam of the New Grey Men did his best to demonstrate his surprise at that. "*Men like us*," he repeated, softly. "Thank you for that, my friend. No one has ever gone out of his way to pronounce such a phrase before."

It was at that moment that the sheer bizarrerie of the occasion struck Ned with some force. He had been face-to-face with Grey Men before, but those occasions had seemed to be the substance of pure melodrama even at the time. Now, he was sitting in a hotel's bed-alcove while a reanimated corpse was relaxing in a nearby armchair, and the two of them were talking, as if engaged in the most natural conversation in the world, about great poets and vampires.

What an adventurer I have become! Ned thought–but then he broke out into a half-smile as he realized that he really did feel more at ease with this strange creature than he had felt during his first interview with the glo-wering Gregory Temple.

"May we talk about these others of my kind you have seen?" the Grey Adam asked, with scrupulous politeness, after a brief pause. "I had heard that they existed, but I have not yet had the privilege of meeting one. Do you know how many there are altogether?"

"I don't know whether Patou has been able to make any more since leaving England," Ned replied, "but even if he has, I doubt that any them have retained as much presence of mind as you. He has hit a snag there, it seem, that your own maker contrived to avoid."

"It's a common problem, it seems," murmured the other. "I've heard rumor of more than one so-called vampire who can pass for human, but I'm far from sure that I can trust the second account, even if the first is true. There are a great many who are less than beasts."

"Patou certainly had not given up hope of restoring more of his patients to full self-awareness and ordinary intelligence," Ned observed. "Had he not been trying so hard to facilitate their re-education, I would never have run into Sawney and become entangled in this business. Given time to experiment, and improve his methods, who knows what he might achieve? In time, it might be possible to replenish all the lost humanity of the reani-mated dead."

"In time," the Grey Adam said, equably, "it might be possible to do far better than that–if we are only given the chance."

That possibility had not occurred to Ned. He chided himself silently; he had, after all, met General Mortdieu and seen evidence of *his* vaulting ambition. "Who are you, my friend?" he asked. "Or should I ask who you *were*, when you were alive?"

"I was no one when I was alive," the Grey Man retorted, "and I'm no one now–but I'm not a monster now, any more than the tenant of this body was when he was alive. I wish I could tell you that my predecessor had been a man of note, but he died too young to make his mark."

Ned took careful note of the fact that the Grey Adam now saw himself as a person distinct and different from the one he had been before his death, but took leave to wonder how that could really be the case. "You must have had a name, though," he objected.

"I did–but I gave it up when I died, and never troubled to invent another. I certainly never thought to call myself Mortdieu, or the Vampire King. If you need a name by which to think of me, though, you might call me Lazarus–I dare say that some such analogy has already cropped up in your private thoughts."

"Of course," Ned murmured. "It was too much to hope, I dare say, that you might have been someone renowned, who would have been at or near the head of any list of those deserving to be brought back from the dead–Tom Paine, for example."

"It's not the rights of man that concern me," the new Lazarus replied, seemingly conscious of taking a risk, "but the rights of the undead."

"You'll not achieve the second without first establishing the first, my dear Lazarus," Ned said. "If you and I are to be allies, that must be understood and agreed."

"I have not asked for an alliance," the Grey Man pointed out. "It was you who invited me to your room and made me welcome. Do you really want to be my friend, given that I am being hunted by men with pistols and muskets, who seem to be prepared to shoot on sight even in a law-abiding town like Spezia?"

69

"Of course," Ned said. "In my youth, in St. Giles's, all my friends and almost all my acquaintances were hunted men, endangered by the rope if not by bullets. I've lost more than I can count, including those I loved most dearly of all. I made a new friend today, who seems very likely to go the way of all the rest. Death and I are far from strangers–and whatever Ned Knob can do to assist in the war of science against death, you can be very certain that he will not hesitate. You have not asked for an alliance, it's true–but you were following me, were you not, in the hope that I might be useful to you?"

The new Lazarus did not deny it. "I hope and trust that a reconciliation with my maker might be possible," he said, "but it might be better if the initial approach were made through an intermediary. I dare not approach Walton, because I'm far from sure what his attitude to me might be. I would have risked an interview with Shelley, despite his wife's opinion, if that had been the best course–but when I saw you come from the house, not long after my maker had gone in, I thought there might be another opportunity worth investigating. I was still wary, as you saw, but I'm glad now that I followed my impulse. You might want to be wary too, though–as you've seen, I'm not without enemies."

"Your maker told me that he and his conspirators have enemies of whom I knew nothing," Ned observed. "In retrospect, though, it's possible that he might have been thinking of you."

"It's possible," the Grey Man conceded, sadly. "I'm not his enemy, though. I'm determined to make my peace with him if I can–but it might not be easy, if he has not entirely recovered from the legacy of his delirium. Are you willing to help me, Mr. Knob?"

"As it happens," Ned said, "it would suit me very well to become your ambassador. It wouldn't be fair to let you think that I am agreeing to your request for purely altruistic reasons."

"I had taken it for granted that you have your own reasons for being here," the new Lazarus replied, graciously. "That is your business–always provided that you mean no harm to my maker or his friends."

"I mean no harm to anyone, at present," Ned assured him. "Although I might want to make some exception to the rule in future. If the mysterious Guido really is a vampire's minion... but perhaps I'm jumping to conclusions. Perhaps vampires are no more deserving of the reputation that Gothic fiction has given them than the reanimate dead."

"I must reserve my own judgment on that score," the Grey Man said. "The term *vampire* appears to be local, though. In the Caribbean, I'm told, the reanimated dead are called *zombis*. The rumors are unclear as to whether they're natural or artificial, although they're said to be very stupid, without exception. You'll go to my maker on my behalf, then?"

"Yes I will, this very afternoon," Ned said. "You had best stay here, for the time being, but if one of the hotel servants comes in, or Guido decides to pay me another surreptitious visit, you might find it diplomatic to leave in a hurry. If so, try to make your way to San Terenzo again, and hide within view of the *Don Juan*– the boat I hid behind when you shouted your warning. I'll look for you there."

"Thank you, Mr. Knob," said Lazarus, extending his hand to be shaken. "You're a true gentleman."

Ned shook the hand willingly. "I had such pretensions once," he said, with a sigh, "but I'm a hardened radical now, who deem all men to be strictly equal, in terms of their innate quality."

Chapter Seven
Wheels Within Wheels

When Ned set out for the house he had been watching for the last few days, the Sun was still some way above the western horizon, reddening in hue but shining very fiercely. The atmosphere was thick and heavy, more somnolent than it had been during the siesta hour, and the world seemed very still and perfectly content.

Ned walked with a confident and satisfied step, thinking furiously about what he ought to say to the new Adam's maker and Robert Walton, and any other conspirators who might be with them. Shelley, he knew, would not be there unless he had taken a turn for the worse, so he would probably meet a wall of hostility–but he had an ace up his sleeve now.

As he approached the house, he looked up at the vantage point where Guido had placed himself on previous days, but found it empty. That put him slightly on his guard, but wariness was not enough to prevent misfortune. He was within ten yards of the gate into the grounds when a man stepped out of the shadows to his right, moving swiftly to block his way.

Ned did not recognize the man, but his costume and the way he moved–like a man accustomed to moving stealthily and to combat–strongly suggested that he must be one of the *banditti* who had been hunting the Grey Man earlier in the day. He had no weapon in his hand, but he had a dagger in his belt and he placed his hand on its hilt suggestively.

"You will come with me, please," he said, in Italian.

The relative mildness of the request suggested that the *banditti* were now showing a certain circumspection, at least while operating in this respectable neighborhood, but Ned had no reason think that help would arrive swiftly if he called for it.

"I think not," Ned said, continuing to move forward, with his hands ready to grapple the bandit's wrist if the knife were drawn. Instead, the other man fell back two paces–but that was a tactical move, for Ned heard footsteps running up behind him. He turned round, and then leapt forward to meet his second assailant, who was wielding a cudgel. He managed to deflect the first thrust of the cudgel, and kicked backwards in anticipation of the other man's closing movement. Had his leg been a handspan longer the maneuver might just have worked, but for once his short stature was his undoing. He put himself off balance without striking a wounding blow at either of his attackers.

He screamed for help then, with all his might, but–as he had anticipated–no help came, at least not swiftly enough to lend him any useful assistance. He hit out with both fists, and tried another kick in the Parisian style, but his opponents were accomplished brawlers. Had they been intent on killing him, they would have slit his throat within five seconds, but they were not. The fact that they only intended to knock him out gave him a full quarter-minute to make his displeasure felt, but he knew before the last blow landed that he had not hurt either one of them significantly.

When he woke up with a roaring headache, he could not estimate how much time had elapsed. It was quite dark, but that told him nothing, since he seemed to be in an enclosed space, with his body lying on a thick carpet and his head on bare boards. His hands were tied behind him, and his ankles were bound too.

As he began struggling against his bonds, Ned tripped a cord attached to a little bell. As soon as it rang,he suspended his struggle, realizing that someone would undoubtedly come in response to the summons. He wanted to compose himself for the confrontation.

A door opened somewhere to his left and two men came in, one of them carrying a tray on which a lighted candle was mounted. It was a tallow candle of no great dimension, and it was held at arm's length, but Ned would have been able to recognize either face by its light, had he ever seen it before. He had not—but neither man was dressed in the manner of the *banditti* who had chased the new Lazarus and kidnapped Ned. Their clothing was simple and severe, but not cheap or well-worn.

While they stared down at him, Ned took the opportunity to look around the room. There was no furniture, although indentations in the carpet suggested that there had once been a sofa, a sideboard and several chairs. The walls had been cleared of pictures, whose outlines still showed there in the stains on the surface. The empty bed-alcove was now home to a large crucifix, though, and there was a slab of slate set beneath it as a kneeling-platform.

The man holding the candle had obviously followed the flicker of his gaze. "Have you a religion, Monsieur Knob?" he asked, quietly, in French.

Ned ignored the question. "It seems that I am the only person involved in this business who readily owns

75

up to his true name," he observed, instead. "In consequence, everyone seems to know it, while I languish in ignorance as to theirs."

"An embarrassing situation, for a spy," the man said. He seemed to be very old and exceedingly thin, but also quite fit and strong–a near-paradoxical combination that Ned had observed before in men of a certain kind. "I am not at all reluctant to tell you my true name. I am Malo de Treguern, of the Order of St. John of Jerusalem."[3]

"The Hospitaller knights?" Ned retorted, skeptically, trying unsuccessfully to squirm into a sitting position. "That Order was disbanded, I believe, when Napoleon captured Malta more than 20 years ago."

"Many of Bonaparte's commands have been reversed in recent years," the warrior monk replied. "Some less ostentatiously than others. If you had come peacefully, as you were asked to do, you would not have been hurt. You were fortunate that we had given our assistants such strict instructions–they are the kind of men who would not normally hesitate to kill someone who attacked them."

"It was they who attacked me, when they blocked my way," Ned said. "If you intend to engage a man in polite conversation, you should not have your invitation delivered by bandits–even bandits who represent themselves as resistance fighters against non-existent oppression."

Malo de Treguern set the candle down beside Ned and stepped back, as if to appraise his condition. "You may have a point," he conceded, "but we are only two,

[3] A character introduced in Paul Féval's *Revenants* (Black Coat Press, 2003, ISBN 978-1-932983-70-8).

and far from home. It was necessary for us to find local allies, and we selected the men we bought because they already had a grievance against the individual we were seeking, and have been fortunate enough to find. Now, alas, the opportunity for politeness seems to have passed. If you will oblige me by answering my questions honestly, we might yet be friends. If not... Well, let us not get sidetracked."

Treguern knelt down then, to help Ned assume a sitting position, with his back to the wall. This allowed the old man to look Ned more fully in the face, while his younger companion remained standing. "*Have* you a religion?" Treguern repeated. The question seemed genuinely important to him.

"I'm no Calvinist," Ned answered, warily, "if that's what concerns you." Frankenstein, he knew, was Genevese, and hence reckonable as a Calvinist no matter what his actual beliefs might be. Shelley was reputed to be an atheist. Neither persuasion was likely to be congenial to an ex-Knight of Malta.

"But have you a religion?" Malo de Treguern repeated.

"No," Ned finally consented to answer. "I have not."

His interrogator nodded, as if he had merely wanted to make certain of his suspicion. "Is that why the demon came to you?" he asked.

"He's not a demon but a man," Ned said, bluntly. "He has been dead, and is alive again, but he is a man regardless. He followed me because he hoped to find a friend. He did. Why were your hirelings attempting to kill him?"

"How can a man who is already dead be *killed*?" the self-supposed Hospitaller countered. "No more banter, please. Was it on the demon's behalf that you were going to the necromancer's house?"

"Ostensibly," Ned said, deciding that it was hardly worth the bother of protesting that Victor Frankenstein was a man of science, not a necromancer. "But it was on my own behalf as much as his. I wanted news of my countryman, Percy Shelley. He fell ill this morning on his boat, the *Don Juan*, and I carried him back to his house. Walton's colleague came to attend him there, because there was no doctor close at hand. I was interested to know the result of his examination."

Malo de Treguern's weathered face gave not the slightest hint of any reaction to this statement, although he undoubtedly suspected that Ned had more reasons to make contact with Walton than the one he had specified. "Who was the man with you when the demon ran towards you this morning?" the Churchman asked.

Ned took leave to regret that the dutiful Lazarus had shouted out his well-meant warning. If only the Adam of the Grey Race had kept quiet, the *banditti* might not have leapt to the conclusion that there was a link between Ned and his rival spy. "He calls himself Guido," he replied, shaking his head in a vain attempt to clear it, "but I doubt that it is his real name."

"Are you working together?"

"No."

"Who are you working for?"

"The King of England," Ned replied, with a certain emphasis.

His interlocutor laughed dryly, although he did not accompany the laugh with a smile. "That will win you no credit in these parts," he said. "There's no lingering love for Bonaparte's lackeys in this region, but that does not make the appalling George more popular than any other foreign king. Is Guido in the employ of His Majesty too?"

"No," Ned said. He almost stopped at that, but could not resist the temptation to make one more attempt to stir a reaction from those wrinkled features, which seemed as hard and polished as teak. "I took him for a Turkish spy at first," he added, "but it seems that he's a magyar, minion of some vampire king."

Ned half-expected another dry laugh, perhaps slightly more vitriolic than the first, but none came.

"That's an awkward complication," muttered the standing man.

"Please be quiet, Simeon!" said Malo de Treguern. To Ned, he said: "Will the necromancer attempt to bring Shelley back to life if he dies?"

"I'd dearly like to know the answer to that myself," Ned said. "Unfortunately, your bully-boys stopped me as I was on my way to find out."

"You talked to Shelley, though," the questioner pointed out. "Is he determined to be brought back, if he should die?"

"He didn't mention the possibility," Ned said, "but I can't imagine that he would prefer to remain dead, if there's a chance that he might not. Did Masi try to kill him in order to provide the man of science with a suitable subject with which to resume his work?"

"You'd have to ask Masi's masters that," the Hospitaller consented to reply, in a neutral tone, after a slight hesitation. "You might ask the boat-builder Roberts the same question–nor would I very confident in trusting the Irishman, Taaffe, if I were your friend Shelley. Someone there is, it seems, who imagines that poets and atheists are ideal subjects for this kind of devilry."

"You might be stretching the imagined conspiracy too far," Ned said, "although I can understand how you might, given the circumstances. Is the reborn Order of St. John commissioned as a new Inquisition, then, hot on the trail of a new breed of heretics? Have you news of *Civitas Solis*?"

That was a chance shot, and a reckless one, but it struck home. For a moment, his interrogator's previous-ly-expressionless face showed such blatant alarm that Ned could easily have believed that the man really was an inquisitor terrified by the imagined threat of legen-dary heresy. "What do you know of *Civitas Solis*?" the kneeling man asked, sharply.

"What does anyone know of *Civitas Solis*?" Ned countered, blandly. "It's a phantom, the stuff of supersti-tion–like vampires, zombis and poor fugitive Lazarus."

"If we were like the inquisitors of old," Malo de Treguern told him, "we would doubtless feel entitled to use less tender methods to discipline your sarcastic ton-gue. Perhaps we are, but we still feel obliged to give you the opportunity to make a free confession before we be-gin heating the irons and crushing your fingers. At any rate, as you have obviously deduced from my questions, we do not approve of atheism or of necromancy. Given that you seem to be involved with known advocates of both, you might want to be a little more wary of offend-ing us."

"I have nothing against true Christians," Ned told him, sincerely, "but I would not count any torturer, how-ever pious he might pretend to be, as a true Christian. You didn't bring me here to hurt me, or your tame *ban-ditti* wouldn't have been so careful, and you certainly didn't bring me here to instruct me to beware of atheism or necromancy. Why not proceed directly to the matter of bribery? I'm a spy, after all, ever ready to work for hire."

"Will you sell us the demon, then? Do you know where he is?"

"How much is he worth?" Ned countered. "I'll need more than the traditional 30 pieces of silver, mind. Gold is more in my line."

"Fifty sovereigns," said the kneeling man, promptly. Inquisitors, Ned remembered, were reputed to be specially licensed to lie to their victims.

"Done," said Ned. "He's in my room at the hotel, waiting for my return." This too was a chance shot, but he felt quite certain that if these supposed Hospitallers had sent two *banditti* to intercept him, they must also have sent others to his room. What he wanted was confirmation that his ally had escaped them.

"Where did you arrange to meet him?" the kneeling man countered, harshly, tacitly providing the desired confirmation.

"Has he already escaped, then?" Ned asked, insouciantly. "Your *banditti* are by no means the cream of the crop, are they? Fra Diavolo must be weeping tears of shame in his Corsican grave, if rumors of his death have not been exaggerated."

"Leave him here, Malo," the standing man advised. "He won't tell us anything useful, even if he knows anything, which I doubt. In two days, it will all be over and we can let him go. He's harmless enough. We ought to provide him with a little company, though, if this Guido really is working for the vampire."

Ned took due note of the fact that the man his interrogator had called Simeon had said "*the* vampire," not "*a* vampire." These gentle inquisitors seemed to be demon-hunters rather than heresy-hunters, and might well have been badly misled as to the manner of creature they were chasing. Perhaps, he thought, they too had read *Frankenstein*. The *banditti* evidently knew Lazarus of old, though, well enough to harbor a long-held grudge against him. They must know that he was no wild beast or imp of Hell.

"We'd better make room for more company than that, if that's the way we intend to go," Malo de Treguern replied, with a hint of annoyance. As he turned to speak to the standing ma, he looked up, thus tilting his head back and allowing Ned to glimpse his tonsure.

He really is a monk of sorts, then, Ned thought, scrupulously. *Perhaps he really was a member of the Order of St. John, and perhaps some relic of the Order really does survive, just as relics of* Civitas Solis *survive. It may well be, though, that the ex-Knights of Malta are, and perhaps always were, affiliates of* Civitas Solis. *Even if Henri has succeeded in infiltrating that Order, he might have provoked grave mistrust as well as keen interest among its factions.*

"You should have answered our request and our questions politely," Malo de Treguern said to Ned, again–although Ned took some slight offense at that, having thought his responses reasonably polite as well as reasonably honest. "That way, we might have been prepared to let you go."

In a pig's eye, Ned thought. Aloud, he said: "I'm no man's enemy, and I don't bear grudges after the fashion of your local hirelings. I can do you no harm, in any case, although I'll have to be careful now that I don't lead you to my friend–unless, of course, you can come up with the 50 sovereigns."

Malo de Treguern stood up, picking up the candle-tray as he did so. Looking down at his captive, he said:

"I'm glad to hear that you'll bear no grudge. I'll let you go in two days, as Simeon suggests, provided that we've succeeded in our mission by then. I'll send you water and food when I have time to spare. I'm sorry to have inconvenienced you–you're a mere fly, after all, whose buzz is no more than a tiny nuisance–but matters are already moving too quickly for my liking, and the last thing I need is another loose cannon rolling around the deck. In case you're minded to try to escape, I must warn you that I shall instruct my hirelings that they need not handle you so tenderly if you get in our way again."

"If one of the great minds of his era were to die an untimely death," Ned said, making no attempt to hide his annoyance in the face of this sententious threat, "and your intention were to prevent his being resurrected, and his intelligence preserved to the extent that can be contrived, I might bear a grudge for that."

"Our intentions go a great deal further than that," the aged warrior monk told him, with more than a hint of renewed threat in his voice, as he and his companion moved towards the door, "and we are not to be intimidated by the grudges of dwarfs. Be grateful that we have removed you from the game–it's now a field of play where not-so-innocent bystanders are very likely to get hurt."

The door closed, plunging Ned into total darkness again.

He immediately began to worry the cords binding his wrists, hopeful that he could get free, given time. He rather liked the idea of being a loose cannon rolling around the deck, albeit one that wanted to prevent injury rather than inflicting it. At any rate, he liked the analogy far better than the one that had likened him to a fly whose buzz was only a tiny nuisance.

Chapter Eight
The Necromancer's Den

Ned struggled for an hour in pitch darkness, attempting to extricate his wrists from the tightly-knotted cords, but whoever had tied them knew his business, and Ned was coming close to despair when the door swung open again and faint candlelight poured through it.

The man who entered, bearing a candlestick, was Guido, the "vampire's minion." He looked down at Ned with a wry smile on his face.

"You trapped me very neatly by the shore," he said, in a low voice, "but it seems that you've run into trouble yourself."

Ned did not bother to correct the other's slight misapprehension. "Have you come to taunt me or to set me free?" he asked, keeping his own voice low.

"To set you free," said Guido, with the slightest of sighs, setting the candlestick down and starting work on the knots binding Ned's ankles, "although you don't entirely deserve such generous treatment. We still have enemies in common, Monsieur Knob, and ought to make what alliances we can."

"How did you know where to find me?" Ned asked.

"I have not been idle since I woke up with a sore head. I thought that I had every chance of making friends with the *banditti*, if I were to dispense a little coin; I hardly thought to find them in the employ of Mother Church, avid to do violence to her enemies. We live in strange times, my friend. Anyhow, I found out easily enough where the bandits' masters were lodged, and I saw you carried in unconscious. We're only a few hundred meters from Walton's house, in another covert on the same irregular terrace. I would have come to you sooner, but I had to make perfectly certain that the coast was clear. There are only two Churchmen, it seems, but they have more than a dozen bandits at their beck and call. One party is watching Walton's house, while a larger one has gone to San Terenzo, perhaps hoping to find the demon there–not that he is actually a demon, of course, as you must know as well as I do."

"Any more than your own master is a actually a vampire, I suppose," Ned retorted, rolling over so that Guido could get a better purchase on the cords securing his wrists.

"Did the Churchmen tell you that?" Guido asked.

"Everyone seems to have known it but me," Ned admitted. "I'd assumed that you were in the pay of the Turks, but it seems that I was naive."

"My master would be amused to hear that," Guido said. "The Sultan hates vampires even more virulently than the Pope–mercifully, neither has much say in Hungary nowadays. The last relic of the Holy Roman Empire is neither very holy nor very Roman. There!"

Ned sat up and rubbed his wrists to restore the circulation to his numb hands.

"Do you know who the Churchmen are?" Guido asked.

Ned hesitated, but decided that he owed the other that much. "They claim to be members of the Order of St. John of Jerusalem," he said, "reformed in secret since the fall of Malta. One calls himself Malo de Treguern; he addressed the other as Simeon. Do you know them?"

Guido shrugged. "The name means nothing," he said, "but there are rumors a-plenty of a new crusade against so-called necromancy. Thus far, its operations are clandestine–but if they were able to capture a man returned from the dead, of whatever sort, they might elect to put him on show in order to rouse mobs to continue their work. They would not dare put Frankenstein on trial, given that he is a Swiss citizen with a magistrate for a father, but few people know that he is here, or even that he is alive and nearly sane; if he were to vanish, I doubt that anyone in authority would exert themselves overmuch to find him. We need to prevent that, if we can."

Ned was duly grateful for the fact that his supposed ally really did seem disposed now to share what information he had. There would be no more nonsense about bomb-factories. "Shelley and Byron know that he is here," he pointed out, "and they are famous men."

"For which reason the Hospitallers will not lay a finger on them," Guido said. "But that will not mean that anyone will take them seriously if they were bold enough to tell their story. Their discretion thus far suggests that they are keenly aware of that–genius has the reputation of being perilously close to madness and I doubt that they would be able to win support from the likes of Davy and Darwin without incontrovertible proof of the contention that the dead may return. Frankenstein and Patou have been very wise, I think, to try their hardest to perfect the process before granting it any publicity, given that they want to inspire hope rather than horror. We need to leave now, and must be careful. There was no one downstairs when I came in, but they might send someone back at any moment to make sure that you are safe."

Ned nodded, and followed Guido through the door and along a corridor to a flight of wooden steps. There was no light in the house save for Guido's candle, and they made their way outside without any difficulty. Once they were outside, Guido extinguished the candle, although the Moon was far from full and the stars were partly obscured by drifting clouds.

Ned did not recognize the street, but they were high enough on the hill for him to estimate their location within the town; Guido had been reasonably accurate in his estimate of its distance from Walton's house. Guido started walking in that direction.

"What do you intend to do?" Ned asked him.

"If Walton has any sense, he must have sent a messenger to Pisa to summon as many of the conspirators as possible. If you did not scare them sufficiently by barging into Casa Magni this morning, the sight of that pursuit down the hill and along the strand will certainly have brought them to a fine pitch of alarm. If Walton recognized the demon, as he might well have done, they will know that all hope of proceeding in secret is now gone. They'll probably take flight, but they'll gather at the house first. If there's to be a siege or a pitched battle, it will be as well for us to weigh in before the larger party returns from San Terenzo. If we can help Frankenstein to get away while there's still time..."

"They can't take flight," Ned objected. "Shelley and his wife aren't well enough to travel."

"Then they'll be left behind," Guido said, simply. "Williams and his wife might stay to care for them, but the rest will have to go, and go quickly. I can help, especially in the matter of finding a new place of safety."

"I don't think..." Ned began. He had several objections to raise, and strong reservations to express regarding the wisdom of accepting guarantees of safe conduct from the minion of a vampire, but Guido cut him off and silenced him with an abrupt gesture. They were coming close to Walton's house now, and had to complete their approach silently. Ned wondered briefly whether he ought to have passed on Malo de Treguern's warning about giving the bandits permission to use any and all violent means, but decided that it was unnecessary. Guido did not seem the type to be squeamish in such matters himself.

Ned had no weapon, and Guido only had his stiletto–that being why he had had to untie Ned rather than simply slicing through the cords that bound him–but Ned had no hesitation about going forward regardless. He was not afraid. If the *banditti* were widely scattered, as they probably were, given the size of the tract of land they had to surround, it might well be possible to take them one by one and appropriate their arms. Ned still had questions that he wanted to ask his currently-obliging informant, especially concerning his mysterious vampire master, but that would have to wait.

They found the first bandit easily enough, on the very spot where Guido had stationed himself to watch the house–an understandable coincidence, given that it was a natural coign of vantage. The bandit was not standing up, though–he was laid out flat on his back, unconscious, and he had already been deprived of his weapons.

Guido let out his breath with a slight sigh of delight. Ned, too, was more delighted than surprised. If this was not the work of one of Frankenstein's more muscular friends–Trelawny, perhaps–than it could only be the work of the new Lazarus. Either way, it suggested that the battle had already been joined, and that the right side had seized an early advantage.

The second bandit they contrived to locate was, however, awake and alert. Guido crept up behind him and used one of the cords that he had taken from Ned's wrists as a garrote, preventing him from calling out. Whether he released the strangling-cord before the man had choked to death, Ned could not tell, and he could not afford to care overmuch. Guido took the man's pistol for himself, and handed his poniard to Ned.

Then the silence was broken by an alarm call–not occasioned by Guido or Ned–and there was a sudden flurry of movement all around the house. Ned and Guido separated, hurrying to assist in the burgeoning conflict. Ned had evidently chosen a bad direction, for he found his path suddenly blocked by one man, while another immediately tried to circle behind him. This time, they were obviously not acting under orders to be discreet.

One of the attackers fired a pistol, whose ball whirred above Ned's head, while the other tried to stab him in the throat. Ned avoided the knife-thrust, rather to narrowly for comfort, and hurled himself forward to butt his nearer assailant in the midriff. They went down in an untidy heap, but Ned was able to get a grip on the hand that held the knife and force it away from his body.

He heard a dull thud as the other bandit fell, struck from behind. No more than a second elapsed before strong hands reached down to push him out of the way, before a heavy boot came down on the knife-wielder's throat, crushing the bandit's Adam's apple.

"Into the house, quickly!" said a voice he recognized readily enough as that of Lazarus.

Ned allowed himself to be bundled toward the main entrance of Walton's house and through the open doorway. The corridor within was dark, but he was hurried along it, then pushed up against a wall and told to be still. Others were now hastening through the door, which was abruptly slammed. Then a light was struck and a candle lit.

There were seven men gathered in the corridor, counting Ned and Lazarus. Walton was there, and John Taaffe; Ned also recognized Edward Trelawny, who had visited the house on several occasions, and a man with a terrible wound on his face, whom he took to be Captain Hay. The seventh man was a prisoner, who had evidently been seized by Taaffe and Hay; it was Malo de Treguern.

"Guido's still out there!" Ned was quick to say. "He's no Turkish spy, but a friend—he took care of at least one of the *banditti* for you."

"He'll come to no harm," Lazarus was quick to say. "If he wants to come in, he may—but one of the bandits, at least, ran away down the hill. He'll be in San Terenzo within the hour, and the whole gang may well be back within two. We've no time to waste."

Malo de Treguern looked at Ned, with a steely glint in his eye, which suggested that he might be regretting his clemency. He had seemed perfectly reasonable on his own ground, when all was going according to his plan, but there was a wildness about him now. "The fact that you have a hostage will not deter them from attacking," the Hospitaller said. "They will rely on God to protect me—and rightly so."

The Churchman was not the center of the group's attention, however. The others—Walton and Trelawny in particular—were staring at Lazarus mistrustfully, although they had to know that he had helped them in the skirmish.

"It was *you* who brought down this swarm of hornets upon us," Walton said, angrily. "If you knew how hard we have struggled to avoid any possibility of being thought to be in league with demons, you would surely have stayed away."

"I am not a demon," Lazaruis repeated, yet again. "If the work is to begin again, I have more right to interest myself in its progress than any one of you."

"We have no time for this," said Trelawny, putting his hand on Walton's arm. "Bring them both into the laboratory. Hay, guard the door–and watch out for the man who is not, after all, a Turkish spy, since he seems to be on our side. Let him in if he asks to come in–we may yet need every man and every weapon we can muster."

In the absence of any specific instruction, Ned followed as Trelawny and Taaffe hustled Malo de Treguern into a room at the rear of the house, where the equipment that Victor Frankenstein had been gathering was accumulated, much of it not yet removed from its packaging, Ned's heart sank as he realized how very unready Frankenstein was to resume his experiments, even in the simplest terms. No wonder Shelley had become alarmed by the danger threatening his wife–and so much the worse for him, if the wound in his head could not be healed.

Victor Frankenstein was there, perched on a stool. Malo de Treguern shook off Trelawny's arm and immediately stepped forward to confront him, although Ned could see that the confrontation would be futile. Frankenstein's eyes were glued to his "creature," and his face showed a bewildering confusion of emotions. The man of science clearly did not have the slightest idea what he ought to think or feel about his "creation," let alone what to say to him.

"Vile necromancer!" said the warrior monk, in English, for all the world as if his curse might have real injurious power. "Blasphemous maker of demons! You shall rue this day!" He seemed mad with frustrated rage, having lost every vestige of the calmness and method that he had brought to his earlier examination.

Frankenstein continued staring at his "daemon," who stepped forward and offered his hand. "*Bonjour*, Victor," he said, pausing slightly before withdrawing the unaccepted hand and continuing, in French: "It's good to see you again, and to find you better than before. I came to help you with your work, but I seem to have arrived at the same time as your enemies. It's too late to hide, I fear–in mainland Europe, at least. Will you let me help you find a safer refuge, and assist you in your work?"

Malo de Treguern was amazed, and seemed to have taken great offense at being ignored. He took hold of the small wooden crucifix he wore suspended about his neck and brandished it, as if he were about to attempt an exorcism.

It was, Ned thought, purely because Victor Frankenstein could no longer bear to meet his creature's calm eyes that the man of science turned his gaze aside momentarily to look his angry accuser up and down, with frank disdain–as John Calvin himself might have studied a Romanist friar. Then the alleged necromancer turned to look at Lazarus again, with tears welling in his eyes. "You should have let me alone," he said, in a voice hardly above a whisper. "How many times have I begged you to stay away?"

"I tended you when you first fell ill, Victor," the Adam of the new race replied, quietly. "I was kind, and faithful, although I had recovered but half my wits. Would you rather I had been the monster your delirium proclaimed me to be? Was it so very hard to bear that you found yourself helpless in my arms, like a child? Was it such a terrible blow to your godlike pride? Do you really believe that your future subjects will be more thankful and more docile than me?"

"We have no time for this," Trelawny said, in an anguished tone. "We must act, and quickly. We must leave Spezia–the only question is, where shall we go? Even if Byron brings the *Bolivar* tonight, it may be too risky to go down to the shore, given that the remaining *banditti* are scouring San Terenzo for this fellow. We have a chance to strike inland and make our way to Pisa–I say that we should take it."

"We'd have to hire horses," Walton said, "and carriages too, if we intend to save any of this apparatus. If we can defend ourselves until daylight..."

"We'll get no help from the authorities," Taaffe said. "They sent Masi to deliver that message in brutal fashion. They had no idea what we were planning to do, but they simply didn't want us here. If we fight the *banditti* we'll do it alone, and if anyone's to pay the law for the blood that's shed, it's likely to be us."

"Patou might have been wise to set sail for some remote island," Frankenstein muttered. "I tried to do the same myself, once, but Scotland was not remote enough."

"It's your decision, Victor," Trelawny said. "If you say the word, we'll fight."

"Going inland wouldn't save us," Walton said. "Pisa is full of Churchmen. This one may be a rogue element, but..."

"There's not a man in Italy whose hand would not be raised against you if he knew what you were about," Malo de Treguern shouted, insistently. "The Church has its reasons for discretion, but if you force its hand, ana-thema will be declared against you."

"What about Shelley?" Ned put in, although he knew that his intervention might be far from welcome. "Do you propose to abandon him?"

"Byron's bringing the *Bolivar*," Walton said. "He and Williams can take ship if they wish, with their wives and servants. If not, they'll still have the *Don Juan*."

"Setting to sea too soon might be the death of Shel-ley and his wife," Ned objected. "What hope will there be for them, if Frankenstein is not on hand to inter-vene?"

The man of science turned to look at Ned then, his tearful and bloodshot eyes full of anguish. "I am not ready!" he said, hoarsely. "I wish to God that I were, but *I am not ready.*"

"He's talking about his state of mind, not his appa-ratus," Lazarus put in. "We could get that ready in a mat-ter of hours–except that we don't seem to have hours to spare. *I* am ready, though, Mr. Knob–will you follow my lead, no matter what these men decide to do?"

Ned was astonished by this, but he tried not to show it. "If Shelley grows worse," he said, "and there's a chance of saving him, then I'll seize it–no matter what the risks might be."

"Even a man with no religion ought not ally himself with the Devil," said Malo de Treguern, sententiously.

"It might be General Mortdieu who had the right of it, after all," Ned murmured, distinctly enough to be heard. In a louder voice, he added: "But we are here, and must make our stand in Spezia or San Terenzo. I'll glad-ly follow Lazarus, if he has a plan, and I'm sure that the vampire's minion will do likewise. With four more men to support us, with or without a hostage, I'll wager that

94

we can put the *banditti* to flight–and we can certainly defend Casa Magni thereafter, even if the *Bolivar* takes several days to come to our aid. If the worst comes to the worst, we'd still have the *Don Juan*. I say that we should make a stand, win the fight, and then take the equipment down to Casa Magni–if we can."

Trelawny snorted at the mention of Shelley's boat, suggesting that his opinion of the *Don Juan*'s seaworthiness was no higher than Guido's, but he did not protest against the whole of Ned's speech, despite having been the proponent of the opposite plan. It was Frankenstein who took exception to the notion of following his creature's lead.

"Am I cursed to be haunted forever?" the man of science demanded. "I'm for Pisa, and thence to God knows where–the East, perhaps. India, or the Ile de France."

"You'll never replace and replenish your apparatus there," Walton objected. "We are bound to civilization, if only by technical necessity. Best to head north, don't you think? To Protestant lands where warrior monks will find no sympathy at all. The most important thing is not to be divided. The dwarf's right about one thing–together, we might force the bandits to retreat. If we split up, we'll surely play into their hands."

"To Casa Magni, then!" Ned said. "Lock up the laboratory, so that we can recover the equipment later, but let's be on our way, while we still have a chance of taking the enemy unawares and driving them down the hill into the sea." Lazarus made no objection to Ned voicing this plan, having presumably recognized that his own voice roused reflexive opposition.

"Victor?" said Trelawny, again deferring to the scientist, but with an edge in his voice that testified to his change of mind.

Frankenstein looked at Lazarus, with an eerie dread in his eyes–but in the end, he said: "Very well. We should not desert Shelley, however meager the help might be that we can offer him..."

He would certainly have said more, but the door to the laboratory opened at that moment to reveal John Hay, in a state of high anxiety. "You'd best come immediately," he said. "We're surrounded–and they seem to be demanding a parley."

Chapter Nine
The Power of Desire

When John Hay declared that the house was "surrounded," Ned took the inference–as everyone else presumably did–that the remainder of Malo de Treguern's
hirelings had returned from the shore. The Hospitaller
certainly jumped to that conclusion, for he was seized by
a visible thrill of excitement and triumph. It was he who
led the charge to the main door, and no one sought to
hold him back, preferring to shelter behind him for the
moment–but when he arrived at the door and flung it
wide open, Treguern stopped in confusion just beyond
the threshold, utterly nonplussed by the sight that met his
eyes.

Frankenstein and Walton hung back warily, while
Lazarus maintained his usual careful discretion, but Hay
had already stepped outdoors and Ned had to step out
too in order to see what was happening–with the result
that he and Malo de Treguern ended up side by side,
while Trelawny moved tentatively out on one flank and
Hay on the other.

The house did, indeed, appear to be literally surrounded–but not by any mere dozen bandits strung out
along the hedge and lurking in the olive grove. Ned
could not count the crowd, but it looked to be at least a
hundred strong. Many, but not all, of its members were
armed with guns or blades, but there were women and
children there as well as men, and the attitude of the

whole did not seem to be menacing. In the immediate instance, at least, they seemed quite content to watch and wait.

The townspeople of Spezia, Ned realized–or a substantial fraction of their number–had abandoned their habitual reserve, and had stopped pretending that they and their English guests were living in parallel worlds. For a moment or two, he assumed that they had simply become impatient with the armed *banditti* running through their streets, and wanted to put an end to the private battle that had flared up on the edge of their town– but then he realized that he was quite mistaken, and that the truth was far more complicated.

There was a moment's pause before Malo de Treguern seized the initiative, and began haranguing the crowd in what seemed to Ned to be very fluent Italian. Ned could not understand that language well enough to follow every detail of what the warrior monk was saying, but he knew that Treguern was calling them to action, appealing to them as loyal Catholics. The former Knight of Malta demanded that the people of Spezia should seize the demon, the necromancer and their English lackeys, and deliver them, bound and helpless, into the care of the Church's designated representatives.

It took at least three minutes for the rant to falter, but Treguern finally realized that he was not getting any response.

Someone stepped forward then from the group clustered about the gate. He spoke too rapidly for Ned to be able to grasp all of what he was saying, but there were others in Walton's party who knew even less Italian than he, and they looked at one another in anxious bewilderment until Trelawny took it upon himself to translate.

"They're demanding to see the man who has been raised from the dead," Trelawny said, uncertainly. "I don't understand..."

"I believe that I do," said Lazarus, mildly. He had to step past Walton and Frankenstein as well as the advance party, but no one attempted to interrupt him as he moved forward. "Bring me a lantern," he ordered.

Ned ran back into the house in search of the brightest lantern he could find, and hurried back with it. The Grey Man was now standing three paces ahead of Malo de Treguern, and Ned went to stand beside him, holding the lantern as high as he could.

Lazarus did not say anything, at first, but merely removed his hat. He was no longer wearing his scarf over the lower part of his face, but he unwound it from his neck, and opened his shirt to display his torso. He held up his gloveless hands, fingers widespread. After displaying himself for a few seconds, he began to speak, in a calm and measured fashion. His Italian seemed to be almost as fluent as Treguern's.

Ned understood that the Grey Man was telling the crowd something of his history, and that he was referring repeatedly to Victor Frankenstein as a great man: not a necromancer but a miracle-worker. He understood, too, that the principal reason for the speech was to assure the crowd that a man returned from the dead could, in fact, speak, with all the intelligence that might be expected of a cultured person. The Grey Man did, however, take the trouble to warn them that he was not representative of those who had so far returned from the dead, and that many of the others were stupid and confused.

It was at that moment that Malo de Treguern realized, belatedly, what was happening. The Churchman began shouting again, but Ned knew that the argument was already lost. At first, that seemed astounding–but he immediately began to see the logic of the situation. In the gloom, he picked out the three men beside the gate who were carrying dead bodies in their arms–three *banditti*, who had been struck down in the ferocious struggle that had take place half an hour before. Bandits, he realized, were no different from other men in having mothers and grandmothers, brothers and cousins. Outlaws the dead men might have become, unable to return wholly to the bosom of society following the years they had spent as guerillas, but they had been born in the neighborhood and it was not simply their reputation as heroes that kept them safe when they came into town. Few of their former neighbors returned their salutes nowadays, but everyone who had known them as children felt entitled to take an interest in their deaths–and Malo de Treguern had made certain when he first employed them that everyone would come to know the cause for which they had recklessly given their lives.

Ned did not doubt for a moment that the people in the crowd were good Catholics–as good, in their own quiet fashion, as Malo de Treguern–but they were also veterans, again in their own quiet fashion, of the war into which Napoleon Bonaparte had plunged the whole of Europe. Although Spezia bore no obvious cannon-scars, the order of these people's lives had been rudely overturned, and peace had not restored it to its former clarity. They were, as Ned had earlier observed, still *stunned* by the experience, uncertain as to what the future might hold, and what they ought to expect or demand of it.

In simple terms, the people of Spezia–or those among them who has taken the trouble to put a stop to the latest battle waged by foreigners on their soil–had withheld the judgment that Malo de Treguern found so easy to make. They believed in God, in the Devil, and in necromancy and miracles too, but the idea that there was a man in their midst who had raised the dead, and was eager to repeat the experiment, had not aroused in them the kind of reflexive horror that it struck into men like Treguern. They had dead men of their own on hand, and they wanted to put Frankenstein to the test. They were not about to descend upon his house like a mad mob, to put its inhabitants to the sword and its furniture to the torch. They were in a very different mood. They wanted to know whether Victor Frankenstein really could do what was claimed–and, if so, they wanted him to do it *for them*.

"We have all been too fearful," Ned murmured, addressing himself primarily to Lazarus, although the others were able to hear him now that Treguern's tirade was dissolving into inarticulate confusion for a second time. "The world is already changed. Whatever people in authority might dread, common people are not so foolish.

"I am not ready," Frankenstein said, fretfully. "I cannot do as they ask."

"You certainly cannot refuse them," Lazarus said. "They will be patient if they see that we are making what effort we can, but we must certainly make what effort we can. Ready or not, we must attempt to resurrect those three men. The crowd may well be tolerant if we are not wholly successful, but they will not brook cowardice and will be direly disappointed by total failure. We must all work together, as hard as we can, and our many hands must make swift progress. These people will protect us while we work from any further interference–and that is a security to be treasured, however brief it might prove to be."

Frankenstein opened his mouth again, but did not speak. After a pause, he nodded his head. He knew that he had no alternative.

Lazarus spoke to the crowd again. He asked them to bring the three dead men into the house, and he went on to ask a great deal more than that. Ned did not even try to follow the details. Instead, he confronted Malo de Treguern, and said to him, in French: "You must not waste time in further protest, my friend. You must seize this chance, even if you cannot yet see it as anything more than a chance to see necromancy in action. You need not help us, and cannot hinder us, but you have an opportunity now that has not been granted to any man since the first Lazarus rose and walked."

The Churchman looked at him bleakly. "I have spent more time in the company of revenants than you can know," he said.

"Perhaps you have," Ned said, "but even you, aged and wizened as you are, might live long enough to see a world in which revenants are familiar to everyone, and death has lost its dominion on Earth, as well as in Heaven."

Malo de Treguern stared at the crowd again, as if he were now beginning to absorb the implications of its gathering and its attitude. All of humankind was there, in microcosm, and the understanding seemed for a moment to be dawning in him that the mass of men, faced by a real possibility, would welcome a new way to defy death. Then his expression changed, though. "This is the Devil's work," he told Ned, stubbornly. "No good can come of it, and much evil must. You have no notion of what you are doing, boy. Had you a religion, and a mind unperverted by silly lies, you would have recognized this Victor Frankenstein as the prophesied Antichrist, and you would have shielded your eyes against his seductions."

"Be that as it may," Ned said, with a sigh, "you would do well to observe what happens. Now, I have work to do and no time to waste. In the past, I have only witnessed a resurrection; now I must help to contrive a whole series on them. I am very glad to have the opportunity."

"Imp of Satan!" was the warrior monk's reply to that. "Hell shall claim you all!"

Given that the bulk of the equipment that Frankenstein had gathered was not even unpacked, there was a great deal of work to be done, and it had to be admitted that the many hands available to help him did not make such light work as Lazarus has hoped. Indeed, the presence of so many inexperienced hands in a restricted space led to a good deal of clumsiness and confusion. The lack of clear and efficient leadership made the problem worse.

Initially, everyone looked to Frankenstein to take the lead in imposing order upon the chaos, determining what had to be done, by whom, and according to what timetable, but Frankenstein was too distracted to play the general. When Lazarus took it upon himself to assume command, Frankenstein was not the only one who seemed unready to obey him, but Ned weighed in again, taking the Grey Man's orders and relaying them. The Englishmen, at least, seemed willing to do as he said, perhaps telling themselves that he was, after all, an agent of their King.

Once the work was well underway, in a reasonably disciplined fashion, Frankenstein began to lose his hectic manner and warm to the task in hand. Gradually, and without opposition, he took back his stolen authority. He had to send the townspeople scurrying to their homes and workplaces to bring him tin baths and various household implements, and to plunder more electrical cells from the ships in dock, but they were ready enough to help. The laboratory gradually filled up with apparatus that was carefully assembled into intricate networks. The assemblies looked untidy and rather precarious, but there was a stern order within the makeshift, and Ned felt confident that the delicately-poised towers of acid-filled batteries were fit for purpose.

For the first few hours, everyone involved in the project toiled together, but Walton eventually had to devise a shift pattern that prevented Frankenstein's helpers from getting in one another's way and allowed them time to rest. For the whole of the night and most of the morning the breaks, they took were short, but as the *siesta* hour approached it became obvious that everyone was in need of sleep. Taaffe, Hay, Walton and Trelawny were dispatched by turns to the villa's bedrooms, and in mid-afternoon Ned finally consented to be sent back to the hotel, with instructions not to return for at least four hours. Ned was quite ready by then to obey this command in letter and spirit alike, and he was not best pleased to find Guido waiting for him in his room.

"This," Guido said, shaking is head slowly to signify his incredulity, "is not a situation that my master could ever have anticipated. Had it really been the case, I suppose, that a vampire's bite could confer a kind of conditional immortality, his kind might not have been forced by idiot superstition to lurk in the shadows, but the Age of Enlightenment has not yet begun to penetrate the mysteries surrounding them. If only you could have persuaded Frankenstein to come with me..."

"You would have had to persuade me first," Ned said, grimly. "Your master does not seem to lack friends and loyal servants, who do not seem to fear him any more than servants usually fear an exacting master."

"You should not judge me as typical," Guido replied. "If I appear uncommonly cheerful and content, that's partly because I am so far away from him. If I like my work, that's because it so often takes me away. You are not mistaken, though–because I know what he really is, I am not prey to the same exaggerated dread as the greater number of my fellows. I know that he does not really feed on blood, any more than the South Sea islanders are really cannibals... but he is not a noble and innocently virtuous individual, either, as Rousseau would have us believe that men unspoiled by civilization would be."

"He will be able to step into the daylight soon enough," Ned said. "The Grey Men will not have to hide themselves away much longer."

"Don't be too optimistic," Guido said. "You have not yet seen the outcome of your current experiment. You know well enough, I think, how exceptional Frankenstein's Adam is."

"The process is in dire need of perfection," Ned agreed, "but once experiments can be carried out on a grand scale, in adequate security, progress will be swift."

"And within two or three generations," Guido said, skeptically, "the reanimated dead will outnumber the living, and will set the world to rights. We've a great deal of trouble to endure, my friend, before the empires of the living will condescend to live alongside the empires of the dead. These Tuscan craftsmen may want their beloved stray sheep back, but do you really believe that they would rejoice in the news that Bonaparte and all his hawkish generals might return? Not, you understand, that I am making the mistake of assuming that your General Mortdieu *is* Bonaparte, merely because he is dwelling in Bonaparte's dead body."

"It seems that our alliance has been a modest success after all," Ned observed, mildly, "despite its shaky start. We are scattering our secrets recklessly now–but I'd like to know a good deal more about your master before I agree to act as his emissary and spokesman."

"I dare say that we still have a few secrets in reserve," Guido said. "We are spies after all. I'd like to know a good deal more about *your* second paymaster, before I make him an offer of amity on my master's behalf."

"I don't even know the name of your vampire," Ned pointed out, feeling obliged to play the careful diplomat, in spite of his physical exhaustion.

"He calls himself Szandor, and poses as a Count– but I do not suppose that the name and the title were his before he died. That does not matter–you must have discovered by now that men successfully resurrected from the dead do not consider themselves to be the same men they were when they were alive."

Ned had, in fact, taken due note of the fact that "Lazarus" preferred a obvious pseudonym to the name he had owned in life. "The world is overfull of imaginary Counts," he said, still dutifully beating around the bush. "What the French Revolutionaries began, Bonaparte completed–the old aristocracy is gone, and the new one is open to anyone who can make his claim persuasive. I do want to open negotiations with you, on behalf of Comte Henri de Belcamp–which is only one of my own employer's many names–but I wonder whether it can wait until I've had a few hours' sleep. My first prior-

106

ity is to be able to work as hard and efficiently as I can to make Frankenstein's new experiment a success. May we postpone the remainder of this conversation until tomorrow?"

"Yes, if that's your wish. You do seem very tired. If the Tuscan army puts in an appearance, though, I might be forced to retreat. If so, tell Frankenstein, his Grey Adam and your Comte that my Count would be very interested in a meeting, to discuss matters of mutual interest. Paris might be the most suitable venue. I'll find you again, when I can."

"Do you think the Tuscan army is likely to intervene?" Ned asked.

"They are a good deal more likely to do so now that half of Spezia has taken up arms," Guido told him. "A few foreigners dabbling in conspiracy can be regarded as a matter of marginal concern, but local populations forming associations of self-interest is something else. Don't get carried away by your enthusiasm, Monsieur Knob. You might be full of optimism just now, because of the strange turn that events have taken here, but the Church has sharper blades than Malo de Treguern, and the many political wounds inflicted by the war are still very sore. The individuals we represent must make what alliances they can against the new crusade. You and I must try to keep in touch."

"I'll do my best," Ned agreed. "Is your Count Szandor also interested in meeting Gregory Temple, then?"

"I suspect that Temple and his political masters will be more ready to align themselves with Treguern, for all that they are Protestants. For the time being, it will surely be sufficient to bring the parties I named together."

"Do you know how Shelley is?" Ned asked, abruptly.

"Bearing up, I believe. No worse, at any rate. His wife is said to be improving too–but it's too soon to tell whether or not they'll need Frankenstein's services, as it's too soon to tell whether he'll still be able to offer them this time tomorrow. You'd better sleep now–I'll try to find out what the other Hospitaller is doing, and hinder him if I can."

The rival spy left by means of the door, his slippered feet making hardly any noise on the wooden stairway as he went downstairs. Ned drank a cupful of water and then lay down on his bed, fully dressed. Exhaustion sent him to sleep without delay, in spite of the fact that he had not eaten for more than 24 hours.

Chapter Ten
Between Death and Life

By the time Ned was able to return to Walton's house, dusk was falling. The crowd surrounding the grounds parted silently to let him through. He found Malo de Treguern sitting on the step of the main door, haggard and dispirited. The warrior monk did not reply to Ned's polite greeting.

The stove in Frankenstein's laboratory was blazing, and the room was exceedingly hot, although the French windows opening to the rear of the house had been thrown open to the light breeze that drifted down the steep hillside towards the cooling waters of the Ligurian Sea. Trelawny, Walton and Hay were all in the garden outside, talking in low voices.

All the carefully-stacked supportive apparatus had now been established around the three large enameled bathtubs in the center of the room. The wires carrying the electrical fluid had been gathered into clumps and tied in bundles, but still seemed to be running back and forth in chaotic confusion. Only a few of them were attached to the arrays electrodes immersed in the liquid that each bath contained. Lazarus and Frankenstein were working steadily to put the final touches on this phase of the labor, apparently in perfect harmony.

Ned was delighted to see the Grey Man and his maker united in their purpose. The man of science no longer seemed haunted or unready for anything; he was fully absorbed in his quest again, working with calm determination. Lazarus was at ease too, as if this were his vocation too–as well it might be, Ned supposed, given that he was bravely working for the better future of his own kind in a hostile world.

The apparatus Ned had seen in Patou's cellar in Purfleet had seemed makeshift enough, but the many polished relics of James Graham's pretentious "Temples of Health and Hygiene" that Patou had acquired had given the ensemble a certain style and grandeur, and the cellar itself had been large enough to allow the individual units to be sensibly spaced out. There was no style or grandeur here; all the equipment communicated an impression of hasty improvisation, and the sitting-room that had adapted for use as a laboratory seemed decidedly cramped and inappropriately overcrowded now that so much metal and so many ponderous ceramic vessels had been accumulated within it.

The viscous liquid in the baths was conspicuously darker in hue than the fluid Ned had seen in Patou's baths, but it did not seem, as yet, to be alive in its own right. Patou's life-endowing fluid had resembled brightly streaming protoplasm observed with the assistance of strong light and a magnifying lens, but this was more like sullen molasses accumulated in the gutters of a sugar refinery.

The three dead bodies had not yet been immersed in the baths; they were still laid out on a table adjacent to the wall opposite the French windows. Their congealed blood had been re-liquefied and drained from their bodies into huge jars; while Ned watched, waiting to discover whether there was anything his hands and mind could usefully contribute, Frankenstein set about replacing it with a different fluid, whose function was not to embalm the bodies but to assist in their revitalization.

Lazarus stood up and nodded to Ned. "It looks ugly," he said, "but I believe that it will work." The Grey Man's voice now had a tremor of anxious excitement in it, but there was none of the nervous agitation that possessed Frankenstein.

"What do you want me to do?" Ned asked.

"Help Frankenstein with the injections," Lazarus said. "Your fingers are nimbler than mine, and he's almost ready to drop."

Ned moved to do as he was asked. The bodies were largely unmarked. Ned recognized the one Guido had strangled and the one whose throat Lazarus had crushed. The third man had been stabbed in the heart, but the wound was not gaping, and seemed as if might disappear altogether if its edges were carefully placed together.

Frankenstein looked up as Ned appeared by his side. "This requires expert hands," the scientist said. "Thank you, but I'd better do it myself." In the end, though, once Ned had watched him subject the first body to the necessary preparations, he reluctantly accepted that his weariness was beginning to get the better of him, and contented himself with watching Ned repeat the operation twice more under his instruction.

I am a resurrectionist now! Ned thought, exultantly. *I am a true collaborator in the great work. I have surely seen and understood enough, now, to direct such an operation myself, when the need and opportunity arise.* He knew that he was assuming and claiming a little too much, but his spirit was over-full of enthusiasm and ambition.

"When you're done," Frankenstein told him, "we must place the bodies in the fluid. After that, there'll be

111

little to do but wait, and hope. With luck, at least one or two of them will recover some semblance of life–and we shall have to pray that the crowd outside find enough to satisfy them in that appearance." His voice became noticeably less robust as this speech was concluded; the man of science seemed to be faltering in his resolve again now that his work was almost complete. When Ned finally set the last syringe down and turned to look at his instructor, he saw a slight flash of resentment in Frankenstein's bloodshot eyes. It was as if Frankenstein saw something in Ned's fervent determination to carry the resurrectionist cause forward that made him jealous.

Ned went back to Lazarus, who was testing the tangled wiring. "Will there be sufficient electrical fluid?" Ned asked.

"We must hope so," the Grey Man replied, in a low voice. "Frankenstein's provision in that regard was barely adequate, but the extra batteries the townspeople secured should give us a margin for error. My maker has concentrated his recent research on the chemical aspects of the revivifying process, as is only to be expected."

"Why is that?" Ned asked.

The Grey Man hesitated momentarily, but then said: "Because the resurrection of the dead can only be a preliminary and partial goal, so far as he is concerned. His ultimate objective has always been the preservation of the living against the possibility of death, to the extent that such preservation might be possible."

"The discovery of an elixir of life, you mean?"

"Yes–or, perhaps, an elixir of metamorphosis, which would permit a living body to remake its own substance, greatly augmenting its resilience in respect of disease and injury."

"Alchemists and magicians sought such a device in vain for centuries," Ned reminded him.

"Their chemistry was fatally flawed. They had not even begun to understand the chemistry of life. We have only made a beginning, even now, but at least we have begun. I am the living proof of the rewards that may flow from progress yet to be made. Let us hope that we can show the people outside a little more, while they are still hungry for it. They have opened a window of opportunity for us, and it will be a tragedy if we cannot keep it open. If Frankenstein were able to continue to work here in peace, under the protection of his neighbors, it would be very advantageous to our cause."

"I admire your optimism," murmured a newcomer to their conversation, "but conspicuous success in this endeavor might prove more disastrous than total failure."

Ned looked round, and found himself looking up into Robert Walton's anxious eyes. "In what way?" he asked.

"As King George's spy, you should understand that quite well," Walton told him, bitterly. "If Victor's method demonstrates its worth publicly, at this relatively early stage in his research, the Church's objections to necromancy will be the least of our problems. Do you think that the Tuscan authorities, or any other government, will be content to let us be, so that we may revive bandits and the poor? What do you think the fate would have been of any alchemist who actually discovered the rudiments of a method of making gold or the elements of a technique that might deliver immortality? It was not for fear of madmen like Treguern that we set out to operate in secret, but for fear of possessive monopolists who might fight for our custody like starving dogs over a joint of meat, in order to reserve the proceeds of our further progress for their own profit. Whatever the result of this experiment is, we need to get out of here and vanish as soon as we can." The last remark was aimed at Lazarus, who could not now be excluded from Walton's narrow conception of "we."

"Guido seems to be thinking along the same lines," Ned said, uneasily.

"We can surely deal with properly constituted authorities by diplomatic means," Lazarus said to Walton. "We may yet have cause to be thankful that we have a representative of His Majesty's government here."

Remembering what Guido had said about the side that Gregory Temple and his political masters might take, Ned was not so sure that His Majesty's government would be behind him, or even that it would be as readily amenable to diplomacy as the Grey Man naively assumed—but he did not say so.

"Time is on our side now," Lazarus said, "provided that Treguern's companion cannot summon reinforcements."

"The Tuscan Light Horse is a greater danger by far," Walton opined. "A detachment could ride from Pisa in a matter of hours. They already have a score to settle with us, and might not be in a mood to negotiate. If they do come, Trelawny, Taaffe and Hay agree with me that the vital thing is to spirit you and Frankenstein away—on the *Bolivar* if that is possible, the *Don Juan* if not."

"San Terenzo is conveniently close," Ned observed, addressing himself to Lazarus, "for a man who can walk freely and at his leisure. In a chase or a hunt, as you've already had occasion to notice, the same distance might seem a very long way."

"It's the only escape route we have," Walton stated, baldly. "What's King George's position on the matter,

Mr. Knob? Would he rather we surrendered to the local authorities, or that we killed a few in making good our escape?" He spoke the King's name with a contemptuous curl of his lip. Ned knew that the King and Lord Byron had once been on good terms, in the days when the Prince had not yet surrendered himself completely to a life of idle debauchery, but no one seemed to like him now that he had ascended to the throne.

"In His Majesty's absence," Ned said, airily, "I must obviously act on my own initiative. I'll help you, to the extent that I can–but I'd rather we didn't have to kill anyone, if that's possible, even if we are forced to run."

"Good," said Walton. "I'll pass the word along." He turned and strode back through the open French windows, leaving Lazarus and Ned to assist Frankenstein in moving the bodies into the tanks. Walton brought his companions in from the garden while the three bodies were being carefully immersed and the electrodes connected. Lazarus and Frankenstein made the final adjustments, and then there was nothing to do but wait.

Lazarus went out to tell the crowd that everything had been done that needed to be done, but that no result could be expected for at least 12 hours, and perhaps 24.

The crowd began to disperse, but left a cohort behind that was more than sufficient to form a cordon around the house. These guardians did not prevent John Taaffe from leaving, in order to carry news to Casa Magni, but they grew far more attentive when Frankenstein stepped out for a breath of air, and Ned deduced that they knew exactly what the value of each of their hostages was.

Ned felt duty-bound to go to Frankenstein and say: "If you care to come to England, sir, I can guarantee you the protection of Gregory Temple, who is a man of considerable influence and ability."

"Perhaps you could," Frankenstein said. "The government of Switzerland would probably do more, given that I'm a citizen of Geneva, and I'd be sure of a welcome in Prussia, too–but I'm too much a Calvinist to tolerate overseers of my conscience, whoever they might be."

"I'm a radical myself, sir, despite my profession," Ned said, "and I sympathize with your position."

When Lazarus came back indoors, Ned went to sit with him, and asked the Grey Adam to tell him the true story behind the melodrama of *Frankenstein*. Lazarus did so, and also undertook to complete Ned's practical education in the art and science of resurrection by telling him everything he knew and supposed about the process by which Grey Men were made. All this took several hours, but the new Adam did not pause or hesitate–nor, seemingly, did he hold any anything in reserve. "Take all that to England, if you will," he said, when he had finished. "Make a full report to Gregory Temple, by all means–but if anything should happen to my maker and myself as this particular affair proceeds to its culmination, make sure the information reaches Humphry Davy and Erasmus Darwin. I don't know whether the Royal Society or the Lunar Society will be the better motivated to use it, but one of them must."

"I'll do that," Ned promised.

As with Walton and Trelawny, no move was made to stop Ned when he went back to the hotel again to get something more to eat. He was not so lucky, though, when he tried to leave the dining-room to go back to his bed, for the young men from Sussex were there, making merry before yet another whoring expedition. They knew that something very strange was afoot in the town, and had found out that he was caught up in it.

He told them the truth, in synoptic form, but they laughed uproariously and called him a fine romancer. They, at least, were still trapped within the narrow span of their own limited dimension, which hardly touched the world through which they moved as idle tourists.

"Have you seen Master Shelley at Casa Magni?" one of them asked him. "He could probably make a fine epic poem out of a story like that."

"Where do you suppose the little man got it from?" scoffed another of the good companions. "It's all borrowed from that garish horror tale he published anonymously back in '18."

"No, that was Byron," said yet another, "and it was in '19, in *Blackwood's*."

"The tale of the vampire is another story," Ned said, apologetically, "which I have yet to learn in full. In time, though, lads, in time..." And with that, he contrived to extricate himself from their company, and went back to bed.

Chapter Eleven
The Tuscan Light Horse

Ned did not intend to sleep late, but exhaustion got the better of him again, and the morning sunlight was streaming through his window when he finally staggered out of bed. He bathed and ate a hearty breakfast before making his way yet again to the house behind the olive grove under the harsh light of a blazing Sun that was no more than two hours from its zenith.

He found Frankenstein poring over one of the three corpses, vibrant with excitement, while Walton and Lazarus looked on. "It's definitely working!" the man of science said. "The fluid is beginning to flow in his veins, albeit sluggishly and his flesh is maintaining its consistency remarkably well. Decay had hardly set in, so there's less work to be done..."

"Can you wake him?" Walton asked, impatiently.

"Not yet," said the Grey Man, answering for his maker. "For his sake, it will be better not to hurry."

"I don't care about the bandit," Walton said, brutally. "The point is to satisfy that mob, and get out of here while we can. It might be better if he doesn't recover his wits, in my opinion. How soon will he be in a fit state to put on parade?"

Frankenstein pursed his lips, but made no comment on Walton's attitude. He pushed his right hand into the slimy liquid again to test the flesh of the dead man's arm.

"The signs of life he's showing won't be sustainable outside the fluid for six hours, at least," the man of science opined. "Even then, he might not be able to walk or talk if we hauled him out. We have to leave him immersed until dusk, at least."

Walton consulted his watch. Dusk, Ned knew, was a full nine hours away. "Time for a division of the infantry to arrive in force," Walton muttered, "let alone a detachment of cavalry—but we wouldn't be wise to make a move before nightfall, unless it's absolutely necessary. I can't stand all this *waiting*, though."

"Go to Casa Magni, then," said Frankenstein. "The crowd won't bar your way. Change the dressing on Shelley's wound. Comfort Mary—and tell Williams to be ready to put to sea at a moment's notice."

Walton shook his head. He was determined to stay. If trouble did materialize, that would be the time for him to assume command.

Once the night became dark, Ned knew, Gregory Temple's courier would return to the hotel, expecting to collect another report. At the same time—or a little beforehand, if his ship had caught a favorable wind—Henri de Belcamp's courier would station himself on the approach to the quay at much the same time. The thought of encoding everything he had to write, twice over, was distinctly tiresome, although he knew that he ought to send some word, in case he did not get the chance again. Assuming that he still had time in hand, though, he went out of the main door into the sunlight. Malo de Treguern was still sitting on the step, as if he were hoping that God might somehow contrive to send down a lightning-bolt from the cloudless sky, to obliterate the Antichrist's lair.

"Have you had anything to eat, Brother Malo?" Ned asked him, sitting down beside him.

"I have fasted for 40 days and 40 nights in my time," the ex-Knight of Malta informed him, stiffly.

"They will let you leave, I think," Ned said. "It's only Frankenstein and the Grey Man they're holding prisoner, and Walton won't try to hold you any longer against your will. You'll probably find your friend waiting for you in San Terenzo–although I'm surprised that he hasn't come here to make sure that you're unhurt."

"You will not obtain any advantage by pretended amity," Treguern told him, bluntly.

Ned ignored the rebuke. "You think he's gone for help, then," he said, as if thinking aloud. "But where to? Not to Rome, that's for sure. *Civitas Solis* had convents within a day's ride of Paris, but I doubt that the same is true of any Italian city."

Mention of *Civitas Solis* made Treguern turn his head slightly to look more sharply at his interlocutor, but the warrior monk was as good as his word, and gave nothing away.

"It would not be unprecedented for two orders of the Church to be at loggerheads," Ned went on, "especially when one, at least, could easily be deemed heretical. On the other hand, you seem to me to be every inch the scholar, probably as conscientiously esoteric in his chosen fields of study as Victor Frankenstein. If I were to guess, I'd guess that the relic of the Order of St. John is now under the protection and supervision of the revitalized *Civitas Solis*–unlike my old friend John Devil, whose application for membership was probably rejected, although a certain Jesuitical caution might have prevented your masters from telling him outright. On the other hand, *Civitas Solis* may be a mere myth, like vampires and the elixir of life, unworthy of serious consideration by intelligent men."

Treguern deigned to comment at last. "A buzzing fly," he said. "The slightest irritation imaginable."

"You are entitled to your opinion of me," Ned said, equably, "but I'm not an unreasonable man, Brother Malo. Even though I have no religion, I'm also a passably virtuous one. If and when you find out where the *Outremort* has made landfall, I have information to trade that might make it worth your while to let me in on the secret. I'm usually in London or Paris, and will not be too hard to find in either city for a man with your resources."

"I have spent more time than I deserved in the company of revenants, working patiently for the fulfillment of prophecies," Treguern said, enigmatically but with perfect equanimity. "I'm an old man, and my time of rest cannot be long delayed–but if God still has work for me to do, then he will succor me. You'd do well to be wary, if you're as easy to find as you say."

"I'm sure that the Lord will lend you the assistance you need," Ned told him. "Remember, though, that He works in mysterious ways. Given the company you've been keeping of late, death might be no more than a punctuation mark in the ongoing story of your life, and you might be required to do the Lord's work for a long time thereafter. The road to Heavenly indolence might not be as easy to negotiate as you presently suppose."

That finally got an emotional reaction from the Churchman. "Vile korrigan!" he exclaimed–but then the expression in his fiery eyes changed from wrath to exultation as he saw something beyond the hedge. Ned immediately stood up to see what it was.

It was as if a flock of birds with impossibly ornate tails were fluttering in the unkempt branches at the crown of the hedge. It required two seconds and an anxious murmur from the waiting crowd for Ned to realize that they were actually the plumes of military helmets.

The Tuscan Light Horse had arrived.

Ned promptly turned back to Malo de Treguern, and contrived to pronounce the single syllable "Don't..." before he realized how futile any such plea would be.

Having lost the loyalty of his hirelings and failed to sway the Spezian mob, the soldier in God's Army still had high hopes of claiming the loyal support of a secular military unit. He had already come to his feet and was drawing in a deep breath.

Ned did not linger, but darted inside the house, calling for Walton and Trelawny. This time, he knew, the Grey Man would not be the right spokesman to represent the conspiracy.

By the time Walton had run outside, though, followed by Trelawny, Malo de Treguern had already embarked upon his new clarion call–and he was more in control of himself now than he had been when he had ranted at the sullen crowd in the gloom.

The officer in charge of the cavalry detachment had been followed through the gate by three other riders, but once he had come to a halt, there was no room on the path for any more, so the others were grouping in the narrow lane beyond the hedge. The members of the loosely-knit crowd, somewhat circumspect in the presence of bright uniforms and sturdy sabers, had hesitated between pressing forward and retreating into the shadows; they had already sacrificed the opportunity to seem intimidatingly resolute.

Malo de Treguern pointed a bony finger at Walton, rattling out a string of accusations that had nothing to do with necromancy. Ned knew that the cavalrymen were already ill-disposed towards the Englishmen, even though it had been their own man who had picked the quarrel some weeks before. In all probability, none of these riders knew that Masi had been acting under orders, and they very probably had their own ideas as to what had happened and why. Malo de Treguern knew all of that too, and know how to make his pitch to the mind of officialdom.

Walton ran forward and began to shout as loudly as Treguern, denying the accusations leveled against him and demanding to be left in peace. Ned had enormous difficulty following the overlapping tirades, but he understood well enough when Treguern set off on a new tack, complaining about the desecration of the bodies of good Italians and good Catholics, and demanding that the corpses be recovered for proper burial. Walton immediately launched into a stream of protest, but Ned could see that the pre-emptive strike had taken effect on both the officer and his men.

The crowd realized that too, and its ringleaders made a belated decision to exercise its power–but the artisans had delayed too long to make any effective attempt to demonstrate conclusively that they were the superior force and the ultimate arbiters of the situation, and thus deter the soldiers from any belligerence. When the Spezians attempted to gather in a tentatively threatening manner, the Pisan calvarymen were quick to draw their sabers and muster a formation.

There was a brief moment when the crowd's ringleaders might have drawn back, to form their own men up in quasi-military ranks and put on a countervailing display of potential strength, which might have made the officer pause to reflect–but the moment was lost. The mounted soldiers urged their horses forward, as they had probably done a dozen times before when breaking up crowds in Pisa, fully expecting the men on foot to scatter and run. The Spezians were, however, made of sterner stuff.

Ned wanted to join in the shouting, in order to beg the men of Spezia to mass by the door of the house and block the entrance, but his Italian was not up to the task, and he could not have made himself heard even if they had been willing and able to listen to him. The Tuscan Light Horse had evidently been given grounds for a grudge or two in their time, and as soon as the impression was created that they were actually attacking the common people, with no good reason and without sufficient numbers to be sure of victory, the incipient conflict turned into a disorderly riot.

The officer's reaction–natural enough, on tactical grounds–was to look for a defense. The door of the house stood wide open, with no one to defend it but a handful of unarmed men. The officer yelled an order at his men, and charged straight for it.

It was, unfortunately, a capacious doorway; there was plenty of room for a horse and rider to pass through it, without the rider having to duck too low. Walton was bowled over by the officer's horse. Ned had no alternative but to imitate Trelawny and dive sideways to avoid his thrusting saber and the iron-shod hooves of his mount.

Ned got to his feet as quickly as he could, but there was nothing he could do as five more horses swept past him, one by one. They galloped straight along the corridor towards Victor Frankenstein's laboratory.

Ned had to imagine what would happen when they arrived there, but it was not hard. In his mind's eye, he saw the sturdy but delicately-balanced equipment tumbling, its brittler elements smashing on the tiled floor, and also saw the multitudinous wires dragged hither and yon, ripped from their connections. The baths would not be upset; nor, in all probability, would the calvarymen pause to drag the men who were suspended between death and new life from their fluid in which they were immersed–but all hope of their eventual resurrection was lost now.

The remainder of the cavalry troop was caught up in the seething crowd, whose members were now agitated to fear and fury. There were few screams, and Ned could see that both sides in the battle were exercising a measure of restraint; the horsemen still considered themselves to be engaged in crowd control rather than a massacre, and the men fighting from the crowd were trying to unhorse the soldiers rather than hack them to pieces. Far more bruises were being inflicted than cuts–but even so, the situation was completely out of control. The riot could not be stopped.

Walton barked an order, in English, instructing his own people to execute the emergency scheme he had hatched. There was no alternative. There seemed to be little chance, though, that Frankenstein's friends could form a coherent group in order to protect one another as they retreated in an orderly manner.

Ned ran into the house. The corridor leading to the laboratory was clear now, and there was nothing to obstruct his passage. As he had anticipated, though, the laboratory itself was in a very different state. The horses had passed right through and made their exit by the wide-open French windows, their riders apparently hoping that they might go around the house and tackle the crowd from the rear, but they had done enormous damage as they passed. In the event, three of their riders–

including the officer–had been thrown or forced to dismount, and all three were waving their swords in near-panic, although no one was trying to engage them in combat.

Frankenstein, to his credit, had not only stood his ground bravely but was still doing everything he could to defend the baths where the dead men lay. He was screaming at the soldiers, with his empty hands held high to demonstrate that he was unarmed, but his Italian was not good enough for him to make his message clear; the cavalrymen were extremely unsympathetic to his attempts to block their way, even though they had no idea where they ought to be going, or why. The officer would have run the scientist through had Lazarus not snatched his maker away in the nick of time and dragged him towards the French windows.

Ned would have run to help them if he could have done so, but there was too much debris in the way, and his short legs could not bound over it with sufficient alacrity.

Lazarus caught sight of Ned as he was making good his escape, dragging Frankenstein with him. "Run, Ned!" he shouted. "Get clear as best you can!"

It was good advice, and Ned knew it. He turned on his heel and went back the way he had come. Once he was out of the front door, he put his head down and sprinted for the gate. Once he was out of the gate, he headed for the steepest part of the hill and he went down it with all possible speed.

He did not stop running until he reached the shore, by which time he was completely out of breath. He looked around, hoping that he might see Lazarus and Frankenstein, or any one of the others, running behind him–but he found himself alone. He took two or three leaden steps in the direction of San Terenzo, but paused as he realized that help might be available nearer at hand. He hesitated for a full minute–but then he did catch sight of other running men coming towards him, from the direction of Casa Magni. There were at least three, He cursed as he recognized more of Malo de Treguern's *banditti*. He did not suppose that the orders Treguern had given them two nights before had been countermanded.

Mercifully, he had time to give the bandits the slip.

Fortunately, it also turned out that the boat that had brought Henri de Belcamp's courier to collect his latest report had arrived early.

Unfortunately, that was the last stroke of luck he had for quite some time.

Chapter Twelve
At Sea

Ned intended, once the courier's vessel had cleared the harbor, to sail directly to Casa Magni. That did not happen quickly, though, because the harbormaster insisted on delaying the vessel's departure until it had been cleared by customs officers.

The customs officers were not acting on anyone else's orders, and had not the slightest inkling of what had been happening on the hill above Spezia, far beyond their sphere of interest and influence, but simply by carrying out their ordinary functions in their customary manner, they contrived to hold Ned back for several hours. During that interval, the weather changed drastically.

A violent squall blew up–so violent that the boat's master evoked his privilege and refused to put to sea once he was cleared to do so. Ned had authority enough and anger enough to overrule him, but his insistence turned out to be worse than futile–once out of the harbor, the vessel could make no headway at all towards Casa Magni, even though it was a mere mile away, and was blown out to sea instead. By the time the storm had died, as rapidly as it had been born, it was too late. Ned returned to Casa Magni to find the *Don Juan* gone and the house deserted. He lingered for a while, hoping that Guido might be lurking in the vicinity, but in the end, he consented to be borne away westwards.

At Genoa, Ned wrote his report and translated it in-to code–once only–for the benefit of Gregory Temple. He took it to a dispatch office in the city which handled large volumes of material sent to England by tourists, and entrusted it to the mail-coach. By that time, 48 hours had passed since the vessel had left Spezia, having been forced to put into Riomaggiore to pick up supplies that the captain had not had time to load upon departure. That particular delay proved something of a small bless-ing, though. The Italian courier, who was no stranger to waterfront inns, was able to collect rumors regarding the sensational events in Spezia in Riomaggiore that would not have troubled the more urbane gossips of Genoa. Once the more flagrant fantasies had been discarded, those rumors had allowed him to amend and augment his report to a judicious degree.

What Ned wrote to Gregory Temple, in the clear version, was: *VF forced to abandon new experiment and flee following arrest attempt by Tuscan cavalry, urged on by Malo de Treguern, once Knight of Malta–please investigate. VF's first resurrectee joined company; fled with his maker. No reported English casualties.* Bolivar and Don Juan *both put out to sea, carrying most or all of conspirators, but all their equipment lost. Destination unknown, but should be possible to identify if enough spies alerted. VF will certainly resume work if possible.* Ned was by no means entirely content with this narra-tive, but he resisted the temptation to embellish it fur-ther. There were some things that he would have to con-fide to Temple in person.

By the time Ned finally reached London, a full two weeks later, more news had caught up with him, arriving through the orthodox medium of the French daily news-papers.

Percy Shelley and John Williams, in company with one Charles Vivian, it was reported, had set sail in the *Don Juan* from Leghorn on July 8, intending to take the vessel to San Terenzo. Edward Trelawny had intended to accompany them in the *Bolivar*, but had been retained there by the harbormaster. A storm had blown up that afternoon, and Trelawny had been forced to wait until it cleared to set out after his friends. The *Don Juan* had not arrived at San Terenzo, and the boat's dinghy had been washed up at Viareggio, with other debris. Three days later, two bodies had come ashore, one near the tower of Migliarino and the other near Viareggio. Both had been badly damaged and were partly decomposed; they had been buried in quicklime. One of them had been identified as Shelley's by means of a book of poems by John Keats, contained in the pocket of his jacket; the other was assumed to be Williams. A third body was subsequently found, and buried at the mouth of the Serchio. The body identified as Shelley's was subsequently burned on a pyre, although Trelawny was said to have recovered a heart, miraculously unburnt, from the ashes and had preserved it in brandy.

Ned felt perfectly sure that these reports were false from beginning to end, and he told Gregory Temple that when he finally came face to face with him in his office in Whitehall.

"For one thing," Ned said, "the *Don Juan* was at San Terenzo on the morning of July 8, not Leghorn, and the *Bolivar* was almost certainly there too. If the two boats encountered the storm, as my own did, they probably encountered it together. Mary Shelley and Jane Williams were in Spezia when I arrived at Casa Magni, having presumably been sent there for safety's sake. Having been entirely uninvolved in the events at Walton's house, it is possible that Percy Shelley and Williams remained there with them, but I feel certain that they would have gone with their companions.

"Assuming that they did put out to sea with Frankenstein and the other members of the company, they must have been taken aboard the *Bolivar* if the *Don Juan* really did run into difficulties, but it seems equally probable to me that the debris was thrown overboard deliberately, to give the impression of a catastrophe that did not, in fact, take place. The intention may well have been to persuade the Tuscan authorities, and Malo de Treguern, that Victor Frankenstein and his first subject had drowned in the storm–although the authorities could hardly be expected to publicize that, whether they believed it or not

"I cannot guess whose the three bodies actually were, but I am sure in my own mind that Shelley, Williams and Frankenstein are all alive. This manifest nonsense about the heart being recovered from the funeral pyre must have been put about for the purposes of dissimulation. Even if they are not alive–even if Shelley had already succumbed to the unfortunate reopening of the wound that Masi had inflicted–I feel sure that his body is safe in Frankenstein's custody, not burned on some Italian beach. Whatever Trelawny has in that jar of brandy, it is certainly not Shelley's heart. It cannot be."

"You're an utter fool, Master Knob," Temple told him. "A spy cannot think like that. He must deal in facts, not Romantic fancies and delusions. In any case, there is no need for us to worry about some miserable poet. The point is to determine whether Frankenstein and his creature are alive. If they do contrive to resume their work, even after some delay, when they have made a discreet landfall, we need to know about it. You made a bad mess of this mission, and I'm sorely disappointed in you. You should have discovered where Frankenstein was bound, even if you had to stow away on the vessel that carried him away from Spezia in order to do it. Now we have to find him all over again. It might not be so easy to stop him in his new location as it would have been in Tuscany."

"Stop him?" Ned queried. "Is that the policy of the King and Parliament? Are they so jealous of their petty privileges that they would preserve death's empire in order not upset their own?"

"No more of that radical talk, imbecile!" Temple told him, sternly. "You work for me now, although you're so ridiculously incompetent that I ought to send you back to play the fool in Jenny Paddock's gin-palace until you rot. The King's desires are your desires, and you'd better not forget that."

"I won't forget it," Ned promised. "Did you investigate Treguern, as I suggested?"

"I've obtained reports on your former Knight of Malta from his native Brittany," Temple told him. "They're agreed that he's a good and heroic man, albeit a little crazed. We can work with him, I think, despite his being a Romanist."

Ned shook his head, slowly, but made no verbal protest. He knew that Henri de Belcamp would not have understood, either, why it was so important that Percy Shelley should not have been lost forever, whether he were dead or alive. Nor would Guido, the vampire's minion, have understood it. None of them understood that it was the poets who were the true legislators of the world. None of them was a true Romantic.

Ned had not included any mention of Guido's vampire master in the report he had sent to Gregory Temple from Genoa, and he renewed his decision not to mention it in Whitehall. This was not because he particularly wanted to keep the vampire's existence secret, but because he did not want to damage his credulity and further than it had already been damaged. He had, however, told Henri de Belcamp about the alleged vampire's request for a meeting, on the grounds that John Devil was a man of far more liberal imagination than his former arch-enemy.

I am on no one's side but my own, now, Ned told himself, when Gregory Temple finally dismissed him from the dingy office, after suggesting disdainfully that he might as well go back to his work with Jenny Paddock's petty theater while awaiting further instructions. *No one's side, that is, but that of the unbound Prometheus. If Shelley is really dead, and there is no one left but me who understands how the world ought to be changed, and must be changed, then I must be the one to direct its metamorphosis.*

PART TWO: THE VAMPIRE IN PARIS

Chapter One
Fog in Paris

As Gregory Temple was about to turn the corner of the Rue de la Lanterne he heard a curious sound, something between a hiss and a whistle, which was evidently intended to attract his attention. He turned to look at the dark doorway from which it had come, but the combination of shadow and fog made it impossible to discern the face of the man who was lurking there. He cursed the bad weather; fog was the curse of London, but he appeared to have brought this one with him to the streets of Paris, where it seemed to him to be just as foreign as he was.

"Monsieur Temple!" The man in the door way was evidently impatient.

Temple did not move, although he had stopped dead. If the other man wanted to talk to him, then he would have to step out into the street, where he face would be lit, vaguely at least, by a street-light.

Eventually, the other accepted the necessity. He was a small man but a wiry one, dressed with unusual flamboyance for someone who maintained vigils in dark doorways, although he did not seem to have acquired sophisticated tastes, any more than he was blessed with natural elegance. He might have passed for a dandy in the worst kind of licherie, but he would have been a clownish caricature in the Bois de Boulogne.

"We'd do better to step into the shadows, Monsieur Temple," the caricature said, speaking in vulgar French but obviously expecting to be understood. "You're being followed, and you're not the only visitor that Monsieur Sévérin is expecting tonight. Monsieur Vidocq suggested that I should look out for you, and make contact if I could. Don't worry—we're on the same side."

Temple scowled in dire annoyance. He had not been in the best of tempers for some time, ever since discovering that Ned Knob had held back a considerable fraction of the story of what had happened in the Spezia. It was bad enough to be betrayed by one's own petty low-life spies without having their French equivalents greet him as if he were a brother in arms. He had heard rumors at the Prefecture regarding the gang of ex-convicts who had set up as an arm of the detective police in the Petite Rue de Sainte-Anne, with the reluctant blessing of the Prefect, and was not at all pleased to learn that they had apparently heard rumors of his business—rumors that had evidently been updated as a result of his findings in the Prefecture files, which he had assumed to be known to no one else but himself. "Is that hulking brute dogging my footsteps another of Vidocq's damned *bagne*-sweepings?" he demanded, angrily.

The agent did not seem at all alarmed by his attitude. "Monsieur Vidocq is a great admirer of your work, Monsieur Temple," he said, earnestly. "He considers your book on the art of detection to be a masterpiece. My name is Coco-Lacour. I'm Monsieur Vidocq's most trusted associate—and I can assure you that the person following you is not one of our men. If you will agree to work with Monsieur Vidocq in this matter, we can easily relieve you of the inconvenience of being followed."

Temple suspected that there was probably little competition for the title of "Vidocq's most trusted associate," but he struggled to remove the cutting edge in his voice. Coco-Lacour might be the worst kind of police agent, but he was a policeman nevertheless. "That's very kind of you, Monsieur Lacour," he said, warily. "I shall be pleased to call on Monsieur Vidocq at the Petite Rue de Sainte-Anne when I have the time—perhaps tomorrow."

"Coco-Lacour," the other corrected him, understandably anxious that no one should think that Coco was his forename rather than part of a nickname he had doubtless been given in the *bagne* from which Vidocq had plucked him. "Would you like me to have your follower arrested tonight? I would have to summon several of my colleagues in order to make the arrest, but I could do that if you wish. He'll doubtless linger nearby while you're talking to Monsieur Sévérin."

"Please don't go to any trouble," Temple replied. "If he's not one of your men, he must belong to another branch of the Prefecture, and I wouldn't like to cause Monsieur le Préfet any inconvenience."

"I'm sorry to have to correct you, Monsieur Temple" said Coco-Lacour, who did not sound in the least sorry, "but he has no connection whatsoever with the forces of law and order. I dare say that your presence in Paris is not without interest to the political police, but the *hulking brute*, as you call him, is in the employ of an Englishman. Would you like to know his name?"

"If you've got something to say," Temple retorted, "spit it out."

The *licherie* dandy sighed. "Lord Byron," he said, briefly, immediately adding: "but you probably knew that already."

Temple had not known it already, but he did not find the news surprising. The fact that Byron was in Paris—although there was no suggestion in the reports received in London that Victor Frankenstein was with him—had been one of the factors that had drawn Temple here, although his principal motive had been a desire to consult the Prefecture files with respect to the infamous vampire affair of 1804. Thanks to Ned Knob's disloyalty, he was apparently late on the scene, at least one step behind the other players in the game—including, it now seemed, the vampire himself. It was even possible, Temple thought, that Henri de Belcamp, *alias* John Devil—to whom The perfidious Knob had presumably made a fuller report of his discoveries in Spezia—might be among the people taking a sudden interest in the vampire of Paris, but he was not about to ask one of Vidocq's gang of poachers-turned-gamekeepers about the one man in the world they undoubtedly admired more enthusiastically than himself. "Why are you watching Jean-Pierre Sévérin's house?" he growled, instead.

"Monsieur Sévérin is a very popular man nowadays," Coco-Lacour replied, still seemingly confident that he had the advantage of knowing more than his interlocutor. "If I were to tell you the names of some of those...but I have my duty to the Prefecture to consider, and you're a foreign spy. Our countries are no longer at war, but still...."

"Monsieur Sévérin has always been a much-respected man," Temple said, stiffly. "When he was in charge of the morgue at the Marché-Neuf, he had occasion to meet many influential people. It's remarkable is it not, what a generous cross-section of Parisian society the...what do you call it in France?... the *salle d'exposition* brings out. You and Monsieur Vidocq must be regular visitors yourselves, in search of old friends and adversaries."

"Monsieur Sévérin is not as well-respected as he used to be," Coco-Lacour told him. "The political wind is a little chilly nowadays for old Bonapartists. A little unfair, perhaps, since he was never associated with the Deliverance, and his son-in-law is a *chouan*—but he did know the emperor personally, and that counts as a black mark nowadays. You visited the *salle* more than once yourself in the old days, I believe, war or no war—breakdowns in diplomatic relations are God's gift to the criminal classes, are they not? You were not one to let petty international disputes keep you from maintaining contact with *old friends and adversaries*."

The point was a fair one but Temple was not about to call *touché*. "Goodnight, Monsieur Lacour," he said.

Coco-Lacour frowned "There is no need to be impolite, Monsieur Temple," he said, in a wounded tone. "We are colleagues, after all. Our little band of heroic crime-fighters might well be able to render you invaluable assistance—if you were to get into difficulties."

Temple did not bother to ask whether that was a veiled threat. He was, after all, the man on foreign soil; it was inevitable that the Prefecture should be enthusiastic to maintain a monopoly on detective work conducted in the capital, even of the crazy kind in which he was presently engaged. He could not help wondering, though, why Vidocq's agents—who were supposedly affiliated to the criminal police, although they were rumored to be nothing more than organized criminals themselves—were taking such an interest in a representative of His Majesty's Secret Service.

"I do not anticipate getting into difficulties, Monsieur Lacour," Temple retorted, "and we are not colleagues. I'm no longer employed by Scotland Yard; I have retired from police work and am here in Paris simply to look up a few old friends, of whom Monsieur Séverin is one."

"Oh, have it your own way," Coco-Lacour replied, probably more put out by the continued deliberate mangling of his name than by any disappointed expectations. "Monsieur Vidocq will be disappointed, but he's come to expect such ingratitude." He stepped back into the shadowed doorway so abruptly, that Temple turn round, expecting to see that a third person had come into view further along the street—but if Coco-Lacour had seen someone, the other had been very quick to take evasive action.

Again, Temple cursed the fog. Then he swiftly rounded the corner of the Rue de la Lanterne and sounded the bell of the first house whose door he encountered.

It was not a concierge who answered but a young woman, perhaps seventeen years of age. She had beautiful blonde hair.

Temple told her his name, and asked, in French, to see Jean-Pierre Séverin."[4]

"I'm afraid that Monsieur Séverin is very old, Monsieur," The young woman replied. "He hardly receives visitors at all, and never at this advanced hour."

"He'll see me," Temple said. "I knew him long ago, when he was in charge of...the establishment at the Marché-Neuf. I was a detective at Scotland Yard at the time, but I'm retired now, just as he is."

---

[4] A character introduced in Paul Féval's *The Vampire Countess* (Black Coat Press, 2003, ISBN 978-0-9740711-5-2).

The blonde girl's dark blue eyes looked him up and down, as if estimating his own antiquity, and any worth he might have acquired in consequence. She was not about to be convinced, through.

"I'm afraid…." She began—but was then interrupted.

"It's all right, Angela," said a male voice from the stairway behind her. "This isn't the one we were expecting. I'll handle it."

"Yes, father," the young woman said, meekly. She stepped back, and was replaced in the doorway by a melancholy man with dark hair, who must have been in his late thirties.

"Monsieur de Kervoz, I presume?" Temple was quick to say. The corridor inside the door was too dark to allow him to judge the extent of the other's surprise at hearing his name spoken.

"I don't believe I've had the privilege," René de Kervoz said, in English—with almost as much stiffness as a genuine Briton might have contrived.

"I need to speak to Monsieur Séverin," Temple said, not wanting to stand on the foggy street any longer than necessary. "I'm sorry to call at such a late hour, but I've been busy since my arrival. You will both be interested in what I have to say. It concerns Countess Marcian Gregoryi."

This time, the young man's start of surprise was very clearly visible. "What do you mean?" he demanded.

"I need to see Monsieur Séverin," Temple repeated.

René de Kervoz hesitated, then nodded. "Please go to your room, Angela," he said. "I'll take Monsieur Temple up to see your grandfather. If the other one comes, tell him that Monsieur Séverin is engaged, and cannot possibly see anyone else tonight."

"I'm glad that my unannounced call has provided you with a potentially-useful excuse," Temple murmured, as they mounted the staircase to the first floor. "I shall feel a little less embarrassed by my inability to warn you that I was coming."

Kervoz made no reply, but stood aside politely as he ushered his visitor through the doorway of a bedroom. Jean-Pierre Séverin evidently had no reception-room or study, although he belonged to the respectable ranks of the poor and was the proud possessor of two large bookcases as well as a capacious writing-desk. The bed-curtains were closed, and the retired morgue-keeper was sitting in an armchair by the fireside. He was, as his great-granddaughter had said, very old—but he was not frail, and he stood up to greet Temple with a polite bow, followed by an English handshake.

"Gregory Temple," Séverin said, immediately. "Why, it must be at least five years since I saw you last. How are you?"

"Quite well," Temple lied. "I wanted to come to see you when I was last in Paris, but I was exceedingly busy."

"The affair of the two assassins buried at the Trocadero," Séverin said, as he resumed his own seat and indicated that Temple should take the one opposite the hearth. René de Kervoz fetched a less comfortable chair from the bedside for himself. "The trial at Versailles caused quite a sensation—we followed its course eagerly in the newspapers. Should the young man have been convicted? He came from a very good family, did he not? But he committed suicide immediately after his release, so I suppose he must have had some cause for shame."

"His father's family is a very good one," Temple admitted, not bothering to tell his host that he had been in Paris far more recently than the trial at Versailles, in order to visit the Château de Belcamp and contend with a gang of kidnappers, "but his mother...well, that was another story. Henri de Belcamp was something of a chimera, his dark and light selves seemingly in continual conflict. Yes, he should have been convicted, but no, he did not commit suicide. That was yet another of his see-mingly-miraculous evasions."

"Mr. Temple says that he wants to talk about Countess Marcian Gregoryi," [5] René de Kervoz put in, apparently eager to blight the old man's gladness at seeing an old friend.

Jean-Pierre Séverin did not react with alarm, though, or even with undue astonishment. "I did not know that you were party to that affair," he said, in a voice that was low but perfectly even. "Our countries were not on the best of terms at the time—although such petty disputes did not always prevent you from visiting us, of course."

"I've only read the reports filed at the Prefecture," Temple admitted. "I don't know how accurate the information contained therein might be, given the extreme unreliability of its sources, but I have some reason to suspect that it is not as fanciful as it must have seemed at the time to Monsieur le Préfet."

"Do you, indeed?" murmured Séverin, cocking an eyebrow. "I have not seen the files myself, of course, but I remember that old villain Ezekiel, who must have supplied much of their content. I wish I could say that the

---

[5] A character introduced in Paul Féval's *The Vampire Countess* (Black Coat Press, 2003, ISBN 978-0-9740711-5-2).

Prefecture no longer hires men of that stripe, but I fear that it would not be true."

"There's one watching your house as we speak," Temple told him. "He seems to have been posted to look out for someone else who was intending to pay you a visit tonight—the one you asked your granddaughter to put off."

"I seem to have become somewhat sought-after lately," Sévérin admitted. "Everyone is hungry for information about my old friend Germain Patou. I seem to have convinced people that I have no news of his whereabouts, but I cannot seem to persuade them that I know nothing about his experiments, or that I do not know where he hid any records he might have kept. Even some of my old friends from the morgue can find no other topic to discuss."

"I'm interested in Patou too," Temple admitted. "Obviously, I take your word for the fact that you have no knowledge of any records he kept—but I'm a little concerned to hear that you've attracted the attention of people who might not. Would you mind telling me who you are expecting to call tonight?"

"Not at all," the old man replied. He took up a visiting-card from the occasional table beside his armchair and held it out to Temple. "He did not request an appointment," Sévérin said, with a slight sigh. "He simply asked the Dominican lackey who brought the card to say that he would call on me this evening, if he could. The Church takes the Restoration very seriously, and seems to regard the king's resumption of his throne merely as a symbol of its own renewal."

The name on the card was MALO DE TRE-GUERN. There was no address, but there was a design beneath the name: a red Cross of Calvary, entwined with a thorny briar that might—or might not—have symbolized Christ's crown of thorns.

Temple was considerably intrigued, not so much by the fact that Malo de Treguern wanted to consult Jean-Pierre Sévérin as by the odd circumstance that Monsieur Vidocq had posted one of his men at the corner to watch out for a Churchman operating on the direct authority of a papal warrant. "Do you know this Treguern?" he asked.

"Only by reputation," René de Kervoz put in. "He's a legend in my native province. He was a Knight of Malta before the Emperor disbanded the Order, and then spent many years on a quest to find a fragment lost from the tomb of one of his ancestors. He was thought to be mad, but the object of the quest—the restoration of his family's fortune—was eventually fulfilled, with or without the stone in question. After that, he disappeared from Brittany. It was rumored that he had gone to Rome."

"He did," Temple supplied, feeling that he ought to offer as much of a *quid pro quo* as his duty permitted. "He's working for the Holy Office now."

"As a heresy hunter?" Kervoz said. "What has that to do with us?"

"I don't imagine for a moment that you're under suspicion of heresy," Temple hastened to reassure him. "He has a different quarry in view—the same one, I suspect, that I am pursuing. All my rivals are ahead of me, it seems, and I must count myself fortunate that I seem to have overtaken him, at least."

"What quarry do you have in view?" Jean-Pierre Sévérin asked. "And by what authority are you hunting on French soil?"

"Monsieur le Préfet knows that I am here," Temple said, taking the easier question first. "I have his permission, if not his blessing. I came to Paris to investigate the vampire that terrorized the city eighteen years ago—and was both astonished and alarmed to learn that he seems to have returned."

"She, not he," René de Kervoz put in.

"Countess Marcian Gregoryi," Séverin said, pensively. "Has she returned?" Temple was glad that the old soldier wasted no time with any futile protest that the countess was dead. The old man had seen René de Kervoz shoot her in the head, but he knew now, if he had not then, that the eyes of men were subject to gross deception in the presence of that remarkable woman.

"A woman of that name is now in Paris," Temple told him. "I am not certain that it is the same woman that was here in 1804, since she is said to be in her early twenties, but I have learned to expect the seemingly impossible in this affair. That is one reason for my presence here—I was hoping that you might be able to identify her for me if your memory is good enough. Monsieur de Kervoz's attempted correction might be mistaken, though; if my information is trustworthy—which is, I admit, dubious—the countess you encountered in 1804 was not the actual vampire, properly speaking, but merely his instrument."

"That was not my impression," René de Kervoz murmured, doubtless recalling the fateful day on which the countess had seduced him, while pretending to be her own dark-haired sister, seemingly in order to obtain the secret of his uncle's whereabouts. "But you need have no fear that my memory has faded. If Countess Marcian Gregoryi is indeed in Paris, whether she had aged a full eighteen years or not a day, I will know her as soon as I set eyes on her."

"Is it possible, do you think, Mr. Temple." Jean-Pierre Séverin asked, "that the woman now using the name might be the same one, even though she looks no older?"

"I think it is," Temple said. "It is possible that she is a different person altogether—an innocent instrument, completely in her master's power—and that even if she seems to be the same, that appearance is merely a clever illusion. I really do not know what to expect of this vampire—but I do not think that he is the bloodsucking monster of superstition. He appears to know secrets that science has not yet discovered, which might perhaps have been known to mages of old and then lost—but it is equally possible that he made them himself, if he is as old as the facts suggest."

"There was no rumor of bloodsucking in 1804," the white-haired ex-morgue-keeper said, softly. "The manner of predation attribute to the countess was even more bizarre—but people died nevertheless. Who does the countess intend to marry and murder this time?"

"I doubt that she intends to marry anyone," Temple said. "Her master is in search of the same thing as everyone else: the records of Germain Patou's experiments, and those of Victor Frankenstein, if any exist. I suspect, though, that the so-called vampire, like Malo de Treguern, is more intent on destroying such secrets than making use of them. Like the Church, albeit in a very different fashion, he is probably a would-be monopolist in matters of resurrection."

"You said that asking for our help in deciding whether the present Countess Marcian Gregoryi is the same one that was in Paris before was one reason why you came," Séverin asked. "It seems a trivial one—what are the others?"

"I thought that you would like to know," Temple said, simply. "I thought that you ought to be warned—and…."

René de Kervoz cut him off. "Warned?" the Breton said. "She is the one that ought to be frightened of us. We have a score to settle. I tried to shoot her once, and believed that I had done so; I'll be delighted to have another chance. She killed my beloved Angela—the mother of the girl who answered the door to you just now."

"It would be unwise to shoot her again," Temple said. "It would be reckoned as murder if you succeeded this time, no matter what crimes she might or might not have committed in the past."

"Might or might not?" Kervoz echoed. "Are you saying that she did not kill Angela?"

"I have no reliable information as to that, one way or the other," Temple told him. "Neither, I think, do you."

Kervoz was about to protest, but Séverin silenced him with a gesture. "René was deluded when he was seduced and drugged by the countess, and was in no fit condition to form reliable judgments." the old man said, addressing himself to the Englishman. "What I saw on the river that night—all of which must be neatly recorded in the Prefecture's files—was admittedly impossible, and I have every reason to doubt that my own eyes were telling me the truth. I have had abundant cause to wonder whether I collaborated wholeheartedly in an illusion, because I could not bear the thought that my daughter had committed suicide. She was my step-daughter, as you probably know, but I loved her no less for that. The fact remains, though, that she did die—and that Countess

Marcian Gregoryi *was* responsible, directly or indirectly, for her death."

"If you really did catch a glimpse of a supernatural creature in the river that night," Temple told him, "it might have been the actual vampire rather than his glamorous instrument—I can draw no firm conclusion on the matter until I find out more."

"You were about to give us another reason for your visit when René interrupted you," Séverin said. "Is it that you want our help in trying to find out?"

"Yes," Temple said. "I am alone in this business, mistrusted by my superiors and unable to place the slightest faith in my hirelings. I need assistance if I am to get to the bottom of it. All the other interested parties are ahead of me—including, it seems, the infamous Monsieur Vidocq. I hoped that you might give me the help I need, given that you have your own very powerful reasons for wanting to understand what really happened in 1804. I must warn you both, though, that it may not be possible for you to take your vengeance. If, as I suspect, the vampire has already died at least once, and has powerful means at his disposal to create illusions, he might be more difficult to destroy than you or I can imagine."

"I thought I saw the countess reduced to ashes once, and was then convinced that I had blasted her brains out," René de Kervoz muttered. "Was all that really no more than illusion?"

"I suspect so," Temple said, "but I cannot be entirely sure. There are more things in Heaven and Earth than I once dreamed of—but I need to find out, and I need help that I can rely on."

"I'm glad that you consider us trustworthy," Séverin replied, courteously, "but my granddaughter is always assuring me that I'm far too old for adventuring nowadays. It's a long time since I took my little skiff out on the river. René, on the other hand…."

"René can speak for himself," Kervoz interrupted, sharply. The Breton did not seem enraptured by the prospect of working for an English policeman, even though the prospect of hunting down the vampire that had killed his young wife-to-be was obviously tempting, even after all these years.

"Might I ask you an exceedingly delicate question, Monsieur Sévérin?" Temple said, hastening to interrupt any possible dispute between the two men.

"Of course," Sévérin replied, suggesting by his tone that he was not promising an answer.

"You spent the whole of your working life in the Paris morgue," Temple said, his own tone one of deadly earnest, "And you succeeded your father, who held the same position before the Revolution. There is no one in the world more qualified to give an expert judgment on this matter. Tell me, Monsieur Sévérin: *do the dead ever return to life?*"

"You are the second person to ask me that, in so many words, within a week," Sévérin said, pensively. "Like you, the other was an old acquaintance from my days at the Morgue—a genuinely good man, though, not a polite ghoul like some of those who haunted the *salle*. I told him that I could not be sure, and I will give you the same answer. You must know, of course, that the morgue was first established in consequence of a panic regarding the possibility of premature burials, rather than for its ostensible purpose of allowing the dead to be formally identified. I do not know how much truth there is in the many gruesome tales of men awakening in their coffins and tearing off their fingernails scrabbling hopelessly at the wooden lid, but it must have happened on occasion. It is certainly true that a small number of those brought into the morgue as dead eventually began to move again, and to sit up on their slabs demanding to know where they were.

"The official attitude to such cases has always been that they could not have been truly dead, but only cataleptic, and I have always agreed with that judgment in public...but I *cannot be sure*. Some of the *revenants* did not seem to their relatives to be the same person they had been before. Again, the official attitude to such cases has always been that their brains must have suffered some damage as a result of their catalepsy, which affected their minds, and its is certainly true that most of those undergoing such transformations were damaged beyond repair, having been rendered stupid or mad...but again, *I cannot be sure*. I am not at all certain what a man who really had returned from the dead, or a spirit that had possessed the body of a dead man, would be able to do to persuade an unprejudiced observer that he really had been resurrected, or that he really was a different person from the one who had died.

"If you were to ask me whether I believe in vampires, Mr. Temple I would have to say that I really do not know whether I believe in them or not, simply because I hardly know what I might mean by the word when I pronounce it. Germain did believe in the evidence of his own eyes, wholeheartedly—and, having convinced himself that Countess Marcian Gregoryi really had returned from the dead, he immediately set out to discover a means of restoring *all* the dead to life. He was equally convinced that he had found the road to success, and I was present at some of his earliest demonstrations...but at the end of the day, all that I can truthfully say on my own behalf is that *I cannot be sure*."

"Thank you for your honesty, old friend," said Temple, sincerely. "I appreciate it. I, too, cannot be sure, but I have grown so familiar of late with the notion that the dead can return, with the proper assistance—and sometimes without any assistance whatsoever— that I am no longer certain even of my own uncertainty. Who, by the way, was the other old friend who asked you the question?"

"Colonel Bozzo-Corona—you might have heard of him. He's said to be very rich, and a great philanthropist, although he lives quite modestly in the Rue Thérèse."[6]

It was Temple's turn to be astonished, and slightly alarmed, although he was unable to tell his host why that was the case, and was not entirely certain himself. "Colonel Bozzo-Corona is interested in this affair?" he repeated, playing for time.

"Not in this business with the vampire, or even the matter of Germain's supposed secret—but he did ask the question about the dead returning to life. He has known me for a long time, as I said. He was always interested in the morgue—fearful, I think, of his own mortality. You do know him, then?"

"Yes I do," Temple replied. "He has visited London several times, and had more than one occasion to make himself helpful to the police. He was directly or indirectly responsible for more than one of Scotland Yard's early arrests."

"He does not travel as much nowadays," the old man told him.

Temple had to remind himself to get back to the immediate point of his visit. "I have not yet found out

---

[6] A character introduced in Paul Féval's *The Black Coats* series (several volumes, all from Black Coat Press).

where Countess Marcian Gregoryi is staying in Paris, but I believe that I know where she will be tonight. I shall try to follow her myself, but I am not as young as I once was, and she will doubtless have at least one man with her on her carriage. Monsieur de Kervoz has followed her successfully before, I believe. If we were three instead of one, I think we would stand a greater chance of tracking her to her lair, in spite of the fact that two of us are no longer well-fitted for such work—and we shall certainly be able to learn more about her."

"Where will she be?" Séverin asked.

"I discovered, quite by chance, that she has made an appointment to see a lawyer named Robert Surrisy at his office, not far from the Tuileries. I do not know, as yet, what she wants him to do for her, and it might not be easy to find out once she has told him—he is another old acquaintance of mine, who has occasionally acted on my behalf in French legal matters, but he takes his duty of confidentiality very seriously, and would not have let it slip that she was about to become his client had he imagined that the fact could be of any professional interest to me."

"And how do you propose we get to the Tuileries?" René de Kervoz demanded. "Have you a carriage?"

"No," said Temple, evenly. "We shall have to take a fiacre. We will be followed, but that does not matter. If we split up thereafter, the follower will probably stick with me."

"While I...." Kervoz began—but again he was interrupted by the old man's peremptory gesture.

"We will both go with you," Séverin promised, standing up and reaching for a slender cane that was leaning on the arm of his chair. "If this woman really is Countess Marcian Gregoryi, René will run after her carriage when she leaves the lawyer's office, and he will report back to us here when he has found out where she goes thereafter. But I must ask you one question first, Mr. Temple, since you have not asked it of me: Do you know where Germain Patou is?"

"I have information on that score that I believe to be reliable," Temple replied, without hesitation, "and I have dispatched agents to find out whether it is accurate or not. I wish that I could reassure you that he is safe and well, but I cannot. He left London in very bad company: a small army of Grey Men, led by a veritable demon who calls himself Mortdieu. Did you witness his resurrection, by any chance?"

"No," said Sévérin, who was already in the corridor, retrieving his coat from a stand. "That was not one of his early experiments. Germain left Paris in order to carry out a particular mission, but I do not know what it was—except that, now you mention...." he trailed off, as if struggling hard to recover a memory that had surfaced momentarily and then sunk back into oblivion.

"Except what?" Temple prompted.

"There was a lawyer involved in that negotiation too," Jean-Pierre Sévérin said, as he set off down the stairs with an expected spring in his step, twirling his cane like a dandy in anticipation of some amorous adventure. "Now that I come to think about it, I believe that his name, too, was Surrisy...."

Chapter Two
Three Ladies of Quality

When the hired fiacre set the three men down at the southern end of the Avenue de l'Opéra Gregory Temple's first action was to look back carefully along the thoroughfare, searching for evidence of their likely followers. Coco-Lacour, he presumed, would not have bothered to remain at the corner of the Rue de la Lanterne when he saw the three men come out together, figuring that there was nothing to be learned from watching Malo de Treguern turned away from an empty house. Temple could not see any evidence, however, that any other cab had followed theirs, and there was no sign of the burly man who was reputedly working for Lord Byron. Then he checked his watch, to make sure that they were still in advance of the time that Countess Marcian Gregoryi had fixed for her appointment with Robert Surrisy.

While the three men walked to the side-street in which Surrisy's apartment and business office were located, Temple mulled over the possible consequences of what Jean-Pierre Séverin had told him immediately before they had set out. He had certainly mentioned Germain Patou's name to Robert more than once without obtaining any response whatsoever—which implied that Robert was deliberately hiding something from him, presumably something that the lawyer considered to be protected by his duty of confidentiality. Temple already knew that Patou had entered into some sort of compact with Henri de Belcamp, and if that compact had been negotiated by a lawyer, Henri might well have asked Robert to act for him—though probably not directly, given that Robert was supposed to believe, like everyone else in Paris, that Henri really had shot himself. It would undoubtedly have amused Henri to do that, given the past that he and Robert shared. Robert had been in love with Jeanne Herbet before Henri came home to Miremont, and had even tried to win her back after Henri's disappearance—but she had been determined to remain true to the memory of the father of her son.

The three watchers had no difficulty, in a street almost as badly lit as the Rue de la Lanterne, in finding a covert where they could watch Robert Surrisy's door without the slightest danger of being seen. They had not been waiting a quarter of an hour when a sumptuous carriage pulled up outside the door in question.

"She always did believe in traveling in style," muttered René de Kervoz.

"She's ten minutes early," was Temple's only comment—but then he drew in his breath sharply.

"What's the matter?" Séverin asked.

"That's not the same...." Kervoz began, the disappointment in his voice very obvious as he stared at the woman who had just got down from the carriage while her footman went to knock on the door.

"Shh!" said Temple. In order to forestall questions, he added, in a whisper: "That's Countess Boehm—the former Sarah O'Brien. She's Robert Surrisy's half-sister. She bought the so-called new château in Miremont not so long ago, intending to make a home there, but there was an unfortunate incident some little while ago that gave her pause for thought. I was under the impression that she was intent on returning to her husband's estates

156

in Germany." He did not bother to explain that his source for these items of information was his own daughter, now resident at the Château de Belcamp.

"There's another carriage coming," Kervoz observed, almost as soon as Countess Boehm had disappeared into the house. "This one has a French coat-of arms."

Temple could not quite suppress a curse, which escaped as a half-strangled gasp.

"It's another comtesse, though," the Breton went on, his own voice gaining inconvenient volume as his excitement revived.

"It's the Comtesse de Belcamp," Temple was quick to supply, hardly able to believe his eyes. "Of all the nights to come calling…."

This time, a full quarter of an hour ticked by.

Neither of the two women who had gone into Robert Surrisy's house had come out again, in spite of the fact that he must have told them that he was expecting a client imminently. For a moment, Temple wondered whether Countess Marcian Gregoryi might have cancelled her appointment—but then a third carriage turned the corner, coming from the direction of the *quai*. Far from being early, the vampire's minion was actually five minutes late. Her coachman had to draw to a halt a good thirty meters from Robert Surrisy's door, but the Countess did not seem to mind. She walked along the pavement behind her footman, resplendent in her flowing blonde locks, unrestrained by any hat.

"Mon Dieu!" said René de Kervoz. "She *is* the same! She had dark hair when she seduced me, and claimed the blonde was her twin, but there's no doubt—she's the same, and not a day older!"

"That is the woman I saw in 1804," Jean-Pierre Sévérin confirmed, in a whisper, his tone perfectly sober and rather pensive, "and she has not aged a day in eighteen years. What does it mean, Mr. Temple?"

Temple made no answer, having none to give; he was holding his breath.

When the footman knocked, the door was immediately opened, and the third countess vanished into the interior.

Gregory Temple let out his breath. "She must have summoned them to meet her here!" he said, wonderingly. "Perhaps she *is* after money! But how does she propose to persuade Jeanne and Sarah to hand it over, if that's her objective? The old châteaux is almost as well-protected now as it was in the days when every fine house had to be a fortress, and Jeanne is not in a trustful frame of mind nowadays." Even as he spoke, however, he had a sinking feeling in the pit of his stomach. If Countess Marcian Grigoryi were to persuade Jeanne that she had reliable news of Henri, Jeanne might well be willing to pay for the information—and if the countess really did have such information…."

"Perhaps it's as well, after all, that there are three of us," Sévérin suggested, cutting off Temple's train of thought.

"I already know where the other two live, and I have eyes and ears in that camp" Temple told him. "I wish I were a fly on the wall of Robert's office, though. Jeanne and Sarah have not the slightest idea who this woman is, because I never thought for a minute that I ought to warn them. I can only hope that Robert has had time—and has taken the trouble—to warn them that she is a person of interest to me. That will put them on their guard, if they are not sufficiently suspicious already"

The waiting soon became painful for the detective, who was now in a state of high tension. "You must not lose her, Monsieur de Kervoz," he said to his new acquaintance. "We must know where she is staying, if we are to frustrate her master's plan. We must know everything we can discover, as soon as possible—I might have to go to Vidocq after all."

"You can depend on me," the Breton assured him, grimly.

"Do you know that man, Mr. Temple?" Séverin suddenly asked, using the tip of his slender cane to indicate a passer-by who was walking purposefully along the pavement, as if he were late for an appointment, but who darted sideways glances at all three of the parked carriages as he passed them by.

Temple cursed again. "I met him for the first time tonight," he said. "His name is Coco-Lacour, and he's one of Vidocq's gang—wolves in sheep's clothing, like your old friend Ezekiel. He's good, though—I never caught a glimpse of him following us. I wonder whether my other stalker is also here?"

Having passed the third carriage, Coco-Lacour paused and looked around attentively. Temple groaned. He and his two companions were quite invisible, but a man like Coco-Lacour, once convinced that they were nearby, would have no difficulty at all in identifying their hiding-place. Astonishingly, having picked the spot out, the police agent proceeded to saunter insouciantly across the street to join the three watchers.

"Bonsoir, Mr. Temple," he said. "Monsieur Séverin, Monsieur de Kervoz, you may be interested to know that Malo de Treguern did eventually arrive at your house, but that he went away disappointed. He'll be back, mind—he's a man who knows how to stick to a

159

task, when matters of duty are at stake. It's said that he's far cleverer at appealing to the conscience of the devout in the course of his interrogations than Monsieur Vidocq has ever contrived to be."

"How do you know that Treguern arrived, if you followed us?" Temple demanded, suspiciously.

"I didn't follow you," Coco-Lacour said, with a broad smile. "I already had one of my colleagues close by, in a fiacre—just in case. He drove you here, then reported back to me. You *were* followed, of course—but you already know all about His Lordship's man. Would you care to tell me why the Comtesses Jeanne de Belcamp and Sarah von Boehm are visiting Monsieur Surrisy, and who the third party is who seems to have an assignation with them?"

"No," Temple said, through gritted teeth, "I wouldn't."

"So much for professional courtesy," observed Coco-Lacour. "Do you mind if I wait with you? Professional curiosity will now oblige me to follow the third carriage."

"I'd rather you didn't," was all that Temple could think of to say.

"But this is Paris," Coco-Lacour pointed out, "where I have full authority to act and you merely have permission from the Prefect to go about your business unhindered. It really would be better if you were to accept our co-operation."

"This does not concern you," Temple told him, frostily. "It's not a criminal matter."

"Now there, I must correct you," the agent said. "This is most definitely a criminal matter." He leaned forward, as if to impart of confidence, and said, in a carefully-contrived whisper: "It concerns the Gentlemen of the Night," He pronounced the final phrase in English, his atrocious accent only serving to emphasize the mockery in his tone.

The remark took Temple by surprise, but he controlled his irritation. "Is *that* who you're hunting?" he asked, contemptuously. "I wish you the best of luck, then—I've chased them myself, and only caught smoke."

"Who are the Gentlemen of the Night?" Jean-Pierre Sévérin enquired.

"The name originated as a myth," Temple told him, "invented by the crooked magistrate Jonathan Wild—but it's a myth that continually intrudes upon reality, as one gang of more-or-less organized criminals after another lays claim to the name and its associated reputation, in order to intimidate their recruits and victims alike. Tom Brown, *alias* John Devil, was the head of one such gang. That's dispersed now, but I dare say that someone else is taking over the legend even as we speak—perhaps more than one someone. I thought the equivalent title in Paris was the *Habits Noirs*—although we've had Blackcoats in London too, so I suppose Paris is entitled to its own *Gentilhommes de la Nuit*."

"Will it be light tomorrow?" Coco-Lacour quipped, cheerily. "Yes, I believe that it will, fog or no fog. But there were Ladies of the Night too, were there not? Tom's mother Helen was the real gang-leader, and the operation fell apart when you shipped her off to Australia."

There was nothing surprising in the fact that Vidocq's right-hand man had these items of information on the tip of his tongue, but the fact that he had bothered to repeat them here and now caused Temple some anxiety. Was Vidocq's motley crew of notionally-reformed villains now in the pay of Henri de Belcamp, alias Tom Brown, alias John Devil? Was that why they were keeping an eye on Malo de Treguern? Were they, perhaps, working—knowingly or unknowingly—for *Civitas Solis*?

"If you are intending to slander the Comtesse de Belcamp or Countess Boehm," Temple said, darkly, "you had best be careful."

"I wouldn't dream of it," Coco-Lacour replied. "They are most certainly not Ladies of the Night—but I do not know who the proprietor of that third carriage is, and I do know something of Monsieur Surrisy's reputation. He's a Bonapartist too, Monsieur Sévérin, of a more dangerous type than yourself."

"Bonaparte's dead and buried," Temple said, shortly.

"Dead, yes," Coco-Lacour agreed. "Buried—I'm not so sure. There are rumors."

"There are always rumors," Temple retorted. "Go away, please, and leave us in peace."

"To lurk in the shadows watching over the houses of honest Frenchmen?" Coco-Lacour queried. "I'm a member of the Sûreté, Monsieur Temple—I'm duty bound to prevent such things from happening. I could have you all arrested and thrown into the Conciergerie. Can you give me one good reason why I should not?"

"Because the Prefect would love to have an excuse to throw you out on your ear," Temple retorted, although he was by no means sure of that, "and nine Parisian policemen out of ten would cheer your departure. Now...."

He had no chance to go on. The door of the house he was supposed to be watching had just opened, and three women emerged: three extraordinarily beautiful young women, each one guaranteed to turn heads and attract admiring glances. Of the three, though, Countess Marcian Gregoryi—the only one, presumably, never to have borne a child—probably had the edge. Had Paris of Troy been judging this contest, and judging it fairly, the golden apple would doubtless have gone to her.

The three women seemed to be on very friendly terms. They exchanged kisses on the cheeks as they separated and went to their respective carriages. As each of the three prepared to mount the steps unfolded by their faithful footmen, Countess Marcian Gregoryi called out to the other two: "Remember, I can be contacted at the Hôtel Trianon in the Rue Caumartin."

"That's lucky!" Coco-Lacour observed, in a whisper.

Gregory Temple, who thought the remark far too apposite to have been made by chance, knew that René de Kervoz could not see his face well enough to read his expression, so he had to take it on trust that the younger man would follow the prearranged plan.

When the carriages drew off, René immediately set off to follow the vampire's minion—and so did Coco-Lacour, who was evidently not a trusting man. Gregory Temple stayed where he was, and Jean-Pierre Séverin stayed with him.

"I'm sorry about that," Temple said to his companion, once the three carriages had all disappeared and Vidocq's agent was safely out of earshot. "It's an inconvenience, but not a fatal one. The agent won't do René any harm. This is unfamiliar territory for him—he's more used to picking up petty thieves—and he's improvising as he goes along. I dare say that Vidocq's put him on to this out of simple curiosity—all that stuff about Gentlemen of the Night was probably just bluster."

"You don't need to convince me of anything," Sévérin reminded him. "What do we do now?"

"Now," Temple said, "we go to see Monsieur Surrisy—and hope that he's prepared to give us the information we need. Now that Jeanne and his sister are involved, I should be able to persuade him that there are more important loyalties at stake than his duty of confidentiality."

The two men crossed the road and Temple knocked on the lawyer's door. The concierge who admitted them seemed heartily sick and tired of the continual stream of visitors, but let them in without too much ill grace, and led them to Surrisy's study. Surrrisy did not seem pleased to see them, but he greeted Temple courteously enough.

"Robert," said Gregory Temple, as the lawyer came to shake his hand, "may I introduce Jean-Pierre Sévérin. He's had dealings with Countess Marcian Gregoryi before. If I can't convince you that there's anything uncanny about her, he might be able to do so."

"I've heard your name, Monsieur Sévérin," Robert Surrisy said, bowing and waving his guests to leather-clad armchairs who seats were still slightly warm. "It has a fine reputation in the circles in which I once moved—but I must confess to both of you that the countess seems to me to be perfectly delightful. Jeanne and Sarah evidently like her too—although I confess, too, that I was surprised to see them here. I had no idea that they had been invited to the consultation."

Temple gritted his teeth slightly. Robert Surrisy's attitude made it all too obvious that he had been charmed by his beautiful client, even in the presence of two women he had loved very dearly indeed. It was not going to be easy, now, to persuade the lawyer to co-operate.

"And what was the consultation about?" Temple asked.

"I can't tell you that," Surrisy parried. "I have a duty of confidentiality to my client."

"And I have an offer of collaboration and support from Monsieur Vidocq," Temple told him. "Their interest ought to inform you that something is amiss here. Is Countess Marcian Gregoryi's business such a closely-guarded secret? Did she forbid you to mention it to anyone? You know full well that I can simply ask Jeanne— why not save me a little time?"

Surrisy sighed, but he obviously had no powerful reason to be stubborn. "Countess Marcian Gregoryi merely wants to buy the new château at Miremont," he said. "Even though Sarah has only recently acquired it, she wants to sell up and return to Germany, because of the kidnapping. She has promised that she would not sell it to anyone who might compromise Jeanne's security at the old château, so she invited her to be party to the negotiation as a matter of courtesy. I don't think Jeanne will raise any objection to the new owner now that she's met her, though. Everyone seems perfectly satisfied, and there's nothing in this that could possibly concern you, Mr. Temple, as a detective."

"You may be perfectly certain that Jeanne will raise an objection," Temple said, flatly, "once I have talked to her."

"Once you have told her that the countess is a vampire's minion?" Surrisy's tone had suddenly become firmer, if not exactly hostile. "She might not believe that, Mr. Temple, even from you. You were the one, after all, who once told the old Marquis that Henri was not guilty of General O'Brien's murder. I have not yet forgiven you that lie—and probably never will, given what it did to my mother."

"I apologize for that," Temple said. "My intention was to alleviate a friend's misery, not exacerbate misery in anyone else. You must believe me, though, when I tell you that Countess Marcian Gregoryi is a highly deceptive and thoroughly dishonest person. Monsieur Sévérin can confirm that she is the same individual who visited Paris in 1804, during the vampire panic, and was implicated in several murders—and that she does not seem to have aged a day in the interim."

Surrisy did not even glance at Sévérin in search of that confirmation. "She explained about her mother," he said, shortly.

"Her *mother?*" The incredulous interpolation came from Sévérin.

"Yes—surely you cannot really believe that the Countess Marcian Gregoryi with whom you had dealings some eighteen years ago was the same one as this, who is only a few years older than that? It was to secure the present countess's future that the original countess committed her crimes—which, her daughter assures me, were greatly exaggerated at the time. She was not a multiple murderer, as rumor now claims, or even a serial bigamist."

"Marcian Gregoryi is the name of the supposed Hungarian count to whom the mysterious lady claimed to have been married," Jean-Pierre Sévérin pointed out. "Her daughter would not—could not—have the same name."

"She could," Surrisy countered, "if she were the one and only true Countess Marcian Gregoryi, fully entitled to a name that her mother was not really entitled to wear.

She is, in fact, legitimately married to the son of the man whose mistress the first so-called countess was."

"She is the same woman," Jean-Pierre Sévérin stated, flatly. "I would know her anywhere."

"There is no need to press the point further, Monsieur Sévérin," Temple said, calmly. "There will be no sale—I can guarantee that. Now, Robert—what else did you find out? Did she tell you that she is staying in the Hôtel de Trianon, on the Rue Caumartin?"

"If you already know that," Surrisy countered, "why ask?"

"Because I do not think it is true, and I do not understand why she should take so much trouble to advertise the address" Temple retorted. "Monsieur Sévérin's friend is following her carriage, and so is one of Vidocq's agents. Hopefully, they will discover where she is really staying. Did you, perchance contrive to notice anything that was not a mere show put on for your benefit?"

Temple realized immediately that he had made a mistake in phrasing the question in that mildly insulting manner; his fraught nerves had got the better of him. Robert Surrisy took offence, and became even less ready to help than he had been before. "No," the lawyer said, coldly, "I did not. I repeat that the countess seemed to me to be entirely honest and perfectly charming—and I really ought not to have told you anything that passed between us."

"In fact," Temple said, "you ought to be extremely enthusiastic to give me all the help you can. You should also have told me what dealings you had with Germain Patou before he left Paris some three or four years ago. You mentioned at Miremont that you knew him, but you did not say that you had acted on his behalf."

For a moment, Surrisy seemed genuinely puzzled. Then his face cleared. "But I didn't act on his behalf," he said. "I drew up a contract of partnership for someone else, to which he was a signatory. I only met him once, and everything I know about him is based on hearsay rather than acquaintance. I had no idea at the time that the contract in question had to do with this business of attempting to bring the dead back to life, to which you introduced me a few months ago—and I certainly did not connect it in my mind to this new nonsense about vampires"

"Was the other signatory to the contract Henri de Belcamp?" Temple asked.

"Good Lord, no!" Surrisy replied, his shock seeming quite genuine. "I was still under the impression at that time that Henri was dead. No, I can be absolutely certain that he had nothing to do with it. I was acting for quite a famous man, as it happens—but I really should not tell you who he was, for that would certainly be a breach of trust that could land me in hot water."

Temple knew that he would only have one chance to surprise a reaction from the lawyer; if he guessed wrong the first time, it would put Surrisy on his guard. He only hesitated a moment, though, before saying: "Lord Byron."

Robert Surrisy was too honest for his own good; he could not maintain a blank face. "If you already know the answers to all the questions you're firing at me," he said, resentfully, "why are you even here? And why are you dangling other names before me, when you know they have nothing to do with it?"

"I'm trying to complete an enormously complex jigsaw, Robert," Temple told him. "It's very difficult to see where each piece fits, until it is actually in place.

Henri de Belcamp has everything to do with this, no matter how determined he is to keep a low profile—but Lord Byron has already been mentioned to me tonight, by someone else fishing for pieces of the jigsaw. I already knew that Byron and Shelley were associated with Victor Frankenstein, and that Patou must also have had some communication, however indirect, with Frankenstein, although I had not imagined previously that there was a formal contract involved. What you need to know now, Robert, is that Germain Patou also encountered Countess Marcian Gregoryi in her first incarnation; that was what first set him off on the hunt for the secret of resurrection. Whether he found Frankenstein's associates or they found him, his enquiries evidently led to an alliance of some sort. Lord Byron is in Paris now, and it seems that he is interested in the countess too; he has apparently set someone to follow me, so he is also aware of my interest. If he comes to call on you again, you might end up more deeply embroiled in this business than you want to be. I suppose Lord Byron must be just as enthusiastic to meet the vampire as I am...."

"Perhaps more so, if the rumors that have been circulating of late are true," Surrisy observed, cutting in on Temple's train of thought. "He's reputed to be something of a vampire himself—not that I'm sure, any more, as to what the word is supposed to mean. Are we really talking about reanimated corpses with a thirst for human blood?"

"Reanimated corpses, certainly," Temple said, soberly. "Bloodthirsty, perhaps not literally. Lord Byron is alive, though, and he's no bloodsucker, literal or metaphorical, no matter what Lady Caroline Lamb and John Polidori might allege. If he's trying to track down the vampire, it's not to meet his kin but to find out what the creature knows—and that's a dangerous game, even if he does have Frankenstein's daemon to assist him."

Temple shut up of his own accord then, realizing that he had let his mouth run away with him while thinking aloud. Surrisy did not seem to have taken what he said at all seriously, though; he was still under Countess Marcian Gregoryi's spell.

"I know that you got Sarah's son back from the kidnappers," the lawyer said, "and Jeanne's too, at some risk to your own life. I'm grateful to you on both counts. I feel obliged to warn you, though, that the reputation for madness you gained while pursuing Henri so obsessively still holds firm in Paris, and you will not find many men here willing to entertain this new insanity." As he finished speaking, Surrisy's gaze went to Jean-Pierre Séverin's face, questioningly. Séverin did not rise to the bait, though.

"Henri de Belcamp did his level best to drive me mad," Temple stated, flatly, "but he did not succeed. That did not prevent him asking for my help when he needed it, or trusting me when I gave it. Please be careful, Robert—you cannot get mixed up in this affair without exposing yourself to danger. If Countess Marcian Gregoryi asks anything else of you—and she will, if I cannot stop her—you really ought to refuse, until I have found out what is really going on. Until then you ought, at the very least, to tread exceedingly carefully."

"Thank you for your advice, Mr. Temple—and yours, Monsieur Séverin," Surrisy said, obviously eager to put an end to a conversation that had become distasteful to him. "Now, gentlemen, it is rather later, and if you will forgive me...."

Chapter Three
A Brief Skirmish

"What now?" asked Jean-Pierre Sévérin, as he and Temple paused at the end of the street, where they had the choice of turning towards the Pont Royal or heading back towards the Avenue de l'Opéra. "Shall we return to the Rue de la Lanterne to wait for René?"

"Not yet," said Temple, searching the street for a fiacre, in vain. "It will only take a few minutes to get to the Rue Caumartin. It's probably worth going down to the *quai* to pick up a cab."

"But you don't believe that the countess is staying there."

"No, I don't—but she did go to some trouble to give the address to anyone watching Surrisy's office. I doubt that she knew that you or I would be there, but she might well have expected Vidocq's man, and perhaps someone else."

"Lord Byron's agent—the one you referred to just now as Frankenstein's *daemon*?"

"Perhaps—but a different agent. If it really was Byron who put the Grey Man on my tail—and I'm not prepared simply to take Coco-Lacour's word for that—he's likely to have delegated someone else to follow the countess: Robert Walton, perhaps. The vampire's primary objective, I now suspect, is to make contact with Henri de Belcamp, which might or might not mean making contact with *Civitas Solis*. Countess Marcian Gregoryi has probably made the acquaintance of Sarah and Jeanne with that in view—but he'll certainly be interested in Victor Frankenstein too, so Byron's interest will likely be welcome, however cautious milord is inclined to be. I didn't see anyone else set off after the carriage, so the other watcher, if there was one, probably waited until we went inside to slip away."

By this time they had reached the corner of the *quai*, where there was a fiacre waiting—but it was empty, and Temple had to look around for he missing driver. He spotted the man outside the door of a quayside drinking-den, standing at a small table at which a card-sharp was offering passers by the chance to *cherchez la femme*. The cab driver had just placed a bet and lost it.

Temple strode over to the table, enthusiastic to vent a little of his accumulated bad temper.

"Does Monsieur Vidocq know that you are plying your vile trade within shouting distance of the Tuileries?" Temple enquired of the sharper. He had seen the trick worked in a dozen locations, from Drury Lane to Ascot racecourse, and had long since taken a hearty dislike to its practitioners.

"I should think so," the sharper replied, morosely. "He sends that popinjay Coco-Lacour round once a week to collect his rake-off."

"And does he know that you mention that fact to every English detective you meet?" Temple demanded, stretching the truth a little for the sake of effect. "Now, return this fellow's money immediately—I need him to drive me to the Rue Caumartin."

"No, sir," said the cabman, mournfully. "He won the money fair and square. I was certain that I could find the lady this time, but I couldn't."

"Do you mean that you've fallen for the trick before?" Temple asked, incredulously.

"A dozen times and more," supplied the sharper. "He's one of my regulars. I'm an honest man, sir—I tell them over and over again that the hand is quicker than the eye, but they never will believe me. They insist on believing that if they only look hard enough, they can follow the lady. They just won't accept that it's impossible."

Temple released a strangled impression of disgust, and dragged the cabman back to his vehicle. There did not seem to be any need to waste a moment's anxiety on the question of whether this man too might be one of Vidocq's agents in disguise—although, he reflected, as the cab set off, it might have been as well if he *had* managed to find another policeman in disguise, just in case some kind of trap had been set in the Rue Caumartin to catch anyone showing too much curiosity about Countess Marcian Gregoryi's whereabouts.

The Rue Caumartin was a reasonably respectable street, and the Hôtel Trianon a moderately respectable hotel, much patronized by English visitors. When Temple asked the night-clerk whether Countess Marcian Gregoryi was in residence, the man simply replied, in English: "The Countess is not here at present, sir. If you would care to leave a message, I'll make sure that she gets it when she returns."

Temple hesitated for a moment, then said: "Thank you, no," in his own language. "I really need to see her in person. Tell me, is Lord Byron in his room, by any chance?" The second question was a stab in the dark, but he felt so completely at sea that any amount of guesswork seemed justified.

"I believe that he is, sir," the clerk replied, somewhat to Temple's surprise. "If you would care to give me your card, sir, I'll have it sent up to him."

Temple handed over the card, and then took a seat in the lobby.

"That was a good guess," Jean-Pierre Séverin observed, sitting down beside him, although he did not seem capable of relaxing. "But what does it signify that Byron and the Countess have both retained rooms here? Have they already made some sort of alliance, do you think?"

"If they have," Temple replied, "then we're further behind the game than I thought—and the countess's suggestion could not have been addressed to Lord Byron's man. I might have been wrong to think that her remark could not be aimed at me."

"Is his lordship in danger?" Séverin asked.

"I really don't know," Temple had to confess.

A few minutes passed before the clerk reappeared. "His lordship will see you, Mr. Temple. He's waiting for you in the garden behind the hotel."

"The garden?" Temple queried. "At this time of night?"

"It's a private garden," the clerk told him, as if that somehow explained everything.

Temple shrugged, and allowed the clerk to lead him through the corridors of the ground floor to a rear door that let out into a small, high-walled garden. There was someone sitting on a bench at the far side of the lawn; he was directly beneath a lantern, but the fog made it impossible to make out his face or his costume. The clerk closed the door behind Temple and Séverin as they set out across the lawn.

Temple had only taken half a dozen paces before becoming certain that the man waiting for them was not, in fact, Lord Byron. As soon as he stopped, though, two other men appeared out of the bushes behind the bench, both armed with thick cudgels. As the man on the bench stood up, he lifted up a sword that had been laid horizontally on the bench beside him.

"Monsieur Temple," said the unknown man, in English that was severely tortured by a thick Parisian accent. "We've been expecting you. Who's your friend?"

Jean-Pierre Sévérin had not stopped when Temple did, and was now two paces ahead of him. He was already lifting his cane; it was a perfectly ordinary cane, not a sword-stick, but he was holding it now as if it were an épée. "Jean-Pierre Sévérin, at your service, sir," he said, in perfectly-enunciated English. The excitement in his voice was palpable, and Temple realized that the old man must have been starved of this sort of stimulation for far too long.

To his amazement, Temple saw that all three of the waiting men reacted nervously to the name, with which they were obviously familiar. The ringleader switched back to his own language to say: "It's all right, you fools—he must be seventy, at least, probably nearer eighty. Feet of lead and a wrist like a dry stick." So saying, and without standing on the least ceremony, he lunged forward with his blade, obviously expecting to take Sévérin by surprise.

The tactic did not work. Sévérin deflected the blow with ease—and then he moved forwards.

Temple presumed that the old man must, in fact, be somewhat slower in his paces than he would have been in his heyday, and his thrusts considerably less elegant than they had been at their finest. Even so, the tip of the cane became a mere blur, which would surely have been impossible to follow even in broad daylight. Temple, who had the advantage of watching from a distance, had to presume that its effects must have seemed like pure magic to the clumsy street-brawlers who were facing the flickering stick head on.

It took Jean-Pierre Sévérin less than three full seconds to disarm his three opponents and leave them sprawling on the ground. One of the cudgel-wielders was clutching at his throat in agony and another was shielding his right eye, which must have been badly bruised if not actually punctured. The swordsman was holding himself rigid, hardly daring to lift himself on his elbow, with the point of his own sword poised an inch from his breast, directed at his heart.

"My God!" Temple said. "I heard that you were once the best swordsman in France, but I had no idea...."

"I was never quite the best," Sévérin corrected him, although the denial somehow seemed prouder than any boastful admission could have been, "and am now so poor that I could not stop these poor fellows without doing two of them severe damage. I thought for a moment that I would actually have to run this one through—which would have been a great pity, as you presumably need him in a fit condition to talk. Shall I cut off an ear by way of encouragement, do you think? It will be an untidy job, I fear, for this blade is in a terrible condition. People do not take as much pride in their instruments as they used to."

"No!" the bravo protested. "No one told me that Temple had a protector, let alone one such as you! I was simply hired to do a job—I feel no loyalty to an employer who gave me a mere pittance to do the impossible!"

"What employer?" Temple demanded, harshly.

"Countess Marcian Gregoryi—or her lackey, at any rate. Calls himself Guido, but I doubt that he's Italian. Dirty Magyar, if you ask me."

"And where can I find this Guido?"

"Damned if I know—he came to me. All I know is that that he isn't here himself, curse him. Called away on urgent business, he said—and that certainly seemed to be the way of it. You're not the only one who has to be requested to stay clear, it seems. We never intended to kill you, I swear—our orders were to pink you in the leg, to make sure that you couldn't walk straight for a week or so. That's true, on my mother's life!"

"I believe you," Temple told him, "although I can't say I'm sorry that your friends got worse than they were supposed to give. You know, I suppose, that Monsieur Vidocq's men are also in search of the countess and her lackey?"

The man on the ground groaned; evidently, he had not been warned about that, either. "Don't turn me over, sir," he begged. "Guido told us that you were an Englishman, with far more enemies in Paris than friends. How was I supposed to know that you had such allies?"

"What's your name?" Temple demanded.

"Eugène Fantin. Vidocq knows me well enough—he'll testify that I'm an honest villain, if you care to ask. I've had dealings with the *fait-il jour demain?* brigade—who hasn't?—but I'm just a common arm for hire, nothing more."

"What's all this nonsense about daylight?" Séverin asked, evidently remembering Coco-Lacour's flippant remark.

"I'll explain at another time," Temple told him. "The rumor of this affair has obviously run through the whole of Paris. No one knows the truth of it, but everyone knows that Germain Patou's hypothetical records have now become a precious object of desire. I dare say that there'd be half a dozen forgeries on the market already, if anyone had the slightest idea what to put in them. In the meantime, the vampire is in a hurry to make deals with anyone who has hard information on techniques of resurrection, and seems to be enthusiastic to hobble the competition by any hasty means that comes to hand. If his minions are stooping to this kind of farce, he must be genuinely anxious. Let him up, Monsieur Séverin—I think he's lost his appetite for his appointed role."

Séverin not only allowed Fantin to get to his feet but returned his sword to him. The bravo carefully put it down on the bench, to make it clear that he had no intention of attempting to make further use of it.

"Do you have any idea where Guido went?" Temple demanded, harshly.

"No," Fantin replied. "I only know that it must have been important, else he'd have been here with us, lying in wait for you."

"Damn!" said Temple. "This is worse than I imagined. Come on, Monsieur Séverin—we've been doubly tricked. Perhaps I should have made a deal with Coco-Lacour after all. Better the Devil you know...." While he was speaking, Temple had already set off back to the door through which they had come. It was not locked, and they made their way through the hotel without difficulty. The night-clerk was no longer at his post. The fiacre was still waiting on the Rue Caumartin, although Temple had not retained it.

"Are you one of Vidocq's men, perchance?" Temple demanded of the luckless gambler, although he had little hope of receiving an affirmative answer.

The coachman's surprise seemed perfectly genuine. "Me, sir?" he said "No, sir—I'm an honest man, sir."

"More's the pity," Temple murmured, as he hauled himself into the carriage. "Rue de la Lanterne—and hurry, if your nags are capable of anything more than the gentlest trot."

The driver swore that his horses were a fine pair, thus demonstrating the limits of his supposed honesty, but they did prove capable of a slightly faster pace than many of their sort.

"What is it?" Jean-Pierre Sévérin asked, a hint of anxiety creeping into his tone.

"Evidently, it *was* me they were expecting," Temple told him. "When the countess took care to give the address in such a clear voice, she knew that I would be watching. She must, in consequence, know that Byron's having me followed, and that I came to see you tonight. I fear that she might have taken advantage of the fact that I took you and Monsieur de Kervoz away from home to send Guido in search of German Patou's records—or some leverage that might enable her to demand them as a ransom."

"But I don't have any such records!" Sévérin protested.

"The vampire doesn't know that—and he'll probably stop at nothing to make sure."

The lamp inside the fiacre cast enough light to allow Temple to see that his companion's face had gone pale. "You think they'll take Angela!" he exclaimed. "And demand a price for her return that I can't meet!"

179

"I fear so," Temple said. "Let's hope that I'm wrong."

They said nothing more while the cab completed the journey, but Temple could see that Jean-Pierre Sévérin's hand was tightly wound around his seemingly-inoffensive cane, his fingernails digging into the palm of his hand. He had been excited before, glad of the opportunity to bring back the old days of adventure one last time, but now he was afraid—afraid that history might repeat itself, and that he might lose a second Angela to the dreaded Vampire of Paris.

When they reached the Rue de la Lanterne, however, everything seemed perfectly calm. When Jean-Pierre Sévérin knocked at the door, it was immediately opened, without the necessity of withdrawing the bar or the bolt, by his blonde grand-daughter, who flung herself upon his neck. She, apparently, had been afraid for *his* safety. Temple understood why when he perceived that she was not alone.

He moved past the hugging relatives to confront the man who was lurking in the corridor. "I believe that you answer to the name of Lazarus," Temple said to the creature to whom Frankenstein's sensationalized memoirs referred as a *daemon*. "You have met my employee, Ned Knob."

The Grey Man drew himself up to his full height, which was impressive, in order to be able to look down on Gregory Temple. He also pushed back the hood he was wearing to conceal his face; evidently, he had been reluctant to frighten Angela de Kervoz, but had fewer reservations about alarming the man he had been following for most of the day. "I will answer to that name if you wish, sir," was all that he said.

"Where's Guido?" Temple demanded, not standing on ceremony. "You haven't killed him, I hope?"

"I have not," the giant replied. "I could not prevent his companions from running off—I have only one pair of hands, after all—but I made certain of securing the vampire's chief minion. He is probably the only one who knows where the vampire is. Even Countess Marcian Gregoryi may not be party to that secret, at present."

"She's made contact with Lord Byron, I presume."

"She has attempted to employ her wiles against his lordship," the Grey Man said. "Thus far, he has been very wary. He is certainly intrigued, and vulnerable to temptation—but he does not know what he is dealing with, and he has heard too many terrible tales of vampiric predation to rush in where angels would undoubtedly fear to tread. He is cautious, and feels rather isolated in a city in which he does not know who he can trust."

"His caution must have annoyed her ladyship," Temple observed. "Why, might I ask, is Lord Byron having *me* followed?"

"The principal reason is that he thought your detective skills might locate the vampire before he did," replied the creature who answered to the name of Lazarus.

"And the secondary reason?"

"As I said, his Lordship feels rather isolated, and does not know who he can trust. He has reason enough to be wary of Lord Liverpool's government, and its hirelings. He suspected that you might have been sent to Paris to investigate him."

Temple shrugged his shoulders. "I cannot hold his suspicion against him," he admitted, "but my one and only concern, at this moment, is the vampire. Assure Lord Byron, when you see him, that I am not his enemy."

"And what would you do, Mr. Temple, if you found the vampire?" Lazarus asked, mildly.

Temple scowled at that, because he had no good answer ready. The real question, he knew, was what *could* he do?

Jean-Pierre Sévérin released himself from his granddaughter's embrace in order to step into the breach. "If Mr. Temple were able to confirm that this vampire or his minion is guilty of any of the crimes laid against them in 1804," he said, sternly, "then he would be fully justified in taking justice into his own hands—and I, Jean-Pierre Sévérin, shall be more than ready to stand by his side."

"Ah!" said the Grey Man. "In that case, Mr. Temple, I'm afraid that you and I might be somewhat at odds in this matter—and I regret that I waited for you."

"You're in search of enlightenment regarding your own genesis and nature," Temple deduced, easily enough. "You believe that the vampire might be able to instruct you as to what you are—and what you might become."

"There are textbooks of anatomy that provide some slight clarification of the conventional human reproductive process," the giant observed, with a hint of sarcasm, "but the only books that speak of the risen dead—even those produced by supposed scholars—are far more superstitious in their character. They cannot assist me any more than they console me. Count Szandor is reputedly the most ancient and wisest of nature's grey men—and you should not chide me for hunting for him, any more than you should chide me for seeking enlightenment from Lord Byron and my creator. Remember that I was the one who gave the information to Ned Knob that must have brought you here."

"As it happens," Temple retorted, "Master Knob was a trifle economical with the information he gave me regarding his discoveries in Spezia. I had to find out by another route, and still have not found out what everyone else already seems to know—but I will not be shut out of this affair, by anyone."

Séverin, meanwhile, had been staring at the giant, albeit more in curiosity than amazement—as had Angela, who had obviously not seen him clearly before. Lazarus made as if to raise his hood again and step back into the shadows.

"There is no need to be afraid, Mademoiselle," Temple told the young woman. "This is not the first Grey Man I have seen, and I can assure you that he is a phenomenon of nature, not some supernatural monster. The dead *can* return, Monsieur Séverin, and here is the living proof. Thanks to Victor Frankenstein and Germain Patou, the world is on the brink of a new era—one of unprecedented triumph, if the new knowledge is used responsibly, or horrific chaos, if it is not. Malo de Treguern would have told you that the old era must be protected at all costs—and probably still will—but he is the least of our adversaries at present. The vampire is evidently the worst—and our friend here has contrived to turn the tables on that one, by capturing one of his principal agents." He used the word "friend" hopefully, having taken due note of what Lazarus had said about their being at odds.

"I am honored to make your acquaintance, sir," the giant said to Séverin, respectfully.

"I'm delighted to welcome you as my guest," the old man replied, "in view of the service that you have rendered my granddaughter. I lost her mother to the vampire once…I could never have forgiven myself had it happened again."

"I'm glad that I decided to remain here rather than following Mr. Temple," the Grey Man said. "When I saw that the police agent was not following you, I knew that something else must be about to happen here, and when I saw Malo de Treguern, I feared that others might be hot on his heels—as, indeed, they were."

"We need to interrogate Guido," Temple said. "Where is he?"

"In the cellar," the Grey Man replied. "I have every faith in my knots, but I thought it best to put him in a room with only one issue. I should have taken him away, but…." Without finishing his sentence, the giant led the others to the door leading down to the cellar, unhooking a lantern from the wall as he went.

Jean-Pierre Séverin told Angela to go to her room, but she refused, and he did not press the point. She was involved now, and there was no virtue in trying to pretend otherwise.

The giant's faith in his knots was fully justified. Guido was lying on the stone floor, trussed up so tightly that he could hardly move a muscle, and obviously in considerable distress. When he saw Gregory Temple's face in the light of the Grey Man's lantern, he groaned. "That fool Fantin," he murmured. "I'd have hired someone better if I could, but the Habits Noirs have mobilized the mob tonight, and only left the dregs."

"You recognize me, then?" Temple said, curiously. "I do not believe that we have ever been introduced."

"No," said Guido, with a sigh, "but I was hoping to see someone else—hoping for a rescue, in fact. I never meant to do the young lady any harm. That is not my way."

"Your master is not so scrupulous, by all accounts," Temple replied. "Once you had delivered her into his hands…but that's irrelevant now. What we need to know is where your master is, and we shall brook no delay in obtaining an answer."

"I should have taken the Grey Man to him, when I had the chance," Guido lamented. "I beg your pardon, Monsieur Lazarus, but you cannot blame me for my little stratagem. In fact, the last thing I wanted was to wait until Temple returned before taking you to my master, for I never expected him to return—I was expecting my associates to arrive in his stead. The sensible thing to do now, for both of us, is to come to a private arrangement. Temple is an unnecessary inconvenience that we can both do without."

Temple deduced from this speech that Guido had played for time by promising Lazarus that he would take him to his master when Temple came back—while hoping that his friends might regroup and counter-attack, with or without Fantin's help. Now that Temple and Séverin had returned, and with Fantin out of the game, the men who had been put to flight were highly unlikely to risk another assault.

"That would be rather impolite, don't you think?" said Lazarus to Guido, somewhat to Temple's surprise. "He has surely earned the right to an interview with your master."

He's afraid too! Temple thought, although he kept his face very straight. *Whether we're at odds or not, he wants me with him when he confronts the vampire! He does not want to go alone. I can hardly blame him, though, for I sought out help myself, and was very glad to have it when danger actually threatened.*

"Suit yourself," was Guido's grudging reply. "Perhaps I'll take my chances and remain silent. You'll have to let me go eventually, even if no help comes."

"He seems to think that we won't apply pressure to get him to talk," Temple said to Lazarus. "Are you really that scrupulous? If so, we could always turn him over to Vidocq, who seems to be itching to take a hand in this affair. He has a free hand in dealing with enemy aliens."

That threat worked better than Temple had anticipated. "There's no need to involve Vidocq!" Guido was quick to say. "That's the last thing any of us needs. I'll take you both to see my master, if that's what you really want—but it's a long way to Miremont, and you really ought to let me go if you expect me to be in any fit state to lead you.

"Miremont!" Temple exclaimed. "Your master is in Miremont?"

"He should be, by now," Guido replied. "Don't worry, Mr. Temple—he's not so unsubtle in his methods as the pious brutes of *Civitas Solis*. He'll do no harm to your daughter or your grandchild, or to any of the other innocents of Miremont, but he does need to flush Henri de Belcamp out of hiding—urgently, if possible. Belcamp is the one man who's privy to *all* of Germain Patou's secrets, in spite of the fact that Lord Byron contracted a partnership with the physician. I beg you, please, to let me continue this discussion in less uncomfortable circumstances—I'll give you my word not to try to escape, but I fear that I might lose a limb if the circulation of my blood is interrupted much longer."

"Shall I?" asked the giant. Temple gestured his consent, and the Grey Man plucked Guido from the floor, stood him upright and then set about undoing the knots he had tied. His thick fingers were surprisingly nimble.

By the time that the Magyar was able to start rubbing his wrists and stamping his feet in order to restore normal blood-flow, Temple had collected himself. "Countess Marcian Gregoryi's offer to buy the new château was a means of getting access to Jeanne de Belcamp, was it not?" he said.

"Of course not," Guido replied, his voice dripping with sarcasm. "She fell in love with the mock-classical architecture and the beautiful location."

It occurred to Temple, a trifle belatedly, that he had no idea where Sarah Boehm had been going when her carriage had left the vicinity of the Tuileries. If she were staying in Paris, leaving the new château open for inspection by potential purchasers....

"I'll take you to my master, since I have little alternative," Guido continued, "but I won't guide an army to his hiding-place. I'll take you, Monsieur Lazarus, provided that we leave now. If you want to bring Temple with you, that's up to you, but not Sévérin. If I were you, I'd leave Temple behind too—but you'd best prick his leg to make sure he doesn't follow us or run squealing to Vidocq."

Temple bit his lip to forestall the protest that rose instinctively to his lips—but he need not have worried. "I think I'd prefer it if Mr. Temple were with us," Lazarus replied. "That way, I can keep an eye on him." He too was speaking sarcastically, evidently having realized that Guido was trying to provoke a quarrel between him and Temple.

Guido shrugged his shoulders—rather painfully, it seemed. "Very well," he said. "It's your decision. We must go immediately, though."

"What about René?" asked Jean-Pierre Sévérin. Evidently, the old man was not disposed to argue with

Guido's demand that he be left behind, presumably feeling that his first responsibility was to protect Angela—although Temple assumed that he had taken very careful note of the mention of Miremont.

Temple took his old acquaintance aside and whispered in his ear: "This is another trap, I suspect, although I'm not entirely sure who's setting it for whom. You must decide what to do when René returns—if he does return. Vidocq's men might be inclined to delay him, in order to play their own hand freely, and they have the authority to do it. If I don't come back, you might eventually have to go to Vidocq and tell him everything—you won't get any action out of anyone else at the Prefecture. Byron's party might be more trustworthy allies, but they have no more authority here than I do. The best thing of all would be to play your own hand, if you can."

"That's always been my way," Séverin observed. "I wish I had a better understanding of all this, though."

"So do I," Temple assured him. "There seem to be more pieces in the jigsaw than I could have anticipated—but you and René must concentrate on Countess Marcian Gregoryi, for the time being. At the very least, keep track of her movements, and find out everything you can about her intentions."

In the meantime, Guido and the giant had started climbing the stairs towards the cellar door.

"I had not anticipated that we would have to go as far as Miremont," Lazarus observed. "I have no carriage, and we can hardly hire a fiacre. We'll have to hire horses, if we can find a livery stable that's open at this hour."

Temple looked at Séverin again. "I know where you can obtain horses," the old man said, "Although I'm not sure there's a horse in all Paris capable of carrying the giant more than a kilometer—you might need a Percheron for that."

"We'll hire six and ride them in relay," Temple assured him. "Your part will be the hardest, old friend, for there's nothing you can do for now but wait."

"I'm a patient man," Jean-Pierre Séverin assured him. "I've lived with the dead all my life, and I know how to wait."

Chapter Four
The Ghosts of the Deliverance

The giant tied Guido's hands behind him and secured his ankles to the stirrups of his horse, which Temple kept on a leading-rein along with the three spare mounts. They rode through the barrière not long after midnight, but could not make too much haste thereafter, for the road was very dark. The moon was only half-full and the stars were barely visible through the fog. Once they were in the forest Temple lit a lantern and hung it on a pole which he extended before the lead horse, but it was a poor guide. Fortunately, there had been relatively little autumn rain thus far, and the road was not too badly muddied.

When the time seemed ripe, Temple maneuvered his horse into step with the giant's. "You must have suspected that Guido was merely playing for time," he said. "Why did you wait?"

"I could not be sure," the Grey Man said. "To tell the truth, though, I was uncertain what to do for the best." Temple remembered what he had said about Lord Byron feeling isolated in Paris, and not knowing who to trust—how much worse must his own predicament seem?

"Are you any more certain now?" Temple asked.

"No," the new Adam admitted. "Are you?"

"I have no alternative," Temple told him. "I'm involved now, and cannot let it alone. I must keep going forward, however blindly."

"I know how you feel," the giant said. "My commitment is greater than yours, I believe."

Temple had to concede that point. In spite of what he had just said, he did have the alternative of letting the matter alone; the Grey Man did not. "Ned Knob told me that you and your creator were estranged," he said. "If you're now in Lord Byron's service, I assume that your differences have been reconciled."

"I doubt that Frankenstein will ever be reconciled to my independence of his will," the other replied, dourly, "And I am not in Lord Byron's *service*. Our interests happen to coincide, for the moment. I agreed to follow you because I agreed with his lordship that you might succeed in tracking down the vampire—you do have the reputation of being a great detective as well as a madman."

Temple was disposed to take exception to the last word, but swallowed his pride, knowing that he had a golden opportunity to fish for information. "My detective work has uncovered far more questions than answers, alas," he said, "and the scientists that I have tried to interest in the possibility of resurrection have mostly thrown up their hands in horror, accusing me of ludicrous superstition."

"I have had similar experiences," the Grey Man admitted, "although I did have one fascinating conversation with the Chevalier de Lamarck, who seems glad to have an audience of any sort nowadays."

"But you have the invaluable advantage of experience," Temple said. "What are you, really? Is your condition a matter of a temporarily-dislodged soul repossessing its body? Did it require the reignition of some kind of vital spirit? Or was it some anomalous kind of spontaneous generation—a flaw in the natural pattern of life's origin and development?"

"I wish I knew," the giant said. "What are *you*, Mr. Temple? Are you a soul in a body, a vital spark or a mere routine product of spontaneous generation? Does merely being alive make you an unimpeachable savant in matters of biology?"

"No," Temple admitted.

"We have too poor an understanding, as yet, of what death really means," the giant said, "and how it differs from such states of suspended animation as catalepsy. I hope that the vampire might be able to tell me more, if he is inclined to be generous."

"I fear that he must be alarmed by the reaction that his arrival in Paris has provoked," Temple observed, "and might be regretting his decision to return. You realize, of course, that we are putting our heads into a lion's mouth?"

"Of course—but we have already agreed that we have no alternative but to go forwards. Having stirred up a hornets' nest, the vampire will probably beat a hasty retreat—but he came here in search of knowledge, and might count us precious because of that."

Temple could not help wondering whether the giant's use of the word "us" might be over-generous. He could easily imagine that the vampire might be glad to forge an alliance with the scientific Lazarus—and also that he might have a very different attitude to an aging English spy.

"Do you know why Vidocq is interested in this business," Temple asked. "He must surely be doing someone else's bidding—but whose?"

"I don't know. Lord Byron has made reference to *Habits Noirs*—in London, he says, they're more likely to term themselves Gentlemen of the Night—but I'm not sure that he even believes in them."

"Coco-Lacour attempted to tantalize me with that very phrase, when he took pleasure in telling me that Byron had set you to follow me," Temple said, reflectively. "He was probably just playing games—but there's always a real villain behind such attempts to capitalize on myth and legend: a would-be John Devil or Jean Diable. The Prefect suspects Vidocq himself of being the current Parisian Napoleon of crime, but I can't believe that he's the spider at the center of the web. Tom Brown might be better qualified, but he's been too long away from London and Paris to retain a firm grip on the Underworld of either capital. Someone else must have stepped forward to take on the role, because someone always does—but I don't know who it might be. Are Vidocq's men making things difficult for Byron, too?"

"Very difficult," the giant admitted. "He did not want to come back here at all, but the fiasco in Spezia was an awkward setback. When he heard the rumor that the vampire was coming here…we knew no more than that, alas. If only we had as many spies at our disposal as you must have at yours…."

Temple suppressed an ironic laugh, knowing that there was not a single spy in Europe on whom he could truly rely, and that his own commanders were heartily sick of his escapades. "What contract did Byron make with Germain Patou?" he asked, curiously.

"I'm not free to tell you that, Mr. Temple," Lazarus replied, conscientiously. "I've made a contract with him myself, and am bound by it. I can't tell you my master's secrets, so there's no point in your asking me where

Frankenstein is, any more than there is in my asking you where Germain Patou is. What I will offer to do, though, when our present business is concluded, is to arrange a meeting between you and my master. You have common ground enough to make an agreement, I think—he is English, after all, although his homeland has not been very generous in its treatment of him."

"You have information of your own that you might give me, were you so disposed," Temple pointed out. "You must have found out a great many things while you were estranged from Byron's party. It was you who found out about vampires, if Ned Knob can be trusted— and about the particular vampire we are about to meet."

"I have not been idle," the Grey Man agreed, "but I have only been a Grey Man for a few meager years—not much longer than the infamous Mortdieu. There is a sense in which he and I are both mere infants, however adult we seem. I have been unrelentingly curious—but I cannot lay claim to any settled wisdom. Rumor has it, though, that the vampire who calls himself Szandor has been a Grey Man for centuries, and is certainly not as stupid as the vast majority of his kind. If anyone has learned to refine the process of resurrection—or is able to refine it—he is the most likely candidate. Ned Knob must agree with that judgment."

"I dare say that he does," Temple said, bitterly. "Alas, he was not inclined to share the judgment with me. I think he planned to track the vampire down him-self, or in collaboration with Henri de Belcamp—but I put a stop to that, albeit at the cost of putting him on Pa-tou's trail. Sometimes, I cannot help hoping that his ship will sink in mid-Atlantic, and free me of the little imp forever."

"I rather liked him," the giant admitted.

194

"Nearly everyone does," Temple admitted, gloomily. "It's the child in him, I think. It's almost impossible to hate him, no matter how one tries. He even charmed Tom Brown once, who was very nearly caught in consequence. I have to keep reminding myself that he is all the more useful to me because he also in the pay of my archenemy, and will one day lead me to him."

"Not for a while, though, if he's embarked on a sea voyage," Lazarus observed.

Temple wondered briefly whether he ought to have kept that fact to himself, but he could not believe that Byron did not know it already. The conversation was dying now, because they had reached that hour of the early morning when all energy drains away, even for those who do not give way to sleep "How powerful is the vampire, do you think?" Temple asked, in a desultory tone. "Are you confident that we can stand up to him, if it comes to a contest?"

"If he were powerful in body," the giant replied, after an expansive yawn, "He would not need to hide away so cleverly, or equip his favorite minion with so much glamour and trickery. That he is deceptive I do not doubt, but I do not fear any sort of physical attack." After a pause, he added: "I wish I had brought some food and water from Paris, though, for I shall not be inclined to trust anything that he offers me to eat or drink."

Temple was thirsty too, although he had long since disciplined himself to pay no attention to hunger pangs while he was about his business. Lack of sleep was, however, a more troublesome attrition. "Agreed," he said, and lapsed into silence.

The silence weighed upon him more heavily than the conversation had, and he soon became frustrated with the slowness of their progress—which was not much ameliorated by the fact that the giant switched horses twice as frequently as his companions.

When dawn broke, they were still on the road, having not yet reached the turning that led to Pierre Louchet's former residence—a turning they did not take. They went all the way to Miremont itself, but then deviated from the expected route. Instead of heading for the "new château" they turned on to another path, which led to an isolated cottage by the Oise.

Of course, Temple thought, when he realized what the cottage was. *I should have guessed. Robert's mother lived here, and he retains it as a perverse shrine to her memory. The Knights of the Deliverance once met here, if I remember right, on the night when Henri de Belcamp assumed command of the conspiracy. If only I had known that at the time!*

Temple was somewhat dismayed to find that there were four burly men in the grounds of the cottage, all of them tougher customers than the hirelings that Jean-Pierre Sévérin had put to flight. Guido greeted them cheerily and instructed, in Italian, one of them to come and untie his bonds—an instruction to which Temple and the giant raised no objection. Temple's Italian was far from perfect, but he understood when Guido asked the same man how long it had been since the company arrived. The answer he received was that they had only been there for little more than two hours.

"Is the master asleep?" Guido asked. The reply he received was in the negative; the man who gave it indicated by his attitude that he would have preferred it if the master *had* been asleep.

"You're in luck, gentlemen," Guido said to Temple and the giant, in English. "My master does not like to be woken up when he's asleep, no matter how urgent the reason might be. May I go in before you, to warn him that I've brought him unexpected guests?"

"No," said Temple, shortly, and did not wait for anyone else to go to the cottage door ahead of him. He marched forwards recklessly and opened the door himself, without knocking, leaving Guido and the Grey Men to jostle for position behind him—a contest that the giant inevitably won.

The interior of the cottage was dark. No lamp was lit therein, and the windows were shuttered. The thin beams of wan grey light that filtered through the cracks in the ancient shutters provided some illumination, but Temple's eyes had adapted to the silver glare of the morning mist, and some seconds elapsed before he was able to make out the figure seated at Madeleine Surrisy's old dining-table. In the meantime, he knew, the other would have been able to make a much more efficient assessment of him.

As his slowly-reacting sight gained sensitivity, Temple became aware that the atmosphere within the cottage seemed to be filed with dust, and that the dust was stirring in numerous draughts introduced through breaches in the woodwork, in a rather eerie fashion. For a moment or two, it was not just the grey figure seated at the table that seemed more like a ghost than a solid entity. That central figure seemed, in fact, to be surrounded by a host of other ghosts—almost as if the Knights of the Deliverance had been compelled to return to the scene of their last meeting, following the ultimate failure of their mission and their purpose. It was, however, the central figure that was studying Gregory Temple and Frankenstein's *daemon*, with a stare that seemed inhumanly penetrating.

Temple had to make a positive effort of will to ignore the imaginary ghosts and focus his attention on the one that was real: a surprisingly thin creature, no more than skin and bone, whose skull was so entirely bald, save for a few wisps of white hair, that it did indeed resemble a skull cleansed of all flesh…except for the eyes. The eyes were still there, and their dilated pupils were jet black, although the thin irises surrounding them were so palely grey as to be hardly distinguishable from the whites. The eyes were exceedingly disconcerting, their stare impossible to meet, for the moment—although Temple had a dire suspicion that it might also be impossible to avoid, if the other were that way inclined.

The vampire must have been astonished to see him, but the ghostly head remained quite motionless, as if the creature were literally imperturbable. Temple had come in with considerable impetus, and a determination not to be intimated, but all that vanished like smoke and he too was rendered motionless. He knew, within an instant, that he had overestimated his own capacity to deal with this confrontation—but he was committed, and had to follow through with it.

"My name is Gregory Temple," he contrived to say. "Are you the vampire who calls himself Szandor?"

The vampire's elbows were leaning on the table, while his hands were joined, as if in prayer, in front of his shriveled nose. His fingers were almost all bone, with the articulations clearly visible, but they were still flexible, and they moved so as to grip more tightly as the newcomers took up position side by side, with only the width of the table separating them from the creature. The vampire made no reply to Temple's question, but simply stared at his unexpected guests. It was impossible to tell whether the skeletal creature was smiling, or whether his face was permanently set in a *rictus sardonicus*.

"My lord...." Guido began, attempting unsuccessfully to elbow his way between Temple and the giant.

"Explanations are unnecessary, Guido," said a soft and serpentine voice that might have come from anywhere in the room, speaking in Italian. "You may leave."

Guido seemed glad to have permission to give up his futile struggle and step back. He wasted no time in backing up out of the doorway, closing the door behind him to make the interior of the cottage even gloomier than before.

Temple opened his mouth to speak again, but no words came out. The giant seemed similarly dumbstruck. Temple could no longer believe that he had ever imagined himself equal to this situation, and suspected that he could be struck dead on the spot, if the vampire so wished.

Apparently, the vampire did not wish it—yet. "I see that you have not come equipped with wooden stakes and firebrands," the voice resumed, disturbing the dust as its sibilant sound moved through the unnaturally thick atmosphere, "so I assume that you have come in peace. I confess that I was not expecting you so soon. I congratulate you on your persistence, Mr. Temple, although I really do not think that this business has anything to do with you. You, on the other hand, Monsieur Lazarus, I am glad to welcome to my temporary abode, given that events have moved too quickly for me to contrive a meeting on my own terms. Would you like to sit down, or would you prefer to stand? Many people do prefer to stand in my company, even though I was never the aristocrat that I sometimes claimed to be when I...or the person I once was...was alive."

Temple took no offence at the insulting dismissal of his relevance. His hands, acting without any instruction from his conscious mind, had already pulled out one of the crude dining-chairs, and he sat down, as awkwardly as a puppet in a marionette theatre. The giant followed his example, lowering himself on to a second chair rather gingerly, perhaps because he feared the rickety object might break and perhaps because he was saddle-sore.

"I understand that you have both been searching for me, at least since Guido got into difficulties in Spezia," the vampire continued. "I did not expect you to find me quite so easily, but Paris has changed a great deal since I was last here. Whatever else the Terror achieved, it certainly encouraged men to mind their own business and not enquire too closely into other people's. Nowadays, it seems, the population is a veritable hydra, every head of which has a thousand avid eyes. It is a pity that you have by-passed my most trusted aide, who would have managed everything much more diplomatically, but her first priority was to deal with Lord Byron and Lady de Belcamp. As you can probably imagine, I have poured my heart and soul into her creation. Sometimes, I think that she is now more *me* than I am—but that might be wishful thinking. I am not quite as handsome, I fear. Once your eyes have become accustomed to me, though, you will not find me as fearful."

Temple's eyes were still adjusting, unhurriedly, to the meager light, and the skeletal figure had not yet emerged as fully from the darkness as it ultimately might—but he could not imagine that the sight would be any more pleasing when it did become distinct.

"If it will comfort you to know it, I have no wish to harm anyone in Miremont, or in Paris, on this occasion," the vampire went on. "I have often found it convenient to make superstitious people live in fear of me, and I have killed without compunction for more reasons than you might credit or imagine, but I am not the ravening monster that legend considers vampires to be. We are supposed to be in the heart of civilization, after all, and I ought to behave in a civilized manner, even if my enemies are less inclined to do so. The trap that I set for you at the Hôtel Trianon, Mr. Temple, was a crude and hasty contrivance—but one must sometimes cause a small injury in order not to cause a greater one. You have placed yourself in grave danger by avoiding that trap, not only from me, but from others. You are a brave man, though, and that is your way. I, on the other hand, am a consummate coward. The living have no conception of how fearful of annihilation those who have already died can be. Monsieur Lazarus may not have had time, as yet, to come fully to terms with his condition, but he will learn, with or without my help—always provided that he can survive the fear and loathing of the living."

The voice paused, and Temple felt his chest constrict as his breathing seemed almost to stop. The dust in the air was worse now than the fog outside, and it seemed to him that all the ghosts within that dust were avidly attentive, eager to see him die.

"Sometimes," the voice resumed. "I wish that all the silly tales about a vampire's bite creating more vampires were true. If they were, I'd have raised an army of the dead long ago, to establish an impregnable stronghold if not to conquer the world. If rumor can be trusted, your friend Monsieur Patou has had more success in a few brief years than I ever had in centuries of practical experimentation, although he has inevitably run into the same difficulty that eventually disheartened me. I have known more than a few of the reanimated dead in my time, but never one with whom I could have a decent conversation. I am interested to meet you, Monsieur Lazarus, for that very specific reason—but I ought to warn you that I no longer crave company as much as I once did, and I might be inclining more to jealousy in my second old age. I am a coward, as I say, and I confess that the prospects of this new revolution are alarming. The Church and I might have more in common than I ever suspected, in spite of our diehard enmity. Still, I pride myself on being a rational…individual. I had hoped to create an opportunity to have a few friendly words with Victor Frankenstein. Patou and General Mortdieu are, it seems, out of reach for the time being."

Again the vampire paused. Even in the extremity of his discomfort, Temple found it possible to wonder whether the motionless death's-head might be exactly what it seemed: a mere scarecrow, an inert marionette. Might the real vampire, he wondered, somehow be incarnate in the strangely swirling dust? No sooner had he formed the thought, however, than the skeletal form *did* move, as if to prove him wrong and mock his folly. The chin moved free of the supportive hands, and the terrible stare grew even more intense and menacing. The timbre of the voice remained as soft and sibilant as ever, though.

"I had also hoped to find a way to make contact with Henri de Belcamp," the vampire went on. "Not in the hope that Patou left him some sort of written legacy, for I am far too wise and jaded to believe in convenient treasures of that sort, but simply because he was a witness to so much of Patou's work. I suppose, all things considered, that it might work to my advantage that you have both come to see me, since one of you can probably

202

tell me how to contact Frankenstein and the other has at least one means of getting a message to Henri de Belcamp. For that assistance, I might be prepared to trade a little information, as well as a measure of mercy—but you must not think, if I am disposed to be merciful, and prepared to adopt a mercantile approach, that you are my equals in this matter. If...."

The monster was interrupted then—and the mere fact that he could be interrupted, and that his control of the situation could thus be shown to be less than absolute, seemed to Gregory Temple to be a very welcome revelation. The door to the cottage was hurled back, and a man—not Guido—rushed in, babbling in a language that Temple could not understand. He rushed out again as soon as he had made his seemingly panic-stricken report.

The skeleton remained sitting, though not as languidly as before.

When he claimed to be a coward, Temple thought, *he was not being ironic. And if he is a coward, he must have good cause to be afraid. There are things that can hurt him, things he is obliged to flee, no matter how powerful his mesmeric authority might be when he confronts his adversaries one or two at a time.*

He was breathing more easily now, and knew that the vampire's power over him was already weakening.

I can survive this, he thought, *whether I am his equal or not, I am not helpless in his grip. I might even be able to speak, if I exert myself.*

And when he exerted himself, Temple found that he could, indeed, speak. "Guido ought to have taken better precautions to ensure that we were not followed," he said to the vampire. "No one can make a move in Paris just now without attracting unwelcome attention."

"That's true," Lazarus added. "The Gentlemen of the Night are hot on your heels, it seems, and my guess is that the weight of numbers is one thing with which you cannot cope—like your minion, you only have one pair of eyes. Paris has no shortage of rabble for assembly into unruly mobs, and that rabble has been roused."

Temple joined in again to say: "Monsieur Vidocq will not show his own hand, but he will have given strict orders, in which the words *dead or alive* might well have figured prominently."

For a moment, he thought that he might be struck dead for his temerity, but the vampire was not a hot-tempered creature.

"There's no need to be afraid for me, Mr. Temple," the voice whispered, with more than a hint of mockery. "Your anger is greater than mine!"

Temple tried to stand up then, although he did not know exactly what he intended to do—but as he stood up, he felt an appalling pain his right thigh, as if he had been stabbed.

He collapsed back into the chair, unable to prevent his eyes from closing reflexively in response to the agony. His closed eyes could not, however, shut out the sight of the ghosts that had been drifting in the air, dully resentful of having a vile Englishman in the midst of their Bonapartist company—ghosts that suddenly seemed to gain new authority and new opportunity.

It was not that the superabundant dust-motes gained real substance, but they did gain *impetus*, and they rushed upon him in vengeful millions, blinding him and choking him. Temple flapped his arms madly, although he was aware of the absurdity of the action, which only served to intensify the pain in his leg. A swarm of flies might have been disturbed by his flailing, but the cloud of dust was immune to it.

This is not real! Temple shouted at himself, silently. *This is a trick of magnetic suggestion—and I am not some hysteric young woman, vulnerable to such flummery!*

Hysteric or not, though, he could not fight the dusty ghosts any more than he could fight the psychosomatic pain. Imaginary they might be, but he could not fight the ghosts of the Deliverance or the wound inflicted by an invisible blade. Utterly helpless, in the grip of forces far beyond his control, Temple fell back as his chair tilted and spilled him on the cottage floor.

The dust piled up on his face like a death-mask, consigning him to Hellish darkness and preventing him from—conclusively, this time—from drawing breath.

The detective would have called for help if he could have done so, but his lips were sealed—and he had no reason to expect, in any case, that Frankenstein's new Adam had any interest at all in helping him, even if he were in any condition to help himself.

Chapter Five
On the Sidelines

Gregory Temple awoke as if from a drug-induced sleep, conscious of a dull but nagging pain in his right thigh. He moved to touch the afflicted limb under the blankets that weighed him down—discovering as his hand moved that someone had taken off his clothes and dressed him in a nightshirt—but his probing fingers could find no trace of any cut or contusion. The pain was deep within the flesh; or, more accurately, deep within his treasonous consciousness. He tried to flex the leg, and then made as if to get out of bed, but was left in no doubt that he would be unable to walk, for the time being, even if he could stand up.

He opened his eyes, and tried to figure out where he might be. There was a night-light burning on his bedside table, and the bed-curtains were not drawn, so it was possible to make out the walls of the room and its furniture, but the only thing of which he was sure, to begin with, was that he was not in Madeleine Surrisy's cottage. He was in a much finer house than that, furnished with good taste and a certain effortless luxury.

He had never been in that particular room before, so there was nothing he could actually recognize—but he guessed readily enough where he must be once his head was clear. He seized the little hand-bell set beside the nightlight and agitated it madly. He was not unduly surprised when the person who eventually came in response to the summons was his daughter Suzanne.

He was in the Château de Belcamp—and even though his leg had not been "pinked" by Eugène Fantin's ill-kept sword, he was sure that he would not be able to walk without a limp for some time to come. The vampire had not put him out of the game entirely, but had relegated him to its sidelines. Temple knew that that had been an exercise of mercy, but he could not bring himself to be grateful.

"Daddy!" Suzanne said, as a dutiful daughter was bound to do. "Thank God you're awake, at last! Do you need a doctor? I wanted to call one, but Jeanne said that we ought to wait."

"I need a glass of water," Temple growled. "My mouth feels as if it were full of dust. And I need my clothes." The latter remark brought forth a pang from his leg, as if to remind him, dutifully, that he would not find it easy to dress himself.

There was a pitcher on the dressing-table, and a crystal goblet. Suzanne filled the goblet and brought it to him. He did not empty it at a single draught, in spite of the temptation, but eked it out, using a gradual flow to clear the lingering impression of the ghostly dust. When his mouth felt sufficiently normal again, he said: "Who brought me here?"

"A policeman," she replied.

"The local *garde champêtre?*" he asked, hopefully.

"No—an inspector from Paris. His name is Coco-Lacour."

"*Is?*" Temple repeated. "You don't mean that you *let him in?*"

"We could hardly refuse him entry. You were laid out unconscious in the back of a cart that he was driving.

He apologized profusely for the untidy state of his clothing, but said that his men had been involved in what he called a *razzia*. Some bandits had taken possession of Madeleine Surrisy's old cottage, apparently, and a company of police agents had to be summoned from Paris to capture them—but you must know that, since you were their prisoner. Did the policemen not save your life?"

"The policemen might well be under that impression," Temple admitted, grudgingly. "Where is Coco-Lacour now?"

"Sleeping peacefully in another bedroom," Suzanne told him. "Jeanne could hardly send him packing, in the circumstances—and he's very polite, in spite of his unorthodox style of dress. He says that he needs to question you with regard to your abduction, but that will surely wait until morning—unless you want me to wake him right away."

"No, don't do that," Temple said. "I'm sorry—I never seem to have an opportunity to see you in placid circumstances. How are you? How's Richard, and little Richard?"

"Very well," she assured him, sitting down on the bed. "Which is more than can be said for you, it seems. What on Earth are you doing getting mixed up with bandits in Miremont? I thought that you had done with all that and had become more of a diplomat than a thief-taker?"

"They weren't bandits," Temple grunted. "Well, actually, they probably were—except for their master. Did Coco-Lacour tell you whether his *razzia* was a success?"

"Two villains were killed, he said," Suzanne reported, "and the rest taken prisoner. He seems very pleased with himself."

Temple could not believe that the raiders had actually managed to capture or kill the vampire—and was no longer certain as to whether he ought to wish that they had. If Coco-Lacour was pleased with himself, though, they must at least have managed to deprive the vampire of his remaining human hirelings.

"He's insistent that he needs to see you in order to complete his report," Suzanne continued. "I gather that you're not enthusiastic to talk to him."

"He may carry papers affiliating him to the Prefecture," Temple said, "but he's no better than the thieves he chases, and perhaps worse. His superior has a dark reputation, and my guess is that it's not undeserved. They pretend to be combating organized crime, but I suspect that they're the most organized criminals in Paris, for the time being—or part of some such organization, at least. They've infiltrated the Prefecture, and now they've infiltrated the Château—but I can't believe that they've actually succeeded in killing the adversary they went after. I have to talk to Jeanne, to warn her against…well, against things it might be better for you to know nothing about."

Suzanne slapped him, and did not make any attempt to soften the blow. Fortunately, his astonishment blotted out the stinging pain. She leapt to her feet and placed her hands on her hips, although there were tears in her eyes. "How many times must we go through this?" she complained. "I will not let you do this, Father! I will not let you decide for me what I ought and ought not to know!"

Temple stared at her for a full ten seconds, then shrugged his shoulders. "Against Countess Marcian Gregoryi," he said, simply. "The vampire's minion." He watched the expressions that crossed his daughter's face, more fearfully than inquisitively—and then his heart sank. "Oh my God," he said. "Please don't tell me that she's here too!"

"Not yet," was the slightly discomfited reply. "She's supposed to be coming to Miremont this afternoon, with Sarah. She's buying the new château. Jeanne has been invited to dinner there tonight."

"That plan has probably been abandoned," Temple murmured. "In which case, she won't come. On the other hand...."

"What do you mean, *the vampire's minion?*" Suzanne demanded, before he had time to follow the thought through.

"There is a creature," Temple began, a little uncertainly. "A monster, some might say....but probably only a man, of an admittedly unusual sort. A man returned from the dead—not by any intervention of chemistry and electricity, like others of more recent provenance, but by some accident of nature, long ago. Such accidents are apparently less rare than we have recently supposed. In the distant past, they were credited to miracles or black magic; more recently, they have been dismissed as products of superstition, or cases of catalepsy. The simple fact is, it seems, that death is not always the end—but what succeeds it, when some kind of new life does succeed it, remains something of a mystery, even to its beneficiaries."

"A *vampire?*" Suzanne repeated, her incredulity mingling with fear as she realized that her father was perfectly serious.

"Not the kind that sucks blood," Temple told her, offering what scant reassurance he could. "Dangerous, certainly, but...well, he did not kill me when he had the chance." He thought it best to return to safer ground, and continued: "The point is that Countess Marcian Gregoryi is the vampire's instrument. Their plan has gone badly awry, thanks to the involvement of the *Habits Noirs* and their agents in the Prefecture, but they might not be finished yet. Was there another man with me in Coco-Lacour's cart—another victim of the so-called bandits? Is he here too, perchance?"

Suzanne stared at him, obviously wondering whether he was mad. She had had reason enough to suspect him of that in the past, and he could not blame her for it. Eventually, she shook her head and said: "You were alone. No mention was made of any other victim."

Temple was not surprised. Whether the new Adam was still with the vampire, or had returned to Lord Byron—or even if he was in Vidocq's custody—Coco-Lacour would not have been disposed to mention him to the residents of the Château de Belcamp. Temple was quite ready to consider the Gray Man an ally now, although he knew full well that the only person in whom he could place any real trust was Jean-Pierre Sévérin. He made a mental note to send a message to Sévérin, at least to reassure the old man that he was alive, and as well as could be expected.

Temple's gaze strayed to the bedroom window, and he saw through the crack in the curtains that the sky was turning silver. There was evidently still some mist in the air, but the quality of the light suggested that today would be much brighter than the last day to which he had actually been witness. The Vampire's magnetic powers had obviously put him out of contention for almost twenty-four hours, causing him to miss a whole cycle of daylight. He shifted his leg tentatively, but the movement caused the pain in his right thigh to flare up again.

"It's all in my mind," Temple muttered, addressing himself rather than Suzanne. "The leg itself is perfectly healthy. All I need is the will-power to defy the vampire's suggestive command."

"I'll have the cook make you a good breakfast," Suzanne told him, making no response to what he had said. "You need to get your strength back. You're far too old for this sort of nonsense—but I'll get you some clothes anyway. The ones you were wearing when you were brought in will need extensive mending once they've been washed."

"I'm not as old as Jean-Pierre Séverin," Temple observed, a trifle resentfully. "He can still take on three bravos, armed with nothing but a light cane, and put them all *hors de combat* in a matter of seconds. It's not just the dead who can sometimes renew life, Suzanne—the living can sometimes do it too. That's the real holy grail for which Frankenstein and Patou are searching. If they can understand how the dead return, they might be able to understand how death can be prevented in the first place. That's a goal worth fighting for, even for an old fool like me—and I won't let the vampire toss me casually aside, while I still have the strength to stay in contention. Make sure it's a very hearty breakfast, my darling—I haven't had a bite in almost two full days, and I really do need to get my strength back. Tell Jeanne, as soon as she wakes up, that I need to see her urgently."

Suzanne's temper had calmed, and she left the room quite meekly. It was neither her nor Jeanne who came to see him next, however, but Coco-Lacour.

"Good morning, Mr. Temple," the agent said, cheerfully. "Did I not tell you that you ought to join forces with us? Still, we contrived to rescue you from the vampire's clutches, did we not? We've beaten him out of that particular lair, and eliminated all his minions save one. Paris has a thousand eyes alert for the slightest glimpse of him, and he's quite helpless. Everything is for the best in the best of all possible worlds!"

"You make an unconvincing Dr. Pangloss," Temple observed, dryly.

"So did Dr. Pangloss, in Voltaire's estimation," Co-co-Lacour retorted. "I am a literate man you see—never let it be said that no one ever learns anything in the *bagne*. There really is scope for a man to reform there. One day, I might perhaps rise through the ranks to be Prefect of Police!"

"Have you just come to gloat," Temple asked, "or is there some purpose to your visit?"

"You must forgive me if my natural good spirits give me the appearance of gloating," the agent replied. "I'm here on police business, for the mutual benefit of the Prefecture of Paris and Scotland Yard—a fine example of co-operation for our many untrustful colleagues. Do you know, by any chance, where the vampire and Frankenstein's monster might have gone?"

"They didn't take me into their confidence," Temple said, wishing that it were a lie.

"I suspected as much—but you did meet the vampire, did you not? You can give me a reliable description of him."

"I can tell you what I saw," Temple said, "but I cannot vouch for its reliability. Like you, I have always been a trifle cocksure, and I was always perfectly certain that no Mesmerist charlatan could ever cast a spell on me—but Count Szandor has evidently learned a trick or two in centuries of unnatural life, and he's no charlatan in matters of suggestion. I saw him as an ambulant skeleton, with very little flesh on his ancient bones—but his eye-sockets are by no means blank, and if you ever meet him yourself, you'll find his stare extremely disconcerting."

"That does seem to be a problem," Coco-Lacour admitted. "I had a hundred men at my disposal last night—not all official deputies, I confess—but they couldn't lay hands on him, or even give me any sort of description of him. Lord Byron's pet giant, on the other hand, was all too visible and tangible. He put a dozen men in the hospital, although he seems to have made an effort to be gentle, just as your friend Jean-Pierre did when he gave Fantin a fencing-lesson. Since René de Kervoz will doubtless bring you up to date when he has the chance, I might as well tell you that he and I followed your mystery lady—Countesss Marcian Gregoryi, as I now know her to be—to the Faubourg Saint-German, where she attended a very select dinner-party at the house of the Duchesse de Broglie. She stayed overnight, and apparently has a fistful of similar invitations at her disposal. According to the Duchesse's butler, she is very popular, and is sure to be introduced at court within the week—which puts her far beyond my reach, alas. And yours, of course."

"Except that you also know that she is supposed to be coming to Miremont today, with Sarah Boehm," Temple said, "and you presumably have fifty or sixty hirelings of the *Habits Noirs* available to set in ambush."

"The *Habits Noirs* are a myth, Mr. Temple, as you well know," said Coco-Lacour, serenely, "and I am an agent of the Sûreté, sworn to combat any such evil, were it ever to spring up in reality. Arresting Gentlemen of the Night is my duty and vocation, just as it is yours. There will be no ambush—as I said, the Countess is out of our jurisdiction, and must be left to our friends in high places. In the final analysis, you and I are birds of similar plumage, unable to fly into the rarefied heights of the aristocratic atmosphere."

"We are birds of very different plumage, Monsieur Lacour," Temple retorted. "At the very least, I am determined to persuade the Comtesse de Belcamp not to accept Countess Marcian Gregoryi's dinner invitation—but I might go myself, if I can. I always carry a long spoon with me, in case I'm required to sup with the Devil."

"Monsieur Vidocq told me that you were a very stubborn man," Coco-Lacour observed. "I can see why he admires you. You need not worry about the horses you hired last night, by the way. I sent them back to their owner in Paris—although one is lame, doubtless in consequence of having to carry a giant. Please don't worry about the dinner party either; even if you were to be invited, it would be better for everyone concerned if you were unable to attend. You can easily offer your excuses—say that you sustained some injury in this morning's scuffle." The agent smiled broadly.

Temple scowled. "I can still walk," he said, although he was not at all sure that he could. "I sustained no physical injury, although the vampire was very enthusiastic to score an argumentative point. He simply used his magnetic powers to plant a suggestion in my mind, as much by way of a challenge as a simple disabling move."

"Paris is full of Mesmerists," Coco-Lacour observed, laconically. "Would you like me to summon one to put you in a trance and attempt to overrule the vampire's suggestion?"

"Thank you, no," Temple said. "Since I've been challenged, I feel obliged to accept. Jean-Pierre Séverin would expect no less. Incidentally, since René de Kervoz will tell me anyway, was Lord Byron present at the Duchesse de Broglie's dinner-party?"

"He was," Coco-Lacour admitted. "But he left in his own carriage, under no evident compulsion. He seems to be more resilient than most men to magnetic charms—even more resilient than you, perhaps. He has no difficulty at all in walking, so he will certainly be able to accept his invitation to dine at the new château, if any such gathering actually takes place. Our men will be in the neighborhood, of course, to make sure that the party is not disturbed by…undesirables."

"You still hope to catch the vampire, then?"

"We are agents of the law, Mr. Temple" said Coco-Lacour, stressing the word *we*. "It is our duty to preserve the order of things." He turned towards the door as he spoke; it had opened again.

This time, it really was Temple's breakfast-tray—but the person holding it was neither Suzanne nor a servant. Jeanne de Belcamp had brought it herself. The stare she directed at Coco-Lacour had no magnetic power in it, but was sufficiently intimidating to send him on his way without further ado.

When the door had closed behind the agent, the Comtesse set the tray down on the bed. As responsive as ever to his request, Suzanne had indeed prepared a good breakfast, even by English standards. Gregory Temple wasted no time in getting to work on the bacon and eggs; he was extremely hungry.

Several minutes passed while the Comtesse was content to watch him eat, but in the end she could restrain herself no longer. "Have you seen Henri since you were last here, Mr. Temple?" she asked.

"No," Temple said. "Have you?"

"No. Have you any news of him?"

Temple knew that he was bound by a duty of confidentiality even more powerful than Robert Surrisy's, but he prided himself on knowing a higher duty when he encountered it. "Reliable news, no," he said. "But I do have reason to believe that it was on Henri's instructions that Ned Knob set his conscience aside and agreed to work for Lord Liverpool's secret police. Ned is reporting to him regularly, and believes that I do not know. I have no firm proof, but I believe that Henri is presently in Spain, educating himself in the secrets of *Civitas Solis*, whose agent he has consented to become—at least until he can stage a *coup* and take over the organization. I've packed Ned off to the Caribbean to ascertain the truth of a report that Germain Patou and Mortdieu are there; I presume that *Civitas Solis* will send agents of their own, but I doubt that they'll entrust Henri with the mission. They're undoubtedly monitoring the situation in Paris, but they certainly don't need Henri for that—they have better access to the Faubourg Saint-Germain than any of us, now that the Restoration has revived the Church's fortunes, and they surely have their own means of getting close to Lord Byron. In brief, my lady, we can't rely on Henri's help this time. We must contend with Countess Marcian Gregoryi ourselves."

The Comtesse glanced towards the door through which Coco-Lacour had recently made his exit. "I could not turn him away," she said, simply.

"Of course not," Temple said. "Have you heard from Robert? Has he warned you against the countess?"

"He sent me a note to say that you had warned *him* against the Countess," Jeanne admitted. "He did not seem convinced that your warning was appropriate. She is a very charming woman, and I confess that I would

217

not have dreamed that there was anything suspect about her until I received the note. Robert was even more taken by her, I think."

"There's more to her glamour than mere beauty," Temple told her. "She is an extremely accomplished Mesmerist—more accomplished, I believe, than Mesmer ever was. She is probably much older than she seems. I confess that I do not know exactly what she is, or what to make of her master—but I know that they are both direly dangerous to anyone who gets in the way of their plans."

"And what are their plans—besides acquiring the new château?" Jeanne asked, mildly.

"They must have hoped to do that quietly, without attracting any attention," Temple said, trying to draw inferences as he spoke, "but Paris has changed a great deal since they were last here, eighteen years ago. The rumor has spread like wildfire, faster than even I could have anticipated. In two days, they have been exposed to more danger of detection and destruction than in the previous two decades—perhaps centuries. Szandor, the so-called vampire, has evidently had time to cultivate a good deal of occult wisdom, but he is even further behind the times than *Civitas Solis* or the new arm of the Holy Office. He has been caught off-guard by the scum of the Parisian Underworld—as, I confess, have I. I have no idea what he will do in response, or even whether he can get a message relaying new orders to Countess Marcian Gregoryi, but if she keeps her appointment with Sarah Boehm, there might be trouble."

"I've taken your advice, Mr. Temple," the Comtesse replied, calmly. "I have forty strong men on my staff now, and a series of sturdy fences around my property. The house is very secure, especially the nursery. I can make sure that the children are safe, and I can protect my guests as well."

"That's good," Temple said, "but I'm not in need of protection. The vampire could have killed me, but he wants me alive, probably in the hope that I might eventually lead him to Henri. You must not go to the new château tonight, Jeanne, for he and the Countess will certainly use you in that same cause, if they can."

"I'm not afraid," Jeanne replied.

"I know," Temple told her. "On this occasion, though, fear would not be out of place. This creature does not live on human blood, but he probably has no more compunction about killing the living than the living have about swatting flies or slaughtering livestock. You must not go."

"Very well," she said. "I shall remain in my fortress. What about you?"

"I have no invitation—and I'm not sure that I'd be able to accept if I had—but Coco-Lacour will keep his ruffians close at hand, ready to act if any order comes, and I ought at least to hold myself in readiness too. It is quite possible, by the way, that a man named Jean-Pierre Sévérin will make his way to Miremont, having heard that the vampire is here. If he comes here asking for me, let him in—he can be trusted."

She nodded to signify that she would broadcast the instruction. "If I am to stay meekly at home, though," she said, soberly, "you must keep me fully informed, Mr. Temple. I have been involved in this strange business since the moment when Henri plunged into the mill-stream, with my burning body clutched in his hands. I have cheated death myself, and am well aware of it. Had he let me die that day, he would have become rich, but he could not do it. The angel in him was stronger than the devil then, and it will win in the end."

"Yes, my lady," Temple said, meekly, as the Comtesse turned to leave the room. He was not about to point out that the only way that Henri de Belcamp could have claimed the fortune left by Helen Brown's murdered brothers was to assume the identity of Tom Brown publicly—something that he was, by then, extremely reluctant to do. To marry that fortune, whether as Henri de Belcamp or Percy Balcomb, must have seemed the preferable option on purely rational grounds. Even so, Temple did not doubt for an instant that Henri de Belcamp really had fallen in love with Jeanne Herbet, whatever his *alter ego* Tom Brown might have thought of the match.

As soon as he had finished his breakfast and set aside the tray, Temple threw back the blankets and attempted to ease himself from the bed. He contrived to stand up, but it was agony. He even forced himself to walk a few steps; his legs, as he had anticipated, worked perfectly well—but still, it was agony. He cursed the vampire, although he could not help feeling that he was being somewhat unfair in doing so. If the so-called Count Szandor had merely wished to injure him, he could have done so—and could, of course, have snuffed out his life like a candle-flame—but that was not the point of what he had done to Temple. This really was a challenge as well as a lesson, and it was a challenge that Temple needed to meet.

One way or another, Temple thought as he took a rest, slumped in an armchair, before trying again, *what my deceptive acquaintance Giuseppe Balsamo called the Empire of the Necromancers is about to dawn. The dead will return in ever-greater numbers, no matter what the likes of Malo de Treguern might do to prevent them. They will bring a new enlightenment, as well as a force to be reckoned with, and there is no question in the world more important than the question of who will guide that Empire as it grows and bears fruit. Count Szandor knows that now as well as I do, if he did not know it before. Fate has given him a chance to take a hand in that decision, as it has given a chance to me, and I cannot blame him for wanting to take it. Powerful as he is, though, I must still do my utmost to use my own opportunity well, not on behalf of Lord Liverpool, or King George, or even God Almighty, but on behalf of humankind.*

Chapter Six
An Unexpected Invitation

Had Gregory Temple had full mastery of his legs there were a great many things he might have done that morning. He might well have returned to Paris, in order to go in search of Countess Marcian Gregoryi before she set out for the new château—if that was still her intention—or to seek an interview with Lord Byron, or to confer with Jean-Pierre Sévérin. As things were, however, he could not conquer his psychosomatic pain to the extent that would permit such an excursion. The Vampire had got the better of him, at least for a matter of hours. He was, however, able to refuse his hostess's offer to supply him with a wheelchair and a lackey to push it around the grounds of the château; he contrived to walk short distances, albeit with some difficulty, with the aid of a cane like the one that Sévérin used.

The time was not entirely wasted though; there were bridges to be built and fences to mend within the family, and Temple—unable, for once, to offer an excuse for hurrying away—had no alternative but to take a holiday from his obsession and begin that work of domestic repair. Thus, for the first time ever, he conversed for more than an hour with his little grandson. For the first time in five years, he conversed for more than an hour with his former assistant. For the first time in more than ten years, he conversed for more than an hour with his daughter.

It was, as he had anticipated when he saw the early light of dawn filtering through the curtains, a fine day, with not a hint of fog about it, or any of the stink of the city. The valley of the Oise was green and tranquil, as the whole world always seemed to be in his rare dreams of childhood.

"If you were ever to retire, Father," Suzanne told him, as they sat on the mound that offered the best view of the valley available in the château's grounds, while the sun eventually began to sink again into the west, "you would be very welcome in Miremont—perhaps in the village, if you would prefer that to the château."

"I cannot," Temple told her. "Mine is not the kind of vocation that permits retirement. I shall die in harness, if I do not find a way to go on forever—and even if I die…." He left the sentence unfinished.

"Would you really want to come back from the dead?" she asked him. "The rumors I have head about the Grey Men do not make that sort of resurrection seem an attractive prospect."

"Temple thought about Szandor and what it must be like to live among men as a horrid caricature of human form, loathed and feared in equal measure. "The process must be capable of refinement," he said. "There will doubtless be many failures along the way—but a man might be proud even to be one such failure, I think, provided that he could offer a valuable stepping-stone to eventual success. Germain Patou is a long way away, but Victor Frankenstein is still in Europe, and Lord Byron knows where he is. If and when I have the privilege of meeting his lordship, I shall be glad to volunteer myself as a future test-subject, just as Keats and Shelley were."

Suzanne was beside him, but her hand was resting on his shoulder and he felt her shudder. "Don't be afraid," he said.

"I can't help it," she confessed.

A carriage came in sight then, still very distant, on the hunting-path that led from the woods surrounding the crossroads on the road between Paris and l'Isle Adam to the two châteaux. Temple immediately plucked the Marquis de Belcamp's old field-telescope from his pocket, having purloined it for this very purpose.

"That's Sarah's carriage," Suzanne said, immediately.

Temple trained his instrument upon the vehicle. It was, at first, impossible to guess how many passengers that body of the carriage might contain, especially as the blinds were drawn over its windows, but it seemed obvious enough from its seemingly-perfect condition that the vehicle had not been the focal point of any pitched battle such as might have followed any sort of ambush. It had obviously not been stopped on the road from Paris.

"She's aboard," he murmured. "I feel it in my bones. The vampire is not easily put off, it seems. He must be assuming that the influential friends the countess has gathered with such remarkable rapidity will shield her from any potential harm. I cannot believe that he will actually buy the château, though; he is accustomed to discretion, and surely will not try to establish himself in a known location of that sort. He must be hoping that the countess will be able to make a compact with Byron tonight, before they all disappear. If Frankenstein's Grey Man has returned to his master as a messenger, his lordship might be amenable to that possibility—but he will surely still be wary of the countess's magnetic powers. The last thing he would want is to be reduced to the status of a mere instrument himself."

In the meantime, his right eye remained glued to the telescope's lens, studying the carriage as it made its patient way to the courtyard of the new château; he was eager to see who might descend when it pulled up in front of the perron.

When the suspense was finally ended, three people got down from the carriage: two women and a man. The man seemed to be very old; he had to be helped down by the others.

"Is the lady in the red dress Countess Marcian Gregoryi?" Suzanne asked. Temple was surprised that she was able to see the blood-red evening-gown at all, with the naked eye, given that the Countess was wearing a white fur coat over the top of it, leaving only half a meter visible beneath the coat's hem.

"I've only seen the woman at a much closer distance," Temple told her, scrupulously "but I have not the slightest doubt that it is."

"And who is the man? It's not Robert Surrisy—is it Lord Byron?"

"No, it's not," Temple said. "I can't be absolutely certain, because I haven't seen him for many years, but I believe that it's Colonel Bozzo-Corona. If *he*'s fallen under the countess's spell, then she really does have a firm foothold in the cream of Parisian society, and not just the *haut ton*...."

"There's another carriage," Suzanne interrupted. "And a third, further away—but the third isn't coming up the hill. It's stopped by the old mill."

Temple stood up, wincing as he did so, and swiveled the telescope back and forth. Supporting himself on his cane he watched the second carriage—the one that was climbing the hill. "*That*'s Byron," he said, positively, although he could not quite make out the coat-of-arms on the carriage door. "So she has succeeded in arranging a meeting—I wonder if the colonel helped her to negotiate that.

"Who is Colonel Bozzo-Corona?" Suzanne asked. "I don't know the name."

"He's a much-respected man," Temple told her, "but he lives a somewhat reclusive existence, it seems. I met him in London before the war—he took a keen interest in the founding of Scotland Yard, and said that Paris really ought to have something similar, to protect the interests of honest men. He's met Séverin recently, it seems—to consult him about the possibility that the dead return. If he's taking an interest in the business, Frankenstein will have no lack of funds available to him...."

He trailed off as the second carriage reached the perron, and three men got out. All three were of ordinary stature, but all three were wearing hats that made identification difficult.

"Is it Byron?" Suzanne was avid to know.

"I believe so," said Temple, altering the focus of the telescope slightly. "He's the one bringing up the rear, I think. The other two must be his guests, or his bodyguards—but I can't tell who they might be."

Two of the newcomers, including Lord Byron, went into the house; the third, after a brief consultation with the other two, set off in the direction of the Château de Belcamp.

"Is he coming here?" Suzanne asked.

"Apparently," Temple confirmed. In the meantime, he switched his instrument to the third carriage, which had stopped by the mill, on the near side of the bridge over the Oise. This one was the largest of the three, and seemed to be somewhat loaded down with passengers; it disgorged no less than eight men, who must have been very cramped inside. Temple had no difficulty in recognizing their leader by the slightly bizarre manner of his dress.

"Coco-Lacour," Temple said, shortly. "He must have received new orders from Vidocq. Still hunting for the vampire, no doubt—he probably has at least another dozen men lurking in the vicinity. It's sheer optimism, though; he might as well hope to catch a shadow."

After a brief inspection, the group broke up, and the eight men dispersed. They vanished into the woods soon enough, but Temple guessed that they intended to form a picket around the new château's park, so that they could monitor any traffic in or out.

Temple returned his attention to the lone man making his way toward the gate of the Château de Belcamp. He collapsed the telescope and put it away. "Go back into the house," he said. "I'll go down to the gate to find out what the fellow wants. It's a good opportunity to tell him that the Comtesse is indisposed, and won't be able to come to dinner."

"No," Suzanne said. "I'm coming with you. What if your leg gives out?"

Temple pursed his lips, but made no objection. As he set off, there certainly seemed to be a possibility that his leg *would* give out, but he gathered all his strength and did his utmost to ignore the taunting pain.

Pierre Louchet was already waiting at the gate, with the attitude of a faithful bulldog. Temple joined him and took up a position by his side as the messenger approached. He was well-dressed, in an unmistakably English style

"Bonjour," he said, and continued in French: "My name is Robert Walton. I should like to see the Comtesse de Belcamp, if that's possible."

"I'm afraid it isn't," Temple replied, in English. "The Comtesse has been taken ill. She will not be able to see anyone until tomorrow, at the earliest. Pierre was just about to set out for the new château to express her regrets to Countess Boehm, but you have saved him the trouble. Please ask Countess Boehm to accept her apologies."

Walton looked him in the eyes, with perfect frankness. "Gregory Temple, I presume," he said, "late of Scotland Yard."

"Indeed," said Temple. "This is my daughter Suzanne, who lives here with her husband, Richard Thompson. I was in Paris, and took the opportunity to visit."

"Lord Byron mentioned that you might be here," Walton said, equably. "He also anticipated that the Comtesse might not be able to join us, although I have no idea how he came by the suspicion. We have a doctor in our party—would you like me to ask him to come over to attend to the Comtesse?"

Temple heart skipped a beat. "A doctor?" he said. "You don't, by any chance, mean Victor Frankenstein?"

Walton smiled. "No, Mr. Temple," he said. "Dr. Frankenstein is not in Paris just now. The doctor who is with us tonight is an Italian gentleman by the name of Giuseppe Balsamo. I believe you know him, slightly."

Temple did not know whether that was good news or not. "I believe I do," he said. "I admire his courage in coming here."

"Why so?" Walton asked. "It's a harmless social call, after all." His voice had now taken on a slight hint of irony.

The reason why Temple esteemed it an act of courage for "Giuseppe Balsamo" to visit the new château was that all of Sarah Boehm's staff were affiliated to a *vehm* that had lately been involved in a dispute with the organization to which the man now employing that pseudonym belonged—and they were the kind of men who bore grudges for a long time. Balsamo doubtless thought himself safe in his present company, though.

"Of course it is," was what Temple said aloud. "I hope you have a good dinner, and a pleasant conversation."

"Actually," Walton said, "Lord Byron wondered if *you* might care to join us. I think he would be glad to have another fellow-countryman present."

Temple felt Suzanne jab him in the ribs with her elbow, as if to tell him to follow the advice he had given to Jeanne and refuse—but she knew him well enough to know that there was no chance of that.

"I should be delighted," he said. "Please thank Lord Byron for me—it's a great honor."

"Should we send a carriage to collect you?" Walton asked. "You seem to have injured your leg."

"That won't be necessary," Temple assured him.

"Milord also mentioned another person who might be here, who would also be welcome to join us: a Monsieur Jean-Pierre Sévérin."

So Frankenstein's new Adam did get back to his lordship, Temple thought, *and has told him that if he came to this meeting—as his curiosity was bound to drive him to do—then he ought to recruit trustworthy reinforcements. I'm flattered.* Aloud, he said: "I was hoping that Monsieur Sévérin would contact me today, but he has not done so as yet. If he does arrive, I shall be glad to bring him with me. What time shall I come?"

"As soon as you like," was the reply. "We shall be dining at seven, but I dare say that the conversation will be well advanced by then." Walton took off his hat, bowed politely to Suzanne, and turned to leave.

"Will you go down to the village for me, Pierre?" Temple asked Louchet. "Look for Sévérin—I'm sure he's there somewhere, probably keeping his ear to the ground in the inn. You'll know him easily enough by his white hair and cane—he has one just like this."

"I know Monsieur Sévérin." Pierre Louchet replied. "I had, alas, had more than one occasion to visit the morgue in the days when he was its keeper. He knew the emperor, you know."

"I know," Temple said. "Bring him back, if you can, in a hurry. I'll have to borrow some better clothes—and so will he, I'd guess—but this is an opportunity not to be missed. History might be made tonight. I never thought I'd ever volunteer to serve as Lord Byron's bodyguard, but life is full of surprises, thank God!"

Chapter Seven
A Masquerade with Invisible Masks

Pierre Louchet came back with Jean-Pierre Sévérin before Temple had finished dressing. The old man seemed slightly out of breath after climbing the hill, and he leaned on his cane for support when he paused, but there was a flame of naked excitement in his eye. "Thank you, my friend," he said to Temple, with evident sincerity. "René wanted to come with me, but I would not permit it. Someone has to guard Angela. In any case, he is a trifle hot-headed at times. He does not have our cool maturity—but you're hurt! What happened?"

"The vampire pinked me in the leg after all," Temple told him, "but I think I have the better of the injury now. I can't wield my cane as you wield yours, but it will get me to this diabolical conference. You'll find another old friend of yours there, by the way: Colonel Bozzo-Corona. I suspect that he acted as a broker between Countess Marfcian Gregoryi and Lord Byron—we must make certain, if we can, to protect him as well as Lord Byron."

"Is that our mission now—to protect Lord Byron?" the old warrior asked, uncertainly. "I thought we were here to slay the vampire."

"That may not be possible—but we might hope, at least, to prevent his taking control of this entire business. Here—put this suit on. Like mine, it's more than a trifle old-fashioned, having belonged to the old marquis, but it's respectable."

Séverin put on the marquis' old evening suit, and the two men set off for the new château immediately afterwards. Temple had already given stern instructions to Richard Thompson to keep the house sealed at all costs.

The walk from one residence to the other was not easy, but Temple negotiated it without overmuch discomfort, with the aid of his stick.

As they approached the main gate of the new château two corpulent ruffians armed with naked blades moved out of the bushes to either side of the path, blocking their way. Jean-Pierre Séverin immediately placed himself *en garde*, but the situation was immediately defused when Coco-Lacour came running out of a covert, making hasty signals to his men to stand easy.

"Mr. Temple is a colleague, lads!" he scolded them. "He's one of those we're here to protect, not one of those we're here to arrest—and this is Monsieur Séverin, who was the finest swordsman in France before the Revolution, so you must count yourselves lucky that you did not fee the blunt end of his walking-stick in your overstuffed guts."

Having arrived in front of the two visitors he bowed ostentatiously. "Out of bed already, Mr. Temple!" he said. "I hope I have your powers of perseverance when I reach your age."

"But you'll be the Prefect of Police by then, Monsieur Lacour!" Temple retorted, matching the other's mocking tone. "You'll never have to quit your desk, with fine fellows like these to do your bidding."

"You're too kind, Mr. Temple," Coc-Lacour assured him. Looking Temple and Séverin up and down, he was quick to add: "I had not realized that Countess

Sarah's party was a masquerade—but I have to admit that the mothballs have kept the Marquis' old clothes in good condition." He obviously knew that the insult would carry an extra edge, coming from him.

"A masquerade without masks," Temple replied as lightly as he could. "Or perhaps, more accurately, with invisible masks. Be careful, won't you, not to let any shadows slip past you. There will be vampires abroad, once dusk falls."

That reminder struck home, but Coco-Lacour did not cry *touché*. He simply shoved his men aside to let the Countess's guests pass.

In fact, the pause did Temple good, allowing him to vent a little of his bile and permitting his aching leg a useful truce. He felt quite well again when the door of the new château was opened by a German footman. Temple was not displeased to see that the domestic was a strong man with a military bearing—the presence of the *vehm* would, at least, guarantee that Sarah Boehm would be well defended, and her protection would presumably extend to her guests.

The two newcomers were shown into a reception-room where the assembled company was relaxing in a circle of armchairs. Sarah got up to greet them, and introduced them formally to the circle, beginning with Countess Marcian Gregoryi, whose blood-red dress was now displayed in all its considerable glory, emphasizing the contours of her figure with a skill that only the best Parisian couturiers could achieve.

The vampire's minion met Temple's eyes with a smile that seemed to radiate innocence and purity. Her eyes were bright blue, and her complexion was won-drously clear. "Lord Byron has just been telling us all about you, Mr. Temple," she said, in English. "You were once quite famous in England, it seems, for your expertise in bringing villains to justice. I'm delighted to meet you."

Temple acknowledged the compliment as gracefully as he could.

"And the colonel has told us about you, too, Monsieur Sévérin," she said, turning to his companion. "You are, in his estimation, the last of the great swordsmen of the Revolutionary era."

Jean-Pierre Sévérin glanced sideways at Colonel Bozzo-Corona, perhaps puzzled as to why the old gentleman should describe him in those terms rather than as the one-time keeper of the morgue. Her eyes and her smile did throw him into confusion though. "I met a Countess Marcian Gregoryi once before, in 1804," he said, with a marked edge in his voice, although his tone was perfectly polite.

"That was my mother!" exclaimed the lovely blonde, apparently delighted with the news. "She's dead now, I fear—but she lived to see me earn the right to the name that she coveted so dearly. Poor Marcian is dead too, alas—like our charming hostess, I was unfortunate enough to be widowed young." And with that the lady relaxed back into her seat.

Sarah Boehm continued the round of introductions.

Giuseppe Balsamo nodded in recognition of the fact that he had met Temple before, while Lord Byron, whose impeccable jet black costume made a sharp contrast with Balsamo's slightly rumpled blue one, assured him that he had long wanted to meet the famous detective. Walton's acknowledgement was very brief, but Colonel Bozzo-Corona looked at Temple long and hard, in a slightly quizzical manner, and stood up as if to study him more carefully. "You were a young man when we last met," the colonel said, as if he were surprised to see the extent to which Temple had aged—and Temple had to admit, although he did not want to say so aloud, that the colonel hardly seemed to have aged at all, having already been old before the war began.

"I know, I know," the colonel said, apparently reading Temple's mind. "I am far too old for this kind of diplomatic mission—but I tell myself perpetually that whatever business I am involved in must be my last affair, and never seem able to take my own advice. It is hard to reconcile oneself to growing old, is it not, Monsieur Sévérin? Mentally, we might remain young forever, if only our bodies did not let us down—but I fear that the cure for which Lord Byron's associates are hunting is unlikely to materialize in time to help us."

Jean-Pierre Sévérin had followed Temple around the circle, bowing respectfully to everyone. The old warrior was not at all put out by the prestigious company; indeed, he seemed to make a point of looking everyone straight in the eye, as if he had every right to be as proud of his own heritage as they had of theirs. No one, so far as Temple could see, objected to that; none of them was too proud to meet the gaze of a morgue-keeper's son who had followed in his father's footsteps. Indeed, it seemed that they all warmed to the old man immediately.

The German footman had poured glasses of *kir* for Temple and Sévérin; after serving them, he retired. When Temple and his companion had taken their seats the colonel and Sarah Boehm sat down again too. The conversation immediately became fragmented, individuals chatting with their immediate neighbors—as they had presumably been doing before the two new arrivals had been shown in.

Colonel Bozzo-Corona was, however, still looking at Temple, and Temple looked back at him, still puzzled by the old man's astonishing state of preservation. "The company is almost complete," the colonel remarked, placidly.

Temple glanced around, and saw that there was, indeed, one seat in the circle that had no occupant. Séverin leaned over to whisper in his ear: "Will the vampire come in person, then?"

Temple was almost willing to believe that—although another alternative did occur to him. "Who else are we expecting?" he said to the colonel, unable to contain his impatience.

"Countess Boehm's brother and lawyer, Robert Surrisy," the old man said. "There is a little business to be transacted after dinner it seems—I don't know the exact details."

Temple looked at Countess Marcian Gregoryi, who was talking to Robert Walton while Byron and Balsamo were involved in some hushed exchange. She seemed quite oblivious to his suspicion and hostility—and Walton seemed to be as entranced by her as Robert Surrisy had been. Temple could not help experiencing a pang of regret at the discovery that Henri de Belcamp was not, after all, due to spring one of his surprises.

They did not have long to wait for the company to be completed; less than five minutes had passed before the footman opened the door again and ushered Surrisy in. Sarah moved to greet him, but the young lawyer seemed slightly flustered, and did not greet her as gallantly as might have been expected, and was certainly her due. "Did you know that there's some kind of manhunt going on in the vicinity, Sarah?" he said. "My carriage was actually stopped by some buffoon in a clownish costume, who wanted to search it."

"That is Monsieur Coco-Lacour," Temple supplied. "You might be seeing a lot more of him in future—he is ambitious to rise through the ranks, and might well be chief of the Sûreté one day, even if he never becomes Prefect. Tonight, he's hunting for a vampire."

The pronunciation of the last word would probably have imposed an instant silence on any other social gathering of that size, but there was no reaction in this one. Robert looked at Temple, unable to hide his amazement. "Thank you for your advice, Mr. Temple," he said, insincerely. "I must admit that I did not expect to find you here—and Monsieur Séverin is here too, I see."

"Lord Byron took the liberty of inviting us," Temple explained, taking some relish in the other's evident confusion. "Much to my delight—I've always wanted to meet him."

Byron raised his glass in acknowledgement of that remark, and met Temple's eyes with a gaze that was full of significance. Temple nodded, hoping to convey the reassurance that he and the rebel aristocrat were on the same side, at least for tonight. Byron got up then—which provided a signal to everyone else that it was permissible to move around, and came to take Temple's arm in order to draw him aside.

"A mutual friend told me that you had been hurt," he said, glancing down at the stick. "I was very glad when Walton told me that you were able to come tonight. I might need your counsel—and Monsieur Séverin's too. Weight of numbers, I'm assured, is the best defense against mesmeric wiles."

"The countess has only one pair of eyes," Temple quoted. "Her spell-casting powers are limited—but she

237

might well be prepared to deal honestly with you, if she cannot secure an advantage. Her master seems genuinely curious—but if you do intend to sup with her, in the broader sense...."

"I must use a long spoon," Byron completed. "I had gathered that. You and I should have come to an understanding some time ago, I suppose, but I was reluctant to trust you, in spite of your reputation for honest dealing. You're an agent of parliament, after all—although you seem to have enthusiastic radicals in your employ, and your employers are rumored to disapprove of your recent exploits."

"My superiors have almost reached the end of their tether," Temple admitted. "I might be kicked out of the king's employ at any moment—but that does not mean that I would be content to be anyone else's agent."

"Understood. We both have agents on the *Belleville*, though, and I think they might find common cause before they reach the Carib Sea."

"Master Knob thinks that he is his own man," Temple said, with a sigh. "He makes common cause with all and sundry, when he thinks it suits him. One day, he'll forget what he's doing and stab himself in the back."

Byron nodded to acknowledge the quip, and murmured: "We'll talk again, before we get down to business." Then he allowed himself to be drawn aside by Sarah Boehm, who sat him down on a sofa and then arranged herself beside him, presumably because she was genuinely delighted to meet the greatest poet of the age rather than being motivated by any conspiratorial fervor.

Temple took a quick look around, Jean-Pierre Séverin was standing on his own, his penetrating gaze roaming from one face to another—although his eyes never lingered long on Countess Mercian Gregoryi, who

238

was still flirting with Robert Walton. Perhaps, Temple thought, he was afraid that they might be captured and entranced—which might turn out to be a wise precaution.

Giuseppe Balsamo had taken Robert Surrisy aside, to sit on a window-seat, but they did not appear to be talking business. Colonel Bozzo-Corona was sitting very quietly, seemingly studying the assembled guests with as much attention and intelligence as Temple. Temple stepped back to join Séverin.

"Lord Byron's head is clear," Temple said, speaking out of the corner of his mouth. "He has plenty of supporters here to distract her hypnotic gaze, if and when she turns her attention to him. So has Sarah Boehm, although she has not the same suspicion of the danger she's in. I think we can negotiate our way through the pass, when the danger materializes—but we'd best be careful not to drink too much during dinner."

Séverin did not reply immediately, and Temple turned sideways to look him in the face. The old man's eyes seemed remarkably dark, and Temple was suddenly aware of a sinking feeling in his stomach. He opened his mouth to speak, but was interrupted before he could say a single word.

"Does it not seem to you, Mr. Temple," Séverin said, very mildly, "that the atmosphere in this room is surprisingly dusty, for such a fine and modern house?"

As soon as those words had been voiced, Temple became aware that he was drawing breath with difficulty. It was as if the air had become gradually heavier, by such imperceptible degrees that he had not noticed it until it was pointed out, and was now so thick that it weighed down upon him.

239

There were three chandeliers in the room and a dozen wall-brackets holding candelabra—at least sixty candles, in all, of pure white wax. The light should have been bright, but he realized now that it had been dimming for some time, by similarly imperceptible degrees. Moreover, as Jean-Pierre Séverin had calmly observed, the air was thick with dust...or something that resembled dust.

"Damn it!" muttered Temple, finding it oddly difficult to pronounce the words. "He's here! In spite of Co-co-Lacour's ragged legion and all the German guards, he's here!" His first thought, then, was to warn Sara Boehm—but as he took a step in her direction he saw her lie back languidly against the back of her sofa, as if in a coquettish gesture aimed at the pillar of English Romanticism, and he saw her eyes drift shut.

Temple attempted another curse, but could not get it out. He saw that Byron's eyes were closed too, although the poet was sitting up straight. Having observed that, Temple thought it best to raise the alarm himself, and tried to turn towards the door—but his legs, although there was no longer the least twinge of pain therein, simply refused to obey him. He darted a glance at Balsamo and Surrisy, and saw that they had both slumped against the window, apparently having passed out. Even Colonel Bozzo-Corona had relaxed his patient vigilance, and had closed his eyes as if to rest them.

But this is impossible! Temple thought. *Even if he were here, he only has one pair of eyes! Even if he and Countess Marcian Gregoryi have two pairs, that....*

As he formed the thought, he redirected his glance towards the Countess in the blood-red dress. She was not looking at him, though; she was still staring into Robert Walton's eyes. The seafarer's eyes were still open, but they seemed to Temple to be blind to everything but his immediate companion.

Temple turned back to his own companion, Jean-Pierre Sévérin, hoping that he, at least, was still alert and capable of action. He was—but Temple saw, far too late, that his companion was not Jean-Pierre Sévérin at all.

Where Sévérin had been standing only a moment before there was now a walking skeleton, with hardly an ounce of flesh on his bones, on whom the Marquis de Belcamp's old suit hung like a bizarre shroud.

"Have no fear, Mr. Temple." whispered a sibilant, serpentine voice that might have come from anywhere. "The real Monsieur Sévérin is safe in Paris, where I visited him this morning and found him under clandestine house arrest. It will take a more powerful friend than you or Lord Byron to release him, although Monsieur Coco-Lacour did not seem to know that, if Monsieur Vidocq took the trouble to inform him of that part of his scheme. Don't worry—no one in or near suspected that I was there. I was particularly careful not to trouble the lovely Angela—this time. All that I stole was a mere appearance, for the sake of a little masquerade. I have, as you so dutifully repeated on my behalf, only one pair of eyes—but I think you and Monsieur Lazarus might have underestimated what one pair of eyes might do, if given leave to roam for a while."

I am the Trojan Horse! Temple thought, despairingly. *I brought the enemy here myself, without suspecting it for a moment! What a fool I have been!* "What do you intend to do?" he whispered, hardly able to force the words through his lips.

The room was full of dust now, much thicker than the fog that had afflicted Paris two nights before—and the dust seemed, once again, to be full of hungry ghosts.

Temple remembered that the Deliverance had met here, too, on the night when the organization had met its Waterloo, in spite of the warning delivered by Ned Knob, which had allowed the ringleaders to scatter and save their lives. That was the night that Henri de Belcamp had committed suicide, at least in the deluded eyes of his poor distraught father, while Helen Brown lay dead in an alcove at the other château. Was her ghost here in this insistent crowd, he wondered, hungrier for revenge than all the rest combined?

"You know what I intend to do, Mr. Temple," whispered Count Szandor the vampire, as his lovely alter ego glided across the floor to join him, leaving the hapless Robert Walton behind, slumped unconscious in his chair. "I intend to make contracts and discover secrets—but I intend to make and discover them on my own terms, and no one shall bargain with me, let alone prevent me. Certainly not you, my unwitting friend."

Gregory Temple saw, in that horrible instant, that all was lost: that the vampire had won, in spite of everything that had been done by way of defense. Now, it only remained for him to seize the opportunity he had created, not only to captivate Lord Byron and Robert Walton, but also Sarah Boehm and Robert Surrisy, and Giuseppe Balsamo of *Civitas Solis*—and also, by way of a bonus, Colonel Bozzo-Corona, one of the most highly esteemed men in Paris. All that might take time—in fact, it certainly would take time—for he would have to work on them one by one to obtain that kind of control over them and make them speak, but he *had* time, now, and one pair of eyes would suffice, even if he and his minion only had one effective pair between them.

They obviously intended to start on the very least of their captives, by way of *hors d'oeuvres*. They intended to start by enslaving Gregory Temple, formerly of Scotland Yard.

It was the woman's eyes—the eyes of Countess Marcian Gregoryi—that suddenly filled Temple's with their magical blueness, as infinite as the sky, while the avid ghosts clustered round, gloating. Temple tried with all his might to struggle, but he knew that he could not do it. He was utterly helpless. One pair of eyes was all it took…

He tried to cry for help, but he could not. He prayed, instead, for one of Sarah's servants to come in—but he knew that dinner would not be served for an hour, and that no one would appear if no summoning bell was rung.

Unlike her master, Countess Marcian Gregoryi was extremely beautiful: as beautiful as love itself, if his memory served him right.…

Then, astonishingly, both battens of the reception room were hurled back—and from the utmost corners of his not-yet-bewildered eyes, Temple glimpsed two figures stride in, insistently claiming the attention of the blue eyes that had been about to consume his sight.

The one thing with which a Mesmerist could not deal, Temple reflected, as time seemed to stop, was *weight of numbers*—but that was no mere matter of simple arithmetic. It did not require a host, or even a crowd; it only required weight enough to divide his attention, and throw him momentarily into a quandary, provided that advantage could then be taken of the moment of confusion. Two men would be enough, and a mere split second, provided that the two were sufficiently surprising in their appearance, and sufficiently fast-moving in their action.

The two men who had burst in were not *just* two, in fact—there was a whole company of German guardsmen behind them, alerted and armed and ready to fight—but it was the two who led the charge that broke the vampire's spell.

The two men were both grizzled, having the appearance of men who had outlived their natural span, and ought to have had no natural vitality left—but they were very much alive, and they were ablaze with vitality. They wasted no time in challenges or questions, but hurled themselves forwards into the furious dust-storm that formed around them—and the blades they carried seemed to move like streaks of lightning, cutting through the forms that were trying to take shape there.

This time, Jean-Pierre Sévérin—the *authentic* Jean-Pierre Sévérin—had a real épée, not a cane, and his companion—who must, Temple realized, be none other than Malo de Treguern—had a blade like the Breton knights of the age of chivalry, more broadsword than saber.

Count Szandor reacted immediately, and might still have had the power and presence of mind to turn the tables back if he had only been facing Treguern, or two men like the warrior monk—but Jean-Pierre Sévérin's blade was momentarily unstoppable, and his hand had already demonstrated that it was *much* quicker than any mortal eye. The old man was young again, just for that instant, and he knew exactly what to do. This time, it was not clumsiness that compelled him to seek out his opponent's eye.

Count Szandor had no sooner squared up to his unexpected opponents than he staggered back, wounded: sorely wounded, it seemed, in the right eye. Now, he no longer had even one complete pair of eyes.

Countess Marcian Gregoryi still had two eyes intact, but they were not independent of her master's. Those blue orbs, distracted by the commotion, were no longer staring into Gregory Temple's eyes, and no longer holding him prisoner. Even as he reached out to seize her, though, never taking his own eyes off her incredible lovely face, that face began to crumble, aging a hundred or a thousand years within a fraction of a second—and then she disintegrated into dust, seemingly no different from the hundreds of other ghosts that had been clustering around, but which were fleeing now, panicked by the mighty sweeps of Malo de Treguern's shining blade and the darting thrusts of Jean-Pierre Séverin's épée.

Gradually, the dark and cloying air was clearing and becoming bright again—and when Temple looked down, to where Count Szandor's stricken body should have been, that too appeared to be melting into dust. That ghost fled like all the rest—but it did not dissipate as the others did, maintaining a blurred semblance of shape even as it slid between the two swordsmen and glided through the confused ranks of the German swordsmen, who had no idea how to prevent it. Half-blind or not, Count Szandor still knew how to move in such a way as to deceive the sight of lesser men.

Not dead, Temple thought, *nor even mortally wounded. I doubt that he'll return to Paris for some little while, though, once he's had time to collect himself.*

The candlelight was becoming bright again now, and all the eyes that had closed were opening again, staring into empty space in puzzlement. Sarah Boehm looked at the door of her reception-room, frowning at the unbidden intrusion.

None of them, Temple presumed, had seen the false Séverin change into his skeletal form and then vanish.

They were more than a little surprised to see the true one with a sword in his hand instead of a cane, wearing a completely different costume, while the Marquis de Belcamp's old suit and the vampire's cane lay in an untidy heap on the floor. They were even more surprised, though, by the sight of a warrior monk whose habit bore a huge red cross of Calvary, wound around with thorns.

"Who is this man?" Sarah Boehm demanded of her lackeys, who now seemed somewhat shamefaced by the discovery that no one in the room seemed too be under threat, and obviously had not the slightest idea what had just happened.

"Forgive my lack of ceremony, my lady," the warrior monk said, as he sheathed his improbably large sword. "My name is Malo de Treguern. When I arrived in Miremont just now, in company with Monsieur Séverin, and we were informed that his double had already been summoned to this house, I realized immediately that vile diabolism was at work, and that I had a duty to discharge."

Temple ran his gaze over the Germans, who had obviously yielded to the sheer force of the crusader's personality in letting him in—although the sight of a man whose double was already in the reception-room must have assisted their decision.

"Where's Countess Marcian Gregoryi?" demanded Robert Walton, looking in rapt astonishment at a blood-red evening gown that was extended on the carpet.

"I'm afraid that she had to go," Temple said, suppressing a giggle that would surely have confirmed his reputation for lunacy had he let it out. "She had a reckoning to meet, for crimes committed eighteen years ago—but I fear that Monsieur Vidocq's men will not be able to lay their hands on her."

As he spoke, his eyes met those of Colonel Bozzo-Corona, who was staring at him with an unfathomable expression. "For a moment there, Mr. Temple," the colonel said, almost as if he too were suppressing a giggle, "I feared that it was *getting dark*."

Chapter Eight
When the Dust Had Cleared

"As you can probably imagine," Gregory Temple said to the Comtesse de Belcamp, "Walton and Surrisy were not the only ones who found Malo de Treguern a less delightful dinner companion than Countess Marcian Gregoryi would have been. The man is quite insufferable, and we really could have done without his ranting and raving about entertaining the Devil in our homes and hearts."

"But Treguern's timely arrival did save you from the demon's clutches," the Comtesse observed. She was sitting in her favorite armchair, in the room that had formerly been the Marquis of Belcamp's study: the room in which her husband had supposedly shot himself. The two of them were alone, at her insistence, although Temple fully intended to repeat most of what he had just told the Comtesse to his daughter, in order that she would not think that he was still keeping secrets from her.

"The vampire did not intend to kill anyone," Temple told her, trying hard to make himself comfortable in his own armchair. "He is not the Devil—he is not even evil, in any straightforward sense. He can hardly be blamed for feeling isolated, in a world that regards him with fear and loathing, and for his inability to trust anyone who is not entirely subjugated to his will. He did not come to Paris in search of plunder, this time, but in search of enlightenment—as we all did. It is direly unfortunate, but quite understandable, that he could not imagine any other way to obtain it, without risk to himself, but coercion. There is a certain irony, is there not, in the fact that it was his determination to subjugate his fellow guests as a precondition of negotiation that actually led to his downfall? Malo de Treguern's belated visit to Séverin's house was lucky, though—as Coco-Lacour remarked, it needed a more powerful friend than Lord Byron or myself to relieve him of his unofficial house arrest."

"Fortunately," the Comtesse observed, "the Restoration has not only restored the king to his throne, but the Church to its former prestige."

"On the other hand," Temple pointed out, "if Vidocq had not stuck his oar in, it would have been the real man sitting watchfully in the inn in Miremont, not the masquerader, when Pierre Louchet went in search of him and I would not have been tricked into playing the Trojan Horse, introducing our adversary into our very midst. The chain of coincidences was too elaborate to enable Treguern to claim all the credit for breaking it. Nor will Treguern's intervention make Lord Byron any more trustful, I fear—although I do believe that he and I had reached a better understanding by the time the party broke up."

"But if what you say is true," the Comtesse persisted, "Malo de Treguern is at least correct in thinking that the vampire really is a supernatural being. If he and his female companion can turn themselves into clouds of dust and vanish into not-so-thin air, then they really are demons of a sort, are they not?"

"Alas," said Temple, "I merely reported what I saw—and that is not the same as reporting what actually happened. As Jean-Pierre Séverin has now demonstrated to me twice, and a dozen professional card-sharpers have shown me repeatedly, the hand certainly is quicker than the eye. We put far too much trust in our eyesight, Madame de Belcamp, even when we it has been proven to us that it can and does lie to us. It is not our eyes that see, but our minds—and our minds are far more vulnerable to deception than we would like to believe. We have very little idea, at present, as to what the limits of Mesmeric suggestion and induced hallucination might be, any more than we have a clear idea of the true limits of life and death. Sévérin kept the Paris morgue for most of his working life, and saw the dead come back to life repeatedly—but his mind would not believe it, and he insists to this day that he *cannot be sure* of what he saw. And yet, paradoxical as it undoubtedly is, he cannot quite bring himself to *disbelieve* in what he saw on the river on the night when his daughter died, even though he knows full well that it must have been a hallucination induced by the shock of finding her drowned body in the water.

"Frankenstein's *daemon* deduced, rather cleverly, that the vampire could not cope with weight of numbers, because he only has one pair of eyes with which to confuse them, but it is not a simple matter of vulgar arithmetic. The vampire was easily capable of mesmerizing a dozen people at a time, in hospitable circumstances; all he required was some distraction of their attention. It was easy for him to persuade people—including me—to see him as Sévérin, while they were expecting to see Sévérin...or, at least, not expecting to see someone other than Sévérin. In the right circumstances, he could doubtless mesmerize a multitude and make them see something that did not happen. It was a different matter, though, when he was confronted with more than one person who fully expected to see *him*—not necessarily as he is, but as they believed him to be. That was a different kind of challenge. He could have met it, I think—but Jean-Pierre Séverin's hand was far too quick for him, and far too determined. Yes, I *saw* the vampire and his minion turn to dust and disappear—but that was in my mind's eye. It was not what actually *happened*. That, I did not see at all, even though my actual eyes were open."

"Did you say all this to your fellow guests?" the Comtesse asked.

"No. I did not even tell them what I saw. Nor did Jean-Pierre Séverin. Malo de Treguern undertook to shoulder that responsibility single-handed—and what *he* saw, as I have explained, was the Devil vanquished by the strong arm of the Lord."

"Did the others believe that?"

"I doubt that they were as utterly convinced of it as Treguern is. Sarah Boehm and Surrisy were more credulous than the rest, I think. Giuseppe Balsamo probably has a better understanding of what occurred than I have, and might well inform Lord Byron and Walton, now that they have all had the opportunity to get better acquainted. The evening was not a waste of time, you see—it really did build some significant bridges."

"What about the poor old gentleman? He must have been terrified."

"Oddly enough, no. I don't know how old Colonel Bozzo-Corona is—he seemed quite old when I first met him, so I suppose he must be even older than Séverin—but he has obviously seen enough of the world to take everything in his stride. He seemed remarkably undisturbed by the entire experience. Indeed, he seemed strangely delighted by Malo de Treguern's performance—which he appeared to view as a mere performance, devoid of any real significance. He took a polite interest in all the post-prandial discussions, but I don't believe that he will provide Victor Frankenstein with any financial support, if that is what Byron hoped. I think he eventually came to the conclusion that all the talk of resurrection was just as crazy as Treguern's fervent talk of diabolism."

"You have yet to convince me, Mr. Temple," the Comtesse said, dryly, "that the Churchman's talk of diabolism is as crazy as you seem to believe."

Temple accepted the rebuke. "I know that I sound more than a little crazy myself," he aid, "and I know that I have quite a reputation for it—but I really am doing my best to sort out the reality from the illusion."

"I don't doubt that," his interlocutor murmured, sympathetically. "What will you do now? Will you try to discover where the vampire has fled, and track him down again?"

"No. To tell the truth, I'd be just as happy if he never raised his ugly head again, no matter how much useful information he might be able to give us on the subjects of life after death and magnetism, were he so inclined—but I suspect that he'll get in touch, when he's recovered from his wound and regained his strength. He has an appetite for enlightenment himself, now. We shall have to hope that he adopts a more discreet strategy next time he makes contact. I shall return to London to wait for news from the *Belleville* regarding Germain Patou's whereabouts. If he and Mortdieu really have found a secure place of refuge in the New World, I shall have to seek him out…if my employers will allow it."

"I might acquire a steam-driven yacht myself," the Comtesse observed. "I rather enjoyed my one brief excursion to the South Atlantic, and the Americas have always intrigued me. If you find yourself without employment, Mr. Temple, I might well be able to step into the breach."

Temple knew what she meant. If the report came back that Germain Patou had found a safe haven, then Henri de Belcamp would make haste to join him—and Jeanne de Belcamp still believed that her place was at her husband's side, in spite of his firm determination that it was not. Alas, it was highly likely that, as soon as Patou's haven became known in Europe, it would immediately cease to be safe, especially for innocents like her.

"Thank you, my lady," he said, but could not help adding, a trifle morosely—for he was, after all, an honest man: "I fear, though, that I might not be much use to you. My powers as a detective seem to be on the wane, and my meager achievements in this present affair have been entirely due to good fortune."

"Your timely warning kept me out of the danger zone," she pointed out, "and you are at least a little wiser now than you were before. You might have been tricked by the vampire, but it was you who brought his eventual nemesis into the affair. But for you, the real Jean-Pierre Sévérin might be in Paris still, his ancient ears ringing with Malo de Treguern's dire warnings, while Lord Byron and Giuseppe Balsamo might have been sucked dry of all their secrets…not to mention the poor old Colonel, although I cannot imagine that he has any secrets to keep."

"Everyone has secrets of some sort, Madame de Belcamp," Temple said, mournfully. "That is one of the reasons why our own minds are so ever-ready to delude us, in pretending so relentlessly that the world is other than it is."

BLACK COAT PRESS

M. Allain & P. Souvestre. *The Daughter of Fantômas*
Anicet-Bourgeois. *Rocambole*
Guy d'Armen. *Doc Ardan: The City of Gold and Lepers*
Aloysius Bertrand. *Gaspard de la Nuit*
A. Bisson & G. Livet. *Nick Carter vs. Fantômas*
Félix Bodin. *The Novel of the Future*
Comte de Chousy. *Ignis: The Central Fire*
Lucien Dabril. *Rocambole*
V. Darlay & H. de Gorsse. *Lupin vs. Holmes: The Stage Play*
C.I. Defontenay. *Star (Psi Cassiopeia)*
Charles Derennes: *The People of the Pole*
Harry Dickson. *The Heir of Dracula*
Sâr Dubnotal. *Sâr Dubnotal vs. Jack the Ripper*
Alexandre Dumas. *The Return of Lord Ruthven*
J.-C. Dunyach. *The Night Orchid: Conan Doyle in Toulouse*
J.-C. Dunyach. *The Thieves of Silence*
Paul Féval: *Anne of the Isles*
Paul Féval. *The Blackcoats: The Companions of the Treasure*
Paul Féval. *The Blackcoats: The Invisible Weapon*
Paul Féval. *The Blackcoats: The Parisian Jungle*
Paul Féval. *The Blackcoats: 'Salem Street*
Paul Féval. *Captain Phantom*
Paul Féval. *Gentlemen of the Night*
Paul Féval. *John Devil*
Paul Féval. *Knightshade*
Paul Féval. *Revenants*
Paul Féval. *Vampire City*
Paul Féval. *The Vampire Countess*
Paul Féval. *The Wandering Jew's Daughter*
Paul Féval, *fils. Felifax, the Tiger-Man*
Emile Gaboriau. *Monsieur Lecoq*
Arnould Galopin. *Doctor Omega*
V. Hugo, Foucher & Meurice. *The Hunchback of Notre-Dame*
O. Joncquel & Theo Varlet. *The Martian Epic*
Jean de La Hire. *Enter the Nyctalope*
Jean de La Hire. *The Nyctalope on Mars*
Jean de La Hire. *The Nyctalope vs. Lucifer*
Steve Leadley. *Sherlock Holmes - The Circle of Blood*
Maurice Leblanc. *Lupin vs. Holmes: The Hollow Needle*

Maurice Leblanc. *Lupin vs. Holmes: The Blonde Phantom*
G. Le Faure & H. de Graffigny. *The Extraordinary Adventures of a Russian Scientist Across the Solar System* (2 vols.)
Gustave Le Rouge. *The Vampires of Mars*
Jules Lermina. *Panic in Paris*
Gaston Leroux. *Chéri-Bibi*
Gaston Leroux. *The Phantom of the Opera*
Gaston Leroux. *Rouletabille & the Mystery of the Yellow Room*
Jean-Marc Lofficier. *The Katrina Protocol*
Jean-Marc & Randy Lofficier. *Edgar Allan Poe on Mars*
Jean-Marc & Randy Lofficier. *Robonocchio*
J.-M. & R. Lofficier. *Tales of the Shadowmen (Vols. 1-5)*
G. Marot & L. Pericaud. *Nick Carter vs. Jack the Ripper*
Xavier Mauméjean. *The League of Heroes*
William Patrick Maynard. *The Terror of Fu Manchu*
Frank J. Morlock. *Sherlock Holmes: The Grand Horizontals*
Marie Nizet. *Captain Vampire*
C. Nodier, Beraud & Toussaint-Merle. *Frankenstein*
Charles Nodier. *Lord Ruthven the Vampire*
Henri de Parville. *An Inhabitant of the Planet Mars*
John William Polidori. *Lord Ruthven the Vampire*
P.-A. Ponson du Terrail. *The Vampire and the Devil's Son*
Albert Robida. *The Clock of the Centuries*
Albert Robida. *The Adventures of Saturnin Farandoul*
Eugène Scribe. *Lord Ruthven the Vampire*
Brian Stableford. *Frankenstein and the Vampire Countess*
Brian Stableford. *The Germans on Venus*
Brian Stableford. *News from the Moon*
Brian Stableford. *The New Faust at the Tragicomique*
Brian Stableford. *The Shadow of Frankenstein*
Brian Stableford. *Sherlock Holmes - The Vampires of Eternity*
Brian Stableford. *The Stones of Camelot*
Brian Stableford. *The Wayward Muse*
Villiers de l'Isle-Adam. *The Scaffold*
Villiers de l'Isle-Adam. *The Vampire Soul*
Philippe Ward. *Artahe: The Legacy of Jules de Grandin*
P. de Wattyne & Y. Walter. *Sherlock Holmes vs. Fantômas*
David White. *Fantômas in America*